WITCH ON FIRST

The Jinx Hamilton Series - Book 4

JULIETTE HARPER

Prologue

That summer, we didn't know we were playing a game with the bases loaded. The other team had a man on first, second, *and* third. One home run and they would have turned the whole thing into a grand slam.

Let me tell you about the first time I ever played baseball. I was eight years old. The neighborhood kids got a game together in the Masterson's backyard. Me and my best friend, Tori, were the youngest kids on the block. When the others asked us to join in, I was suspicious we were about to be used for batting practice.

Tori, ever the optimist, accepted the invitation. Neither one of us knew how to play. Worse still, I was that loser kid who missed every ball thrown in her direction regardless of how big that ball might be.

It takes *a lot* of talent not to catch a beach ball.

When it was my turn up at bat, Mr. Masterson, who was the umpire, walked up beside me and gently moved my hands into something approximating a correct grip.

"What do I do?" I whispered, looking up at him in a panic.

"Keep your eye on the ball and swing like you're going to slice it right in two. Got it?"

I had no idea what he was talking about, but good little Southern girl that I was, I said, "Yes, sir."

Davy, the oldest kid on our street, was pitching. Anybody else might have thrown me something easy, but I knew that evil glint in Davy's eye. That baseball heading at me was a guided, eight-year-old-seeking ballistic missile.

I kept my eye on the ball because I was positive that five-ounce chunk of rubber wrapped in cowhide might take my head clean off my shoulders.

Acting out of pure, desperate, self-defense without a shred of athleticism attached, I levered the heavy, awkward club forward.

With a resounding crack, wood hit leather. I watched in astonishment as the ball flew high over left field. I didn't even think to run until I realized everyone in the backyard, including Mr. and Mrs. Masterson, was screaming at me to do just that.

I made it as far as first base when I heard Mr. Masterson yell, "*STOP!*"

As the umpire, I don't think he was supposed to be coaching me, but I needed the help.

In the story I'm about to tell you when it was our turn at bat, we made it to first base too. We took down one of the three threats facing us, but it wasn't because anyone coached us. We got lucky.

The whole mess started over a coffee cup and a chessboard.

The cup seemed like a clever homage to the Wicked Witch of the West from *The Wizard of Oz*. I found it early one morning when I went out to sweep the sidewalk in front of our store in Briar Hollow, North Carolina.

The card inside the box said the cup was a good luck gift from a satisfied customer. To me, the gesture seemed sweet, but from the beginning, something about that cup bothered Tori.

Bothered her to the point that I thought she was unreasonable.

For starters, Tori swore the green-faced witch flying alongside the caption on her broom moved. Sometimes she appeared on the other side of the words, which cautioned that if the witch didn't get her coffee, there would be trouble. I told Tori that was nuts.

"Fine," she declared, "you don't believe me? I'll prove it to you. I'll start taking a picture every day until I catch her."

The cup witch never moved again.

Tori's answer to that?

"She heard me. I'm telling you that cup is possessed or haunted or something."

A haunting we should have been able to handle.

The day my powers awakened, I saw Aunt Fiona's ghost. The experience led me to go to the local cemetery that night and meet a whole herd of spooks, including Colonel Beauregard T. Longworth, who has become one of my closest friends.

Ghosts I can do.

I assured Tori no spirits were attached to the cup. I even used my psychometry on the thing for good measure. When I picked up the cup it projected nothing but Elvis lyrics into my mind.

"You don't think *that's* strange?" Tori said. "A cup that listens to the King?"

"Whoever made the cup probably liked Elvis music," I said. "Trust me; there's nothing more sinister in this cup than some leftover notes of *Heartbreak Hotel* and *Jailhouse Rock*."

Then the chessboard showed up, and I do mean, "showed up."

One day we just found it sitting on a table in the espresso bar.

We already owned two chessboards Tori ordered for our patrons. One features Civil War soldiers, the other opposing football teams. There's no mistaking the third set as something special and likely expensive. The burled wood of the playing surface shines under a hand-rubbed finish. Whoever carved the intricate music-themed pieces achieved superb detail from the quarter note pawns to the ornate bass clef kings.

Several days passed before we noticed that no one played on the new board, yet every morning, the major pieces sat on the table with the pawns arranged in strange patterns across the squares.

That bugged Tori so much she asked Myrtle to examine the board for a haunting.

I have to admit that at this stage of things, I was getting concerned my BFF was snorting too many espresso fumes. Her preoccupation with "haunted" inanimate objects was threatening to get out of hand. If anyone could settle her down it was Myrtle, the ancient Fae spirit that inhabits the fairy mound on which our store sits.

Myrtle is our mentor and friend, charged with helping me to hone my witchcraft and facilitating Tori's study of alchemy. We're both descended from the children of a Cherokee witch named Knasgowa and her two husbands. The women on my side of the family are witches, and our "cousins" in Tori's line are alchemists.

In the South we use "cousin" for relatives we're willing to claim but can't explain.

Unfortunately, instead of providing an answer, Myrtle's examination of the chess set turned into one of the strangest interactions we'd ever had with her.

Although Myrtle is an ageless creature of ethereal beauty, she shows herself to us in the store as an elderly librarian with a gray bun held in place by a No. 2 pencil.

Myrtle did as Tori asked. She walked around the chessboard and looked it over from all angles, bending low to peer through the thick glasses she doesn't need. She picked up the chessmen, running her fingers over the smooth, curved surfaces and shook her head.

"I don't feel anything unusual," Myrtle said. "If a ghost has become attached to this board, it is likely only a residual haunting."

Such apparitions are energy recordings playing on an endless loop. Some supercharged event leaves an imprint on the stream of time. It's like a persistent coffee stain on a linen tablecloth. No matter how many times you wash it, that faint brown circle stays there. Residual hauntings have no awareness. They just play over and over and over again.

When Myrtle finished, Tori and I exchanged a look.

I wasn't in on Tori's broader suspicions yet, but even I thought Myrtle's explanation sounded more like an episode of *Ghost Hunters* than a real answer to our problem.

Summoning all my diplomacy, I said, "Uh, Myrtle, you're an all-powerful ancient Fae. Are you telling us you can't make out the details of a residual haunting?"

Myrtle smiled at me tolerantly. "I hear and feel life in all its forms, Jinx," she said, "even its residue, but some imprints are so tiny and faint they do not register unless I direct all my focus on locating them. For instance, there is a rather large water bug under the display shelf by the counter right now."

At that, Tori and I both jumped a foot.

Unless you're from the south, you may not understand "water bug" translates as, "cockroach big enough to saddle"—and they freaking *fly*.

"I knew it," I said, shuddering, "I told you I've been seeing something flying around down here at night."

Several times over the last few weeks, when I paused at the top of the stairs to switch off the downstairs lights, I'd caught sight of a miniature UFO in the shadows. Even after I set out roach traps, the sightings continued.

"What are we going to do?" Tori said, moving behind me. "Can we shoot it?"

Laugh all you want to; water bugs are almost big enough to shoot.

Making a clucking sound in her throat, Myrtle said, "Oh, for heaven's sake." She held out her hand, and to our horror, an enormous water bug came sliding out from under the case. Myrtle lifted it in the air and levitated it *toward* us.

"Myrtle!" I cried, backing away. "*What* are you doing?"

She brought the bug to a stop a few inches from her face. Its antennae twitched nervously while multiple legs struggled against thin air.

"Calm down," Myrtle commanded quietly.

The insect grew still.

"I know you are expecting to die," she said to the bug, "but I am not going to do that. I do not find you horrifying, but my friends are a different matter. I am going to send you outdoors where you belong, so long as you promise me that you will not return. Do we have an agreement?"

Even with my skin crawling the exchange fascinated me. The damn bug nodded. Myrtle levitated the insect towards the back door, which opened of its own accord. When the roach was out of sight, the door closed, and Myrtle turned back toward us.

"Now," she said calmly, "back to our conversation. If there is any spark of life in this board, it is infinitesimal in comparison to that which animates the insect I just evicted."

Still eyeing the back door as if she half expected the water bug to break it down and charge back inside, Tori said, "So you're telling us the chess set isn't haunted?"

"I'm telling you I do not know," Myrtle said, "but I don't

feel anything from the board. I have no explanation for why the pieces move."

At the time, that was good enough for me.

It wasn't until several hours later that it dawned on me Myrtle didn't seem to *care* that we had an unexplained phenomenon in the middle of our home base.

But before I could talk to Tori about that, and before she could tell me about her doubts, somebody threw a dead man into the mix.

Chapter One

On a crisp Sunday morning in late summer I went downstairs to get the morning paper. When I opened the door, I found my werecat boyfriend Chase McGregor standing on the sidewalk outside his cobbler shop, which isn't strange since our businesses sit side by side on the Briar Hollow town square.

Here's the strange part.

He had his smartphone out and was snapping pictures of someone sitting on the bench. Neither one of them said a word. I was holding a coffee cup in one hand, but I hadn't taken more than a sip. My brain wasn't fully engaged. It took several seconds to process what I was seeing—a knife sticking out of the front of the man's shirt pinning a note against blood-stained denim.

That's when things really went bad.

I dropped my coffee.

Chase must have heard me open the door, but he didn't turn toward me until the cup shattered on the concrete.

Quickly pocketing the phone, he said gravely, "I think someone just sent us a message."

For as much as I didn't want to get a closer look at the body, I *did* want to read that note.

I stepped beside Chase and gasped. I knew the dead man. Fish Pike, the half-mad old coot Brenna Sinclair hired to break into the shop weeks earlier. Deep claw marks raked the length of his torso. The strips of torn flesh revealed shocking flashes of white bone and his throat . . . well, the knife didn't kill him.

Even as my mind scrambled to make sense of the details, I noticed one important thing. There was no blood on the bench or the sidewalk. The murderer killed Fish somewhere else and put him on display for our benefit.

"I . . . I . . . can't make out the note," I said, the quiver in my voice making it hard to get the words out.

"It says, 'the cat's out of the bag,'" Chase replied, staring at the body.

"What the heck is that supposed to mean?" I asked, but cold dread crept over me. Sometimes you know something before it's explained to you.

"It means," he said, "that someone doesn't like me seeing you."

Even as my mouth launched a protest, my mind knew he was right.

"Aren't you jumping to conclusions?" I stammered. "Maybe it has something to do with Brenna."

Looking hopefully into Chase's face, I noticed he hadn't shaved yet. The morning sun threw his profile into relief, making the dark stubble stand out along his jaw where clenched muscles worked restlessly under the tanned skin.

"That dagger," he said, pointing at the knife, "is a sgian-dubh."

Gotta tell you, when the people in my world start using Gaelic? We're in for trouble.

"I don't know what that means."

Chase turned, fixing me with the full force of his attention.

When he spoke, the words came out in a harsh whisper so intense, I stepped back.

"A sgian-dubh is a Scottish dress dagger," he said. "I've already called Sheriff Johnson. He'll be here any minute. I need you to say you stepped out to get the paper and saw me standing here looking at Pike's body. Nothing else. Do you understand?"

"I did step out and find you standing here," I replied with growing confusion. "What else would I say to the Sheriff? Chase, tell me what's going on."

"There's no time," he answered, "It's too complicated. Just do this my way. No extra details. Please trust me."

"Of course, I trust you," I said. "But I don't understand why you're acting this way when you're not even asking me to lie."

"No," Chase said, "I'm not asking you to lie now, but if Sheriff Johnson wants to know if we have any information that might explain why Pike would be left here, that's when the lying needs to start."

Good grief! He was acting like I would conversationally mention to the Sheriff that the dead man had been in the employ of a centuries-old sorceress we killed in the basement earlier that month. I opened my mouth to say something to that effect when the sound of a car door slamming stopped me.

"What in the hell is going on here, Chase?" a man's voice demanded, the words punctuated by heavy steps.

"Good morning, John," Chase said, his voice now perfectly normal. "I have no idea what's going on. I came out to get the morning paper and found the body."

Sheriff John Johnson is a big man with close-cropped graying hair he keeps hidden under Stetson hats. He must have been getting ready for church because he was wearing dress pants and a clean white shirt, his badge haphazardly pinned to the pocket. He stopped beside Chase, swiveling his head back and forth taking in the scene, including my broken cup and the splatter of coffee on the sidewalk.

"Morning, Jinx," the Sheriff said. "Mind if I ask you what you're doing here?"

"Uh, I live here," I said, pointing toward the store, "and good morning."

Johnson looked at the door to my shop, and then he looked me up and down. I was standing there in my pajamas. As obliquely as a man like him can manage, the Sheriff asked, "Whose door did you come out of?"

"My own," I said, an edge coming into my tone. "What is your point, John?"

He regarded me calmly. "My point is that this is . . . what . . . the second or third dead body for you this summer?"

"Hey!" I said indignantly. "I am not to blame that some whack job serial killer left bones around for people to trip over. And, may I remind you that solving that case won your department a citation for excellence from the state police? All I did was walk out my front door to get the paper. Instead, I found Chase staring at a dead man. That kinda got my attention."

The Sheriff didn't say anything for a minute. He rolled his omnipresent, reformed smoker's toothpick from the left side of his mouth to the right. "Reckon it would at that," he said finally. "Guess you didn't get to drink much of that coffee before you dropped it."

"You guess right."

Smart men have the sense not to get on a woman's bad side before she's had her morning coffee, especially when they're asking her if she committed a murder.

Sheriff John Johnson is a smart man. He laughed.

"Fair enough." he said, "I'll let you go get another cup as soon as you tell me if either of you knew this feller?"

"For heaven's sake, John," Chase said, "it's Fish Pike. Everyone in town knows him."

"Fish have any connection to either one of you?"

Chase hadn't asked me to lie about knowing Fish, just to make sure we didn't give away any details that would suggest a real connection. Something told me it wouldn't look right if I didn't admit what I was about to say to Sheriff Johnson.

"Mr. Pike used to drink coffee in our espresso bar until we had to ask him not to come back."

Beside me, Chase stiffened, but remained silent.

"Why'd you ask Pike to stay out of your store?" Johnson asked with a note of interest.

"He was kinda crazy," I said, making it sound as if I was reluctant to speak ill of the dead. "Mr. Pike liked to play chess, but he kept getting into fights with the other old men who sit and drink coffee all afternoon. He wouldn't calm down, so we invited him to drink his coffee elsewhere."

To my immense relief, Johnson nodded, blowing out a long, exasperated breath.

"Sounds like Fish," he said. "You weren't the first folks to throw him out. Fish did like to start fights. Looks like this time he tangled with someone he couldn't handle."

We all turned toward the body. Fish looked like he lost a fight alright, with a circle saw.

The Sheriff pushed his hat back on his head. "Damn. If I didn't know better, I'd swear a mountain lion got a hold of him. Those gashes look like claw marks."

"Well," Chase said smoothly, "I don't think a panther dragged him into town and left him there on the bench."

"Wouldn't say so," Johnson agreed, "and most mountain lions don't leave handwritten notes tacked up with knives."

The Sheriff was so fixated on the body, he didn't notice the way the color drained out of Chase's face at the words "mountain lion." We both knew those marks very well could have been made by a panther. We couldn't tell the Sheriff that, however, or share with him that Fish Pike's grandfather, Jeremiah Pike, had been a werecat like Chase and Festus.

In the elder Pike's case, however, Jeremiah broke with tradition and married a human, violating one of the biggest taboos of werecat society. The children of that union were regarded as halflings. As they grew older, each one went slowly mad because they couldn't make the change into panther form. The instability continued into the next generation, and in Fish's case became worse after the recent death of his wife, Martha Louise.

Obviously, there's a whole lot more to that story, but I didn't know any of it that morning.

"Any idea what the note means?" the Sheriff asked.

"None," Chase replied.

"Me either," I said.

"Well," Johnson said, "standing here speculating won't get us anywhere. Let me wake up my deputy. We need to process the scene and get the body to the coroner. You'll both need to give official statements."

"Can I go put that coffee on now?" I asked. "And can Chase come with me?"

"Yeah, sure," Johnson said absently, leaning closer to Fish to get a better view of the gaping slashes. "I'll be in to take your statements later."

Chase followed me inside the store. I closed the front door, and together we watched as the Sheriff stepped off the sidewalk, opened the trunk of his car, and took out a roll of yellow crime scene tape.

"I think you better get Tori up," Chase said softly. "I'll go through the basement and get Dad."

"Dad's already here," a voice said from the vicinity of our feet. I was so rattled I jumped a foot, glaring down at the scruffy yellow tomcat who had come sneaking up on us.

"Festus," I said, "*don't* do that!"

"Can I help it if you humans can't hear paws on a hardwood floor?" he grumbled. "If you washed your ears out every now and then they might work better."

"Whatever," I said. "Just freaking *announce* yourself already."

"I just did," Festus said, jumping up on the windowsill and peering out at Sheriff Johnson. "Dang, John needs to push the milk bowl away. He's getting a gut on him."

"You're a fine one to talk, Dad," Chase said. "Did you see?"

"First, I smelled," Festus said, "then I saw. It's Fish Pike, isn't it?"

"Yes," Chase said, "he was mauled . . . by one of our kind."

Festus arched his back and flattened his ears. "Then we've got a transient."

"A what?" I asked.

"You don't know anything about the werepanther social structure," Festus said, "and I don't want to have to tell this twice. Make your coffee, get Tori, and come into the storeroom."

Before I could ask him who the heck made him the boss, Festus jumped back down, flicked his tail in our direction, and limped off.

"His manners may be lacking, but he's right," Chase said, starting after his father. "Get Tori."

I went to the door of Tori's micro-apartment and knocked lightly. After a second or two, I heard scuffling feet. Tori opened the door wearing pajamas emblazoned with pink flamingos. She blinked at me blearily.

"Hey," she said, "did I get my days mixed up. This *is* Sunday isn't it?"

"Yes," I said, "but we have a problem."

She arched an eyebrow. "When don't we have a problem?"

"Fish Pike is dead on the bench in front of Chase's store clawed up with a dagger in his chest."

Both eyebrows went up at that.

"*Okay*," she said, "so we have a *big* problem."

"Chase and Festus are in the storeroom. Apparently this is some werecat *thing*," I said. "I'm going to make coffee. Sheriff Johnson is working the crime scene. He'll be coming in to talk to us in a little while."

"Give me five and I'll come help you," Tori said, disappearing into her apartment.

When she re-emerged wearing a t-shirt and jeans, I was measuring out ground coffee. "You want to run upstairs and throw some clothes on?" she asked.

"Yeah, thanks," I said, handing her the scoop. "This stuff is not going to do it for me. I need something high octane."

"You and me both," Tori said, flipping on the espresso machine. "I'll make us the real thing."

I ran upstairs and changed, getting back downstairs in record time. Tori handed me a huge, steaming latte the instant I walked into the espresso bar. Darby, our faithful brownie, was with her, bearing an equally huge platter of doughnuts.

"I'm not going to ask how you managed that, Darby," I said, snagging one with chocolate icing, "but thank you."

"You are welcome, Mistress."

He started out with the doughnuts but stopped when I called to him. "Darby, when you deliver those, would you please go down to the basement and tell Colonel Longworth what's going on? You two stay down there until we join you."

Beau is now our in-house ghost, except he isn't so ghostly these days. We're telling people he's my "uncle" from Tennessee. More on that later.

"Yes, Mistress," Darby said, hurrying off toward the storeroom.

Casting a nervous glance at the front door, I called out softly, "Myrtle? Are you there?"

Silence.

Raising my voice slightly, I tried again. "Myrtle?"

Still nothing.

"What the heck?" Tori said.

Going with "the third time's the charm," I said sharply, "Myrtle!"

A three-note trill sounded over my head.

Finally.

"Are you here in the store?" I asked.

This time, the notes played a tune. *Red River Valley*.

Okay. That answered that question. She was in Shevington.

"Can you tell if our mothers are safe?" I asked urgently.

To my immense relief, the positive trill played again.

At that question, Tori looked up sharply. "Why wouldn't our moms be safe?"

"Chase thinks this has something to do with our relationship," I said, "which means . . . "

"Someone could be after your mom and Festus," Tori finished for me.

"Exactly," I said, watching as she put her cup, a mug for Chase, and a bowl for Festus on a tray.

As we started toward the storeroom together, Tori said, "Is it just me, or are we having a *really* long summer?"

A CABIN HIGH in the Mountains

A PALE CIRCLE of light cast by a camp lantern illuminated the center of the cabin where a man sat hunched over a makeshift table. He found the weathered gray board lying in a pile of rubble outside along with the two five-gallon buckets it now spanned. The same mound of junk yielded up his chair, a rickety wreck he tightened up with his multi-tool and pliable wood shims cut from a sapling.

He was following the rules. His rules.

Always have the tools you need.

Make do with the materials on hand.

Create a routine.

Call it home.

Take it with you wherever you go.

That's how he'd traveled for years with just what he could carry on his back.

Not just traveled—lived well on the contents of his weathered, sturdy pack.

He chose every item it contained thoughtfully. He never had much money, but he didn't allow that to be a problem. That was a rule too.

Never think of yourself as a poor man.

Oh yes, and keep a record.

He checked the can of chili warming over the tiny alcohol stove. It needed a little more time.

Flipping open the side pocket of the pack, he took out his notebook and pen, opened the book to a blank page and began to write in precise, careful strokes.

First the date, then the notation.

"Fish Pike - mercy killing."

There. That was done. Once something is written down, it's true. So now, it wasn't murder. It was mercy.

He could eat his supper with a clear conscience.

Extinguishing the flame, the man carefully removed the can and stirred the contents with his spoon.

His spoon. He liked that.

No one else ever had or ever would eat a single bite with his spoon.

Chewing rhythmically, the man thought about what he'd done.

Fish was a crazy, unhappy old man living alone in a house that was nothing but a moldering monument to his dead wife.

Now, Fish Pike would be famous. The town would talk for years about how the old man showed up dead in front of the cobbler shop.

Before long, they'd be talking about how Chase McGregor was found the same way. Clawed up with a dagger in his chest.

That one would go into the book as an act of justice.

His boss might have other motivations, but he killed for virtue.

Not being able to use the same sgian-dubh again as his signature bothered the man. He hated to think of a good blade lying forgotten in an evidence bag, but there was no help for that.

The blade had a message of its own to deliver. The Sheriff wouldn't get it, but the McGregors would.

Chapter Two

Before we go any further, you have to understand about Festus and my mother, and, well, about Chase and me.

Parents don't *ever* lose the ability to shock their children.

It was one thing to find out mom is a witch too, but the idea that Festus, a carousing, smart-mouthed bad boy was carrying a torch for her?

Mind altering.

Don't get me wrong. Mom is attractive—dark-haired, petite, bright blue eyes—but for most of my life, I've known her as an excitable, nervous woman.

Festus is an *alley* cat. I've seen him passed out drunk on a pool table after too many rounds of the werecats's favorite drinking game, Red Dot.

He's a thoroughgoing old scoundrel and *nothing* like my father.

You want to know how conventional my parents are? That Sunday, they were coming home from a *fishing* convention in Houston.

For the record, Mom doesn't fish, and Dad can't stop.

We're talking intervention level fishing here. Jeremy Wade, the *River Monsters* guy, is Dad's idol. I think Mom tolerates the endless local fishing trips because she hopes it'll keep Dad from hopping an airplane to some remote jungle location to angle for a critter big enough to eat him.

My Dad is also the only person I know who claims to have fishing *dogs*. Six of them he takes with him to the river. Together, he and those worthless mutts catch a lot of fish, but they also do a lot of snoring on the bank.

To be honest, from *my* perspective, dating a werecat is kinda . . . hot.

So the idea of my mother and a werepanther . . .

La la la la la la la.

Excuse me while I douse that mental image in brain bleach.

Such a thing would never even have occurred to me until the night of the big fight with Brenna.

When Festus jumped through the portal and changed into a mountain lion in mid-leap.

I attributed the macho act to the werecat being full of himself after a night of carousing at The Dirty Claw. Then I realized the only thing Festus cared about was getting to *my mother*.

I spent the next several days running over the logistics of werecat relationships in my mind. Their magic repels all other power sets. Even if a werecat marries a human, it all goes wrong. Fish Pike was living . . . well, dead . . . proof of that. The children can't shift, but the longing for the change shatters their minds.

Then there's the matter of age.

Werecat metabolism gives them a lifespan of about 200 years on average.

I handled it well when Chase informed me he'd be 87 on his next birthday, especially considering I'll turn 30 this fall. It helps that we look the same age, but there's still a 57-year gap.

Lifespan isn't something I worry about, which is good because a witch's longevity is tied to the extent of her powers. Mine are still growing. Aunt Fiona told me one time that if you're alive, you're still dying. We all are. Some people just take longer to get to their own funerals.

I concentrate on living in the moments I have, not counting the ones I might never receive.

Festus was born in 1905. He's 110, but that's not what makes him cranky. In 1936 a wizard named Irenaeus Chesterfield lamed Festus with a bolt of lightning. Over the past ten years, arthritis has set in.

Moira tried to help Festus. She can mend broken bones with magic, but none of her attempts to give Festus a new hip joint worked. When he shifts, the damage comes back. If he had a human hip replacement, he could never shift again. That's a price he refuses to pay. Festus may be mixing his feline metaphors when he growls, "a leopard can't change his spots," but I get it.

Festus won't give up his true nature just to save himself a little pain and inconvenience.

He lives as a house cat because it's easier to get around on three legs when you weigh roughly 14 lbs. I saw Festus once in human form. He looks like I imagine Chase will look in another 25 years.

As Festus once pointed out to me, living as a house cat has other advantages as well. He can't very well lounge in the sun on the bench in front of the cobbler shop as a mountain lion, and the old rascal does like to get his ears scratched by cute young chicks.

I tried to put the whole thing about my mother out of my mind. After all, it wasn't any of my business, but then I found myself alone in the lair with Festus.

That's the area to the left of the staircase when you come down into the basement. The space looks like it belongs in an English country manor, complete with wood paneling, floor-to-ceiling bookcases, oriental rugs, a massive work table, and a collection of leather wingback chairs.

Festus was sitting on the hearth, warming his bad hip against the ever-present fire.

The temperature in the basement stays a constant "chilly," and there's always a fire going in the grate. No one tends to it. There aren't any ashes to be taken out. It's just there. Since I'm the kind of person who can sit happily in front of a fire any time of year, I often wander down there late at night when I can't sleep.

I was surprised to find Festus alone in the lair, but then I realized that each of us, in our way, use the fire as therapy.

"Hey," I said, "mind if I join you?"

"As long as you don't hog the hearth, I'm good."

"No problem," I said, sitting down in one of the chairs.

When I didn't say anything else, Festus fixed me with a penetrating feline gaze. "Something, in particular, you want to talk to me about?"

That's one thing I appreciate about Festus. He meets things head on.

"Are you in love with my mother?" I blurted out.

Both of his ears went up. A thinly disguised look of shock came into his normally impassive amber eyes. He picked up his good back leg and used it to scratch his whiskers absently. He was stalling, which was as good as admitting I was right. When he finally finished with his whiskers he just looked at me.

If you know anything about cats, you'll understand that when they have something to tell you, they make direct eye contact.

"Yes," he said finally. "I've been in love with your mother since she was a girl."

Now that I'd asked the question and gotten my answer, I had no idea what to say next. I went with the first thing that came into my mind.

"Does she know?"

"She knows I love her," Festus said, "but she thinks it's simply the affection a werecat has for his charge."

That made me wince. For the most part, I've put it out of my mind that it's Chase's job to protect me. Every now and then, however, I have an insecure moment and wonder if that's the source of his interest in me.

Festus instantly read my expression and made an impatient sound.

"Oh, for Bastet's sake," he said, "stop it. You'd make one hell of a lousy poker player. My boy isn't interested in you just because you're his charge."

Embarrassed by my lingering insecurities, I forged ahead as if that exchange never happened.

"Why didn't you ever tell Mom how you feel?" I asked.

Festus stared off into space as only a cat can.

"Chase's mother died when he was a toddler," he said. "My Jenny was a remarkable woman. As long as she was alive, I never even looked at anyone else."

"What happened to her?" I asked softly. "Chase doesn't talk about his mother."

Festus's eyes tracked toward me. "He doesn't remember much more than her purr and the way he'd sleep cuddled against her."

That startled me. "You mean like a . . . like a . . ."

"Kitten is the word you're looking for," Festus said, his lips pulling into a Cheshire cat smile. "Can't get your head wrapped around that one, can you?"

"Not really," I admitted. "I didn't know werecats change so early in life."

"They can't by themselves," Festus said. "The mother's

magic envelops the kittens so they can be nurtured as both human babies and cats. The maternal instinct is strong and protective in felines. We teach our young basic hunting skills early on. That's what all the pouncing and hissing is about."

I couldn't help it. I did what any girlfriend would do.

"Was Chase a cute kitten?"

Festus snorted. "Little beast was an adorable gray furball with big innocent green eyes he used to get himself out of trouble every time he went up the living room curtains."

Oh. My. God. Was Chase ever getting teased about that.

"Are there pictures?"

"There are," he said. "Next time you're over, bring it up, and we'll gang up on Chase to make him take the albums out."

"Deal."

Silence fell over the room interrupted by the crackling of the fire. I hesitated to break the hush, but Festus seemed to be in a mood to talk. I didn't want to lose the opportunity.

"What happened to your wife?" I prodded gently.

"Jenny saw a little girl dart out into traffic," he said, his voice going harsh. "Werecats are fast. Fast enough that Jenny threw the girl to safety, but the car hit Jenny. She could have changed and saved herself, but it happened in the middle of downtown Raleigh. Jenny sacrificed herself to protect our secret."

"Oh, Festus," I said, my voice rough with unshed tears.

He looked up at me and let the sardonic mask fall away to reveal his grief. "Chase has her heart. That's the kind of fool thing he'd do."

"Yes, I said, it is. Did you stay in Raleigh after she died?"

"We did. My Dad was still here protecting your people. I was on assignment to watch Irenaeus Chesterfield. When he lamed me, Chase was only 8. My father was getting old. I was needed here. Chase's life in Raleigh was normal or at least what passed for normal. I wanted him to have that, so I used the portals like a commuter train to come back and forth."

"There's a portal in Raleigh?" I asked in surprise.

"There are portals everywhere, and more worlds than you care to know about."

He wasn't getting any argument from me on that point. I had all I could handle in the *two* worlds I did know about.

"Your job was to guard my mother?" I asked.

"Your grandmother and her daughters," Festus said, "not that they needed it. No one, and I mean no one, was going to cross your grandmother, Kathleen. She had so much power, your whiskers would curl just being near her."

I shook my head. "I thought she was an old church lady."

To my surprise, Festus hissed at me.

"Don't go making light of your grandmother's beliefs," he snapped. "She was a fine and honorable woman. Her faith in the Universe was strong. It doesn't matter what you call that Power That is Greater Than Us All, girl, it only matters that you *honor* it."

I felt the blood rush to my cheeks.

"I'm sorry, Festus. I didn't mean to be disrespectful."

The fur on his back smoothed down.

"I'm sorry too," he said gruffly. "Your grandmother was my friend and my first charge. She still means a lot to me. What I started to feel for Kelly, happened when she was a young teenager. It wouldn't have been right for me to pursue her until she was older and well, it all seemed disrespectful of Kathleen. I couldn't make up my mind what to do, so I did nothing. Then the accident happened. You know about the accident, right?"

When Mom and Gemma were 15, they wanted to be cheerleaders and foolishly used magic to delay their arch rivals from making the tryouts. There was a car crash, and both the girls were killed. Mom blamed herself. I still don't know all the details, but she had some kind of breakdown. She gave up her magic, and Gemma at least pretended to do the same, all the while honing her abilities in case she ever had to defend them.

So far, I've gotten three versions of my family history from Mom.

Version 1: "Your Aunt Fiona is crazy, and there's no such thing as magic."

Version 2: "I'm a witch, and so is Gemma, but we abandoned our magic after we believed we killed two cheerleaders."

Version 3: "Gemma didn't give up her powers, she kept studying on the sly all these years, and my powers woke up again when yours did."

That latest version is the one I like—a lot. It wasn't Gemma who wielded magic against Brenna. Mom reached deep inside and finished awakening her powers. Together, they fought their way out. Granted they had the help of a gimpy werecat, two Confederate ghosts, a brownie, and a rat, but it was still majorly badass, and the whole thing completely changed how I think about my mom.

Nodding at Festus, I said, "Yes. Mom and Gemma told us about the accident."

"Then you understand. Kelly was a teenager, and I was 70."

"Chase is 87," I pointed out, "and he's with me."

"You're twice the age your mother was then," Festus said. "You're a grown woman. She was a girl in a great deal of pain. To her, I was a friend of the family, the werecat who worked with her mother. I thought I'd let Kelly get older, that I'd try to help her, but then she met your Dad, and that was that."

My heart almost broke when he uttered those last words. He tried to sound matter of fact and failed. Festus had been forced to watch everything that happened in my Mom's life from the position of "family friend," when inside, he'd felt something else entirely. Then, he'd watched again as his chance with her evaporated thanks to my father.

"Festus, I am so sorry."

The old cat cleared his throat and turned his back to me to gaze into the flames.

"Don't be," he said. "It was a long time ago. I was playing with fire even thinking about breaking the taboo. Clan McGregor's job is to protect the Daughters of Knasgowa, so that's what I kept doing even though your mother turned her back on magic. I guarded her and Fiona. Then this fool hip started acting up, and I asked Chase to come take over for me. We moved into the cobbler's shop. That's where we've been ever since."

"This is why you don't want me to get involved with Chase, isn't it?"

"Don't put words in my mouth," Festus said, still staring into the fireplace. "You're both long past grown. I can't stop you, and I'm not going to try. But what you're doing is dangerous, Jinx. Mark my words. It *is* dangerous. Don't be blind to that."

At the time, I had no idea how much foreshadowing that conversation contained. Now, with Fish Pike propped up dead on the front sidewalk, the exchange with Festus came back to me full force.

Chapter Three

Tori and I joined Chase and Festus in the storeroom as the bell on the front door jingled. Festus quickly disappeared behind the file cabinet, and Tori obligingly slid his coffee bowl after him. She dove back on the loveseat when the Sheriff called out, "Anyone here?"

Out of the corner of my eye, I saw Rodney peering from the shadows between the liniment cans that guard the entrance to his quarters.

I gave him a shooing motion with my hand, and he retreated farther away from the edge of the shelf.

Under my breath, I said, "Myrtle, are you listening?"

The lamp beside my chair flickered. Good, everyone but Beau and . . . .

A pale ghostly form floated into the room.

"Beau," I whispered, "what are you doing up here?"

"I am here because I do not wish to be excluded," he said.

Which probably meant Darby was with him.

"Did you bring an invisible friend?"

The words were barely out of my mouth before a voice whispered beside me. "I am here, Mistress."

"Hello?!" the Sheriff's voice boomed louder from the front of the store.

"Sorry, Sheriff," I called out, "we're in the storeroom."

Sheriff Johnson's boots clomped over the wood floor. When he appeared framed in the doorway, his eyes immediately fell on the tray of doughnuts.

"I don't guess there might be a cup of coffee for me?" he asked hopefully.

"Of course, there is, Sheriff," Tori said. "I was waiting to find out how you take it."

"Black with two sugars," Johnson said, sitting down in the sagging armchair opposite me. "May I?" He gestured toward the platter.

"Be my guest," I said.

Johnson helped himself to two glazed doughnuts, tearing through one before Tori could get back with his coffee. When he saw my amused expression, the Sheriff said sheepishly, "My wife's got me on a diet. I'm hungry all the time."

"Your secret is safe with us," I said. Be sure to get all the icing wiped off your face before you go home."

Taking another huge bite of sugary pastry and washing it down with coffee, Johnson said, "Okay, tell me again how you found the body. Chase, you go first."

The Sheriff kept us there for more than an hour. He made Chase and me go through the "we opened the door and there was a body" story three times. Johnson even questioned Tori, who assured him that she'd heard nothing during the night because she fell asleep with her headphones on.

As I listened to the Sheriff talking to her, I knew he was half-heartedly trying to trip us up. I watch enough cop shows to recognize the tactic, but from what I could tell, Johnson didn't think we had anything to do with Fish Pike's death.

Even though it sounded like he was being thorough with his investigation, I suspected the Sheriff had another reason for keeping us so long. While we were sitting there, he went through half a dozen doughnuts *and* conveniently missed the beginning of the sermon over at the First Baptist Church.

"Okay," he said at last, flipping his notebook closed and stifling a burp, "I've got all I need."

"Don't you mean all you can *hold?*" Chase asked, grinning and pointing toward the mostly empty platter.

"Cops and doughnuts," Johnson shrugged, "it's a long-standing association. I'll be back in touch if I have any more questions. In the meantime, keep your doors locked and be on the lookout for anything strange until we get this thing figured out."

As he rose to leave, I said, "Sheriff, can I ask you a question?"

"Sure. What do you want to know?"

"Mr. Pike wasn't killed out there in front of the shop, was he?"

Johnson regarded me thoughtfully. "How do you know that?"

"There wasn't any blood on the bench or the concrete," I said. "He was dead when someone put him there, wasn't he?"

The Sheriff nodded. "Good observation. Yes, he was killed somewhere else and brought here. My best guess is that the time of death was last night, but the coroner will have to confirm that. Why?"

"I'm surprised no one saw anything and reported it," I said. "Last night was a full moon."

Johnson frowned. "It was?"

"Yes," I said. "Before I went to bed, I noticed the moon out the front window upstairs."

Which was only part of the truth.

Chase doesn't go furry once a month. He can change whenever he wants to, but magically, all sorts of things can happen during that time. Even people who don't believe in magic know about the full moon effect. Ask the staff of your local hospital emergency room if you don't believe me.

"Whoever arranged the body got in here quick and left just as fast," Johnson said. "Damn shame this town doesn't have a pot to . . . " He caught himself and backtracked. "Doesn't have enough budget money to pay for surveillance cameras on the square. They'd come in handy long about now."

I got up and followed the Sheriff to the door so I could lock it behind him. As I suspected, word of Fish's death spread fast in the small town. A growing throng of onlookers milled around the courthouse lawn. Once church let out and the lunch rush was over, there would be more. I didn't want any of them getting it in their heads to come knocking on my door, even if we probably could have sold gallons of coffee to the curious. Some profits aren't worth it.

After the Sheriff left, I made sure the "Closed" sign was in place and drew the shades down over the long panes. There were no blinds in the big display windows, but no one could see us if we kept to the storeroom and the rear of the first floor.

When I rejoined the group, I found Beau back in human form.

He came away from our encounter with Brenna sporting an amber amulet holding a single feather from the fabled Phoenix. The enchantment in the stone allows him to move about in the world of the living. But the minute he takes the amulet off he reverts to his pale, bluish, wispy self, which he does at least once a week to go across the street and make an appearance as the local Confederate ghost at the base of the war memorial on the courthouse lawn.

The apparitions are fantastic for tourism, and Beau's dedication to his new calling explains the existence of the Briar Hollow Town Square Business and Paranormal Association—or BHTSBPA (pronounced "bits-pa") as they like to call themselves.

We had to come up with some explanation for Beau's presence in the store, so we concocted the "uncle from Tennessee" story. Tori used her wicked fashion sense to get him out of the uniform and cavalry boots he wore for 151 years and into proper eccentric uncle-garb. Regardless of the weather, the resolute Southern gentleman will not go out by day without a coat, but he's finally comfortable in white shirts and vests for indoor day wear.

We did have a bit of an argument over "cravats," an article of male apparel of which I was blissfully ignorant until Beau pitched a fit about "appearing in the presence of ladies in an open-necked shirt." You can still buy cravats—mainly at bridal shops—but rather than let Beau wander around looking like a lost groomsman, we updated him to ascots, which are just guy scarves, but we don't say that.

The one point on which Beau would not budge, however, were his boots. That's where Chase came to the rescue. He made our stalwart Colonel an updated version of his worn and scarred cavalry boots. As I looked at Beau that morning, one long leg crossed over the other, I couldn't help but appreciate the expanse of ebony leather. You want a good shine on your best boots? Hand the polish over to a 19th-century cavalry officer.

"What's with the ghostly appearance?" I asked him.

"I surmised that you instructed me to remain downstairs because it might still be difficult to explain my presence in the store," he said in his deep drawl, "especially to the local constabulary. Therefore, I removed the difficulty by reverting to spectral form. Darby was kind enough to hold the amulet for me. Now we are, as Miss Tori likes to say, 'all on the same page' regarding this most disturbing turn of events."

As I say frequently, Beau is big with the understatements, and he was right. Everyone, including Rodney, heard the "official" version of our discovery of Fish Pike's body. Now it was time to get unofficial.

"Okay," I said, "so the gang's all here. Festus, you said that I don't know anything about werecat social structure. So talk. What does that have to do with Fish Pike's murder?"

"The Pikes stayed here after Jeremiah married a human because my father allowed it," Festus said. "All this land up to the high reaches of the mountains is McGregor territory. No other werepanthers can be here without my permission."

Tori and I exchanged glances. "*Your* permission?"

Chase shot his father a slightly exasperated look. "This is not like the old days in Scotland, Dad. You don't have to make yourself sound like the clan chieftain."

Festus puffed his chest out. "That's exactly what I am."

"Of a clan with two members unless you count grandpa's ghost," Chase said. "I think you better let me tell this."

"Fine," Festus said, picking up one paw and beginning to lick it with a bored expression, "but I'd tell it with more flair."

"I have no doubt," Chase said, "but I think we've had enough drama for one morning." He turned back toward me. "Werepanthers, like the natural panthers in these hills, are solitary creatures when it comes to territory. There have only been four McGregor men in these mountains since the time of your ancestor, Knasgowa."

"Wait a minute," Tori said, "Alexander Skea came over from Scotland and married Knasgowa in 1787. You're telling us that in . . . " She paused to do the math in her head, "two hundred and twenty-eight years there have only been four of you?"

"The old McGregor men came with the first Shevington settlers in in 1584," Chase said. "My direct ancestors stayed in Scotland until our clan name was outlawed in 1750. Callum McGregor, my great-grandfather joined his kin in Shevington and, well, he did something terrible."

"Which was?"

Chase looked down at the toes of his boots, then as if gathering his resolve, raised his head and looked at me directly. "He murdered Knasgowa's first husband, Degataga."

Oh, great. The story was just getting better and better. "Go on," I said.

Chase explained that when Barnaby Shevington founded The Valley, he recognized the pure magic of the Cherokee and worked to build an alliance with the tribe. The two communities existed in parallel realities, but with significant interaction. Shortly after Callum McGregor arrived in Shevington, he ran into a Cherokee hunting party.

Callum claimed the Cherokee attacked him without provocation. He shifted to protect himself and killed Degataga, leaving Knasgowa a widow with a baby girl named Awenasa from whom I am descended.

Tori traces her family line to Duncan, the child Knasgowa had with Alexander Skea. The Creavit sorceress Brenna Sinclair was Alexander's great-grandmother.

"What was Callum's punishment?" I asked.

"The Clan had no proof that he was lying," Chase said, "but they couldn't risk harming relations with the Cherokee. Callum was ordered to swear fealty to the Daughters of Knasgowa into perpetuity. Callum's act of murder was the beginning of the McGregors's role as the protectors of your family."

Well, it was about time somebody explained that one to me.

"Okay," I said, "not the best way in the world to get a job, but what does that have to do with Fish Pike?"

Festus snorted. "We went soft and sheltered the brat's family."

"Dad!" Chase said. "That's enough of that kind of talk."

The old cat stood his ground. "Say what you will, boy, but

we made enemies of the Pikes by taking Jeremiah in, and you know it."

"Hold it," Tori said. "Slow down and connect the dots here. What exactly did the McGregors do or not do for Jeremiah Pike?"

Festus glared at his son. "Am I allowed to tell this part?"

Chase sat back and crossed his arms over his chest. "Be my guest."

"These mountains used to be divided between two werecat families," Festus explained. "The McGregors and the Pikes. When Jeremiah married a human, the Pikes threw him out, and we took him in. My grandmother, God rest her soul, said she'd have no part of an innocent girl being made to pay for violating a taboo she didn't even understand. Fish Pike's father was born under our roof."

"And I'm guessing the Pikes didn't like that?" I asked.

"Not one bit," Festus said. "They attacked us, and we fought back. Barnaby intervened and brokered a peace."

"What were the terms of the peace?" I asked.

"We were given all the territory here in the mountains because of our pledge to guard the Daughters of Knasgowa," Festus replied. "The Pikes chose to move farther south. Jeremiah stayed here. He continued to go back and forth to the Valley, but none of his children or grandchildren could make the change."

"So they couldn't go to Shevington?" Tori asked.

"That's right," Festus said. "They didn't have the magic they needed to open the portal."

"Couldn't Jeremiah have opened it for them?" I asked.

"It doesn't work like that," Festus said. "They were outcasts."

Something about that didn't set right with me. "I thought Shevington was supposed to be a sanctuary."

"It is," Chase said quietly. "This is a werecat prejudice."

"I didn't say I was proud of it," Festus grumbled. "We might have let them into the Valley, but we're not the only werecats in Shevington. Besides, the younger Pikes had bigger problems."

"Like what?" I asked.

"Jeremiah's son was meaner than a snake," Festus said, narrowing his eyes in distaste. "He's gotten more than one warning from me for hitting his wife and son. Fish never was all that bright, and he was far too curious about his werecat heritage. We could never make him understand why he was an outcast. The fool got it in his head that if he could get to The Valley, he'd be able to shift, and he'd be accepted by the werecat community. That's how Brenna got to him."

Beau cleared his throat. "If I may?" he asked, pausing politely before he continued. "Is it your theory that one of the Pikes who left this area returned to murder Fish?"

"That's one possibility," Festus said, "but I think it's more likely that we have a transient on our hands."

I jumped back into the conversation. "You used that term earlier," I said. "What does it mean?"

"A transient is a werepanther with no territory of his own," Chase said. "Any werecat in human form would have been able to sense Fish's true nature. Leaving the body on our doorstep could be a message that the transient plans to make a move on this territory."

"But why?"

Chase looked uncomfortable. "Other more aggressive werecats would see us as weak for allowing halflings to live here. I have no heirs. Since Dad is lame and there's no one to take my place in time, a young, opportunistic werepanther could see a chance to claim prime territory."

He'd put almost all the cards on the table, but he avoided the wild card.

Me.

I played it for him.

"And you're dating a human," I said flatly. "So the chances that any children we might have could be your real heir are virtually nil."

"Yes," Chase said, his voice going ragged. "That too."

Beau looked at Chase. "This transient would go after those you love," he asked quietly, "in the interest of forcing a confrontation with you while you were at an emotional disadvantage?"

Chase nodded.

"Would somebody mind translating that for me?" I said.

"It is a rather simple but brilliant tactic," Beau replied. "A sort of guerilla warfare. Rather than attack his primary objective— Chase—the transient would attack all his emotional resources in the hopes of making him angry and restless."

"He's trying to make me hunt him," Chase said bluntly. "He's trying to make me mad enough to be stupid, so he started with someone on the periphery of my world. Someone weak who had a history with my family. Next time, he'll be more direct."

I hated to ask the next question since I already knew the answer, but in for a dime, in for a dollar. "Who will he go after next?"

"You," Chase answered. "You're the closest thing I have to a mate. He'll go after you."

Chapter Four

Chase's words touched off a myriad of reactions, ranging from Tori's declaration of, "Oh, *hell* no," to Rodney scampering off the shelf and settling on my shoulder like a 1.5-pound bodyguard. Beau said something about such an outrage never coming to pass. I swear to you his hand went for the saber that no longer rested on his hip.

Chase and I just looked at each other.

"Uh, gang," I said, "a minute here, please?"

Everyone quieted down.

"Chase," I said, "please give Tori your phone so she can transfer the pictures of the body to her laptop. We'll meet all of you down in the lair in a few minutes to have a look at them. Chase and I need to talk in private."

After Chase gave her his phone, Tori held her hand out to Rodney, who dug his claws into the fabric of my t-shirt and shook his head stubbornly.

"Little dude," I said, "go with Tori. I'm fine."

The rat reluctantly stepped onto Tori's palm and ran up to her shoulder, but he looked back at me, whiskers twitching worriedly, as they headed out the door.

Without saying a word to each other, Chase and I both moved over to the loveseat. He put his arm around me, and I leaned back against him. We sat there for a few minutes and then I said, "Okay, so the part about you losing your temper and doing something stupid? Not happening."

"I'll do my best."

"No. You'll do it."

"Dad told me about the talk the two of you had," Chase said. "I didn't know he has feelings for your mother."

"Do you think the two of them could be in danger too?"

Chase shook his head. "Nothing ever came of it. People have seen us together here and in the Valley. We haven't exactly been hiding."

We'd done just the opposite. Our growing affections were clear to anyone who was paying attention. Then I realized the implication of his words.

Shifting to face him, I said, "Wait a minute. You can't be serious. You think the killer could be from the Valley? That place is all unicorns and rainbows."

"Unicorns have horns," Chase pointed out, "and you don't want to meet the leprechauns that guard the end of the rainbow. They're nasty, lying little brutes.'

At first, I thought he was joking. Then I realized he was serious.

"Shevington might be full of beings this world regards as magical," he said, "but magic and negative emotions make for dangerous stuff. Did you ever stop to consider how many of the Valley's inhabitants are there because they asked for sanctuary? Nobody does that unless they need to get away from something or someone."

He was right. I had never thought about it that way. When Myrtle described the Valley as a "sanctuary," my mind went more to "enchanted resort," not "witness protection."

"Do you know why Barnaby left Europe in the first place?" Chase asked.

"Because the Creavit practitioners were getting too much power on the Council of Elders and threatened to obliterate pure magic."

Yeah, well, so much for thinking I'd paid attention in Magical History 101 and so much for believing anything an evil sorceress says. That night in the basement, Brenna Sinclair told the moms she killed Barnaby Shevington's wife, and he fled Europe to escape her wrath. That morning, Chase told me the real story.

On April 6, 1580, a magnitude six earthquake hit the Dover Strait, the narrowest part of the English Channel where approximately 20 miles separate Great Britain from the European continent. The quake toppled chimneys and some of the high parts of Westminster Abbey in London. A couple of people died, and out on the coast, a new section of the famous White Cliffs opened up.

If it happened today? Think disaster-movie with massive CGI special effects.

Ask a geologist about the earthquake and he'll rattle off a bunch of stuff about tectonic plates and the depth of the epicenter. Mechanically, that might be true, but the force that caused the earth to shift originated from a simple man's tortured grief.

At the exact moment, the rock under the cold waters of the Channel convulsed in geologic agony, a wizard named Barnaby Shevington fell to his knees on the floor of his country home in Kent, wailing in rage and pain over the broken body of his murdered wife, Adeline.

Ever seen the movie *Tombstone*?

Kurt Russell plays Wyatt Earp.

He delivers a nice speech while looking down a double-barreled shotgun at a sniveling outlaw.

"You tell 'em I'm coming, and hell's coming with me."

From what Chase told me that morning, Barnaby Shevington called down the thunder as he searched the British Isles and Europe for his wife's killer.

"Why did Brenna lie?" I asked.

"To enhance her reputation," Chase replied. "Barnaby conducted his hunt in disguise. He has the power of transmogrify."

The ability to assume different forms. Now that's some *serious* undercover work.

"How did Brenna use that against him?" I asked.

"Originally, he wanted to track his wife's killer without warning the murderer he was coming, but then Barnaby almost went too far. He thought he'd found someone in service to the wizard who killed Adeline. Things got out of hand."

Barnaby wrapped his hand around the throat of a young wizard with an iron grip. He promised to squeeze either the truth or the life out of him—the apprentice could pick. Moira stood to Barnaby's right, speaking in low tones, reminding him of his principles and ethics. Brenna stood on his left, feeding his anger and grief, taunting Barnaby to kill the terrified boy no matter what answer he gave.

"Why didn't they just use their magic?" I asked.

"Because even in the presence of magic," Chase explained, "we are all creatures of free will. Barnaby had to make a choice as a man, not a wizard. His decision would determine the fate of his soul. If he released the apprentice, he could walk away and make amends for the things he'd done. If he killed him, Barnaby's heart would blacken in his chest, and he would become like Brenna."

"He chose to walk away."

"Yes," Chase replied, "but his actions had already created a terrible dilemma. If Barnaby wanted to remain a leader, he could never confess the ways he'd used magic to hunt Adeline's killer. He needed the trust of those first Shevington settlers. The situation allowed Brenna to claim responsibility for the murder in a way that aggrandized her with the Creavit. It looked as if she'd made one of the greatest wizards in Europe turn tail and run like a craven coward. She told the story so many times she probably came to believe that's how it happened. Brenna got what she deserved when Duncan Skea sealed her up in that cave in the Orkneys in 1679."

"And then she got out," I said.

"Yes," Chase said, "but Knasgowa took care of that. She was protecting Alexander *and* Barnaby when she banished Brenna to limbo."

"You mean until I screwed up and let Brenna out."

"Which set the stage for someone to finally kill her," Chase said. "There are no accidents."

"How long was it after Adeline's death that Barnaby and the settlers came to America?"

"Four years," Chase said. "Barnaby created a haven for peaceful Fae in part to atone for the wrongs he believed he'd committed."

The version of the Magical Reformation Myrtle shared with me made no mention of Barnaby's personal tragedy. The official story is that the rising evil of *Proditor Magicae* or "traitor magic" created "made" witches and wizards hungry for power —which is the truth. Their ambitions knew no limits. To them, murder meant a flick of the wrist, nothing more than a few whispered words in Latin.

To Barnaby, his wife's murder meant the light in his world —in his very soul—almost flickered into extinction.

"How do you know all this?" I asked.

"Barnaby and I have played chess together for years," Chase said. "It's taken decades of brandy and cigars, but he finally told me the whole story. I think part of him needed someone other than Moira to know the truth. Barnaby was the first person who sought sanctuary in the Valley—for himself. Magic can be a great and terrible force, Jinx. Filled with the same passions and prejudices that motivate humans."

"Why are you telling me this now?"

His eyes filled with tears. "Because if I lost you like that, I'm afraid I might not stop until someone paid for your life in blood."

"I repeat," I said, "that's not happening. The losing me part or the blood part. We're going to find out who killed Fish Pike and put a stop to this before it goes any further."

You'd think after my boyfriend threatened to rip someone's throat out for me—a literal possibility when you're dating a werecat—the heroine (me) would swoon over the hero's manly manliness.

You'd be half right.

There was mild swoonage followed by a kiss—and then we had a fight.

This probably won't come as a surprise, but we had problems other than dead Fish. Unfortunately, Chase couldn't know about those problems, especially in light of the morning's discovery. That's why he couldn't understand my reaction when he said we should all go to the Valley immediately, and I said no.

I agreed with him that discussing Fish Pike's murder with Barnaby, Moira, and Myrtle was a good idea. I didn't agree that I should go along.

"You'll be safer In Shevington," he protested. "Pack a bag and stay at the Inn for a few days until we get this sorted out."

"No," I said, "and that's my final answer. I am not leaving everyone here at the store unprotected. Besides, I'm going to the Valley in the morning with my mother. Now, come on, let's go down to the lair and look at those pictures."

"Honey," Chase said, "we found a *body* on the sidewalk. Come along and let me keep you safe."

I'm not sure what set me off, the "come along," which seemed to carry an unspoken addendum—"and don't worry your pretty little head"—or the "let me keep you safe."

Truthfully, my reaction had a whole lot more to do with the jangled state of my nerves than being mad at Chase, but he was straight in the line of fire.

"Chase McGregor," I said hotly, "Don't you 'honey' me. I'm perfectly capable of keeping myself safe. I'm not going to the Valley, and that's final."

He backed off and came downstairs with me, but he wasn't happy.

Tori had her laptop set up on the big worktable. Festus was sitting by the machine, directing Tori to enlarge an image as we came into the room. The old cat looked up, and I saw something flicker across his eyes. His head swiveled from me to Chase and back again, but he had the good sense not to ask if anything was wrong. Instead, he said, "Son, you need to look at this. I don't think a werecat killed Fish."

"Why not?" Chase said, moving to stand behind Tori's chair.

They were looking at a picture of the ragged tears on the dead man's chest. I could plainly see five tracks lying equidistant from each other furrowed into the ruined flesh. I'd had micro versions of that same injury on my arms from more than one irate house cat who needed dosing with the all-purpose "pink stuff" from the vet.

"Do you see it?" Festus asked.

Chase nodded. "I do, but what do you think the killer used for a weapon?"

"Hold it," I said. "The non-felines in the room need an explanation."

Festus held up one front paw and extended his claws. "See how flexible my claws are?" he asked, drawing them in and out.

47

I nodded.

"The slashes should be deeper in the middle and more shallow at the beginning and end of the wound," he said. "This looks like the sharp points were jammed in, dragged through the flesh, and pulled straight out."

Leaning forward, I stared at the picture, but I didn't see what he was talking about. "Sorry, you've lost me."

Festus hopped off the table, scoring a three-point landing, and limped over to one of the leather wingback chairs. Without preamble, he gave it a vicious slash with his right front claws.

"Hey!" I said indignantly. "No scratching the furniture!"

"You'll get over it," Festus said. "Look at the damage."

Glaring at him, I approached the chair, bent down, and considered the mark. The track started with a faint scarring of the leather that grew progressively deeper until stuffing spilled out at the center of the gash, which then petered out to a trail of scratches.

"Okay," I said, "I get it. I think you could have found a better way to demonstrate, but I get it. An animal didn't leave those gashes."

"Oh, no," Festus said, "an animal did carve old Fish up, but that animal was a man."

Point well taken.

"So what does this do to your theory about a transient?"

"I'm not ruling anything out," Festus said. "We don't know enough yet."

"How was the wound in the throat made?" I asked.

"You mean the gaping hole where his throat should be?" Festus corrected me.

"Uh, yeah, that."

"I think his throat was cut," Festus said, "and then the killer used something to expand the wound so it would look like the flesh was torn away."

My stomach roiled, but I swallowed hard and forged ahead. "How can you tell?"

"The flesh is torn," Festus said, "but the portion of the aorta that's left is cleanly sliced."

I sat down heavily on the arm of the chair. "Which was done first, the gashes or the cut throat?"

"That I don't know," Festus said, hobbling back to the table and jumping up to resume his post by the laptop. "But I can tell you that dagger wasn't the murder weapon, the blade is too short."

"Then why use it to pin the note to his chest?" Tori asked.

Chase reached down and clicked the trackpad on the laptop. "That's why."

I got up and joined them. The laptop's screen showed a closeup of the dagger's handle emblazoned with a lion's head wearing a crown.

"What is it?" I asked.

"If you read the proper heraldic description," Chase said, "it's 'a lion's head erased Proper crowned with an antique crown.'"

"Huh?"

"It's the central element of the McGregor family crest," Festus said.

Well, there went any lingering doubt about the intended recipient of the message.

"What about the 'cat in the bag' thing?" Tori asked.

Beau, who was standing by the bookshelves holding a large volume, spoke up. "Although I am familiar with the phrase 'let the cat out of the bag,' I have been endeavoring to determine if there are any alternate meanings. According to the good Mr. Webster, the phrase does indicate the revelation of a secret, but I have discovered a secondary definition suggesting the phrase can be taken to mean the inclusion of an outsider into an inner circle of knowledge."

"It means whoever did this knows I'm a werecat," Chase said. "Choosing to kill Fish Pike has to do with his halfling heritage."

The Colonel closed the book and replaced it on the shelf. "Does it?" he asked, as he rejoined the group. "Perhaps the message is regarding Mr. Pike's association with Brenna Sinclair. Surely it is not a coincidence that the chosen victim was so recently in league with a sorceress who violated these premises. Could the message not be taken to indicate that we are about to learn things we do not wish to know?"

Chase frowned. "Maybe. I don't know. I need to talk to Barnaby. I'm going to the Valley."

He looked at me hopefully, and everyone else in the room seemed to be waiting for me to say something. So I did.

"Be careful. Let me know what you find out."

A shadow of irritation crossed Chase's face, but all he said was, "Okay."

Before he and Festus headed off into the stacks, Chase did hug me, but there was no kiss.

"Well," Tori said, as soon as they were out of earshot, "that went well. *Not.*"

"He's got a lot on his mind," I said. "Come on, let's take a walk. Beau, you're in charge until we get back."

The Colonel, who now had several volumes from the shelves, spread out in front of him on the table, nodded absently, then remembered himself and said, "Is it wise for you to be out of doors with a killer abroad in the land?"

I love it when he talks like some old movie script.

"It's broad daylight," I said, "and Tori will be with me. We won't be gone long."

Tori followed me up the steps and out the back door. We went down the alley, crossed the street behind the grocery store, and continued for another block until we came to a bench left over from the bus line that no longer came through Briar Hollow.

"You okay?" Tori asked.

"A dead body on the front doorstep and a fight with my boyfriend all before lunch? I've been better."

"I guess you noticed Myrtle didn't find any of that important enough to show up?"

"I did."

"Are you sure we can't tell Chase what's going on?" Tori asked.

"We're taking enough of a risk that Myrtle will hear us as is, assuming that she's even listening. Was all the stuff delivered?"

"Yes," she said, "it's in my apartment. How are we going to explain all this to Beau and Darby?"

"We're sticking with the ghost story," I said, "because it might be the truth. We could be blowing this whole thing out of proportion."

"God," she said, running her hand through her short, spiky blond hair, "I really, really, *really* hope we are because I'm pretty sure the unsolved murder is gonna keep us plenty busy."

Before you decide that we had turned into evil rogue agents about to go over to the dark side, let me explain. I couldn't go with Chase that day because Tori and I planned to set up a surveillance camera in the espresso bar. We couldn't risk Myrtle finding out what we were doing, which should have been a difficult thing to do.

The fact that it wasn't difficult—and that she didn't seem to be paying the slightest bit of attention to the dead body on our front doorstep—only made our fears more serious.

Chapter Five

Let me break down the timeline of that weekend for you. Myrtle looked at the chessboard the Friday before we found Fish Pike's body Sunday morning. On Saturday, Tori waited until the end of the day when I was closing up to come over and sit down on the tall stool beside the register. When I finished counting the money, she still hadn't said anything.

"Okay," I said, "what's going on? I know that look."

"Myrtle's in Shevington working with Moira, right?"

"Yeah, she is. Why?"

"Take a walk with me."

For the record, Tori and I don't take random walks. Something was definitely up.

"Uh, okay," I said. "Lead off."

I followed her out the front door and across the street to one of the benches on the courthouse lawn. We both sat down, and Tori got right to the point.

"I think Myrtle is lying to us."

"Whoa!" I said. "Where did that come from?!"

"Look, Jinksy," Tori said, "I'm not happy about this either, but her behavior doesn't add up. Hear me out."

"I'm listening," I said. "Is this about the chessboard?"

"That, and a lot of other things."

If anyone else accused Myrtle of lying, I would have ripped their head off, but I trust Tori. She wouldn't get me out of the store to talk unless something had her bothered.

"What things?" I asked.

"For starters, how come Myrtle didn't know Brenna Sinclair was setting up shop right here on the courthouse square?"

At the time, fresh off spotting Brenna casually leaning against a doorframe across the street, I wanted an answer to the same question. Myrtle explained her reaction away by saying that since Brenna had lost her powers, her energy no longer stood out in the crowd—which is what I said to Tori.

"Fine," Tori countered, "that might explain why Myrtle didn't know Brenna was back. But once Myrtle knew, she acted like it was nothing and dragged us off to Shevington. If Myrtle didn't pick up on Brenna being in town, why didn't Myrtle crank up her bandwidth and figure out *why* she was back?"

I had no answer for that one.

Tori pressed on.

"Why didn't Myrtle do something to keep Brenna out of the store? And why couldn't Myrtle sense the Amulet of the Phoenix? Bling that brings back the dead and it doesn't raise a blip on her radar? Come on. That doesn't even make sense."

The "whys" were starting to add up fast.

"The amulet didn't really bring Beau back to life," I offered.

Even I thought the statement sounded lame.

Tori shot me a cocked eyebrow. "Close enough for government work," she said. "Since Myrtle has been teaching me to play chess, she tells me all the time to look for patterns in the game. Well, I see a pattern alright, and it's full of holes. Myrtle is missing things, and I don't like it."

Neither did I.

Lying to Tori is not one of my superpowers. She had no problem reading my growing doubts.

"Yeah," she said, "you see it too, don't you? Kinda throws a monkey wrench in the whole 'didn't know she was there because she had no powers' excuse, doesn't it?"

"But why would Myrtle lie to us?" I protested. "She's on our side. She's one of the good guys."

"I don't know," Tori said, "but that whole water-bug-whisperer routine she went through yesterday seemed like nothing more than an act to get our minds off the real problem. Something is going on with that chessboard, that creepy coffee cup, and whatever it is you think you see at night. Myrtle is supposed to be this big deal ancient Fae, and she has zero information for us. I mean, seriously, Jinksy, what the heck?"

"That's a good question," I said. "They're all good questions, but I don't have any answers."

"You want to know something else that's weird?"

I sighed. "Why not. What is it?"

"Myrtle refuses to play a game with that chess set," Tori said. "And she's been refusing long before we asked her to check it for an onboard spook."

"Does she say why?"

"Oh, yeah," Tori said. "You're gonna love this. She says the pieces confuse her. Do you know how long she's been playing chess?"

"I'm guessing a really long time?"

"She learned with the Lewis chessmen," Tori said like I was supposed to know what that meant.

"Okay. And that is important why?"

"The Lewis chessmen were made around 1200," Tori said.

"She's been playing 815 years, but she can't figure out the pieces on a novelty board?"

Tori was right. We had a problem. A big one.

Myrtle is the aos si, part of a race of beings known as the Tuatha Dé Danann that dwell in the Otherworld, which runs parallel to our world. She came with Barnaby's original group but took a shortcut—under the Atlantic Ocean not over it. Myrtle tends to think outside the box like that.

The only person I've ever met who radiates anything near the kind of power Myrtle possesses is Moira. They work closely together. In her way Moira is just as much of a knockout, but the women paint a study in contrasts—willowy, golden Myrtle beside sturdy, dark Moira.

If we couldn't trust Myrtle, who else might be lying to us?

"We have to get some answers, Jinx," Tori said. "We can't do the things we're being asked to do if we don't trust the people around us."

Tori was right. But that warm Saturday afternoon, sitting on the courthouse lawn looking across the street at the shop, we had no way of knowing where the search for those answers was about to lead us—right beneath our own home and into the regimental rows of shelves stretching into the blackest corners of the basement.

Before we went back inside, Tori and I agreed to keep everything we'd talked about between us. She ordered a night surveillance camera, and we decided to set it up the next day. For all practical purposes, we wouldn't be lying when we described what we were doing to the others as a good old-fashioned ghost hunt. Tori intended to try a series of EVPs in the espresso bar that night for show.

EVP stands for "electronic voice phenomenon." You hold out a recorder and talk to thin air, asking if any spirits who might be there would like to speak with you. Then you play the recording back and listen for responses. She wasn't expecting to get any results, but she also didn't want to leave any stone unturned. Plus, the EVPs were a great set-up for the camera installation.

What we couldn't tell anyone yet was that if we proved the chessboard was haunted, we would also prove Myrtle was lying. What would we do with that explosive information? We didn't have a clue.

Is it any wonder that I couldn't sleep that night?

Usually on a Saturday evening, Chase and I do something together, but he was up in the mountains checking out some hikers who were getting too close to one of the Shevington entrances. It was doubtful humans could get through the warding spells, or would even know to try, but the Valley hadn't remained hidden for centuries based on shoddy security.

Sometime around midnight, I wandered downstairs to the basement to work out. No, not like in a gym. A magic workout. My practice focused on gaining control of my powers preparatory to extending their reach and accuracy.

Myrtle kept trotting objects out of the archives for me to read with my psychometry. She always knew the right answers, which I hit about 90% of the time. But my telekinesis—moving things with my mind—and channeling energy needed work.

We set up a sort of target range for both, but in different locations. Telekinesis proved to be an indoor sport. Darby found a random assortment of objects of varying sizes and weights and lined them up on a shelf. He marked off distances for me with lines on the floor. I picked something on the shelf and concentrated on making it come to me in a straight line before sending it back to the shelf. My accuracy improved steadily, and I discovered that working on telekinesis calmed me. To get the power to work, I had to direct my thoughts to a quiet place in my mind and stay there.

Channeling energy, which you can read as "hurling energy bolts," required more room and fewer flammable objects nearby. That particular trick we work on in the big meadow up in the Valley. Unlike telekinesis, channeling energy depletes me. After half an hour, I'm ready to eat everything in sight and go down for a long nap.

That night, Beau came out of his bachelor pad and watched me levitate an old oil lamp off the shelf and bring it toward me, settling it perfectly on the floor.

"Brava!" he said, clapping his hands. "You have expanded your range to fifteen feet!"

I dropped a sort of mock curtsy and said, "Thank you, kind sir."

"May I see an example of your abilities with energy?"

"Oh, I don't know, Beau," I said reluctantly. "I might burn the place down."

"That is not at all what I have heard," he said. "Why do you not light the lamp now that you have moved it within reach?"

Yes, I admit it. I am the kind of gal who responds well to dares and Beau knows it.

Looking down at the lantern, and narrowing my vision to the wick, I called up that small, bright spark I've discovered dwells deep in my being. I envisioned turning the spark into a compact, perfectly formed flame. As I concentrated, the fire materialized a few inches over my palm. Very gently, I blew it toward the lamp and watched as it floated downward settling itself on the wick, which caught and glowed brightly.

"Oh, my God, Beau," I whispered. "I did it!"

The Colonel came over to me, leaned down and picked up the lamp. He held it aloft in his left hand. "You have, my dear, created a light into the darkness," he announced with mock solemnity.

"I don't know about that," I laughed, "but I do know I need to sit down. That was a lot harder than it looked."

Beau held out his right arm. I took it and allowed him to escort me gallantly to one of the chairs by the fireplace.

"What are you doing up this late?" I asked.

He sat in the chair opposite me and crossed his legs. "I have been reading a most disturbing tome."

"Really?" I said, thinking he must have been catching up on the war that took his life. "What upset you about it?"

"The 1919 World Series," Beau replied, sounding genuinely aggrieved.

Trying to be as sympathetic as I could over a 96-year-old scandal, I intoned mournfully, "Say it ain't so, Joe."

Beau's face lit up. "You are aware of Shoeless Joe Jackson and the shocking betrayal of the national pastime in the name of filthy lucre?"

"Not exactly," I admitted. "I just saw *Eight Men Out.*"

"Ah, I understand," Beau nodded. "The motion picture made in 1988. It is on Miss Tori's list of baseball films we are to view, but we have not yet reached that title."

"What did you two watch last night?"

"A rather shocking presentation entitled *Bull Durham*," Beau replied, coloring slightly. "Mr. Costner is quite forward with his language, but I confess to finding Miss Sarandon oddly beguiling."

I mentally ran through the monologue from the "I believe" scene in the movie and burst out laughing.

Still blushing, Beau looked uncertain for a minute, and then grinned. "The 21st century truly is quite remarkable in its candor. Miss Tori continues to exhort me to 'loosen up,' which would appear to be necessary as a strategy for avoiding cardiac failure."

Can you guys appreciate why I love Beau Longworth so much? He's kind, insightful, understanding, unswervingly loyal—and starting to display a real sense of humor. His newfound baseball obsession came as a surprise until I learned the sport became popular because of the Civil War. Beau heard about the new game being played by northern regiments before his death, so when Tori showed him *Field of Dreams* Beau's curiosity was piqued.

As a bona fide 19th century gentleman scholar Beau knows how to research. Half a dozen baseball movies and a stack of books later, he's picked his team of choice—the Red Sox, because he couldn't bring himself to support a team called the Yankees—and he started watching clips on YouTube. He's catching on to the 21st century extremely well, but those moments when he runs smack into the culture shock wall are downright adorable.

I would have taken Beau for more of a Julia Roberts kind of guy than Susan Sarandon though. I decided for the time being he didn't need to know about her role in *Rocky Horror*.

Having Beau in corporeal form did present a few initial problems. Myrtle solved the matter of living quarters by creating a furnished bachelor pad to the right of the stairs down in the basement.

Tori instantly ordered a new set of clothes for him on Amazon so they could at least go out together and shop without Beau looking like a Civil War reenactor. The shopping wound up being high comedy. Beau came back laden with bags, ranting about the "shocking cost of daily necessities and the abhorrent state of taxation" in the United States version 2015.

In private, Tori told me they spent a total of $350, a sum that almost sent Beau into a fit of apoplexy.

"The worst part was trying to find him a dip pen and ink," she said. "He's going to have to get that stuff online from now on. I am not taking him into that cute little stationery store in the mall again."

"Why not?"

"Let's say the card rack was too much for him," she

grinned. "He can't fathom our 'oddly incongruent sentimentality directly adjacent to lewd innuendo.'"

"You want to run that by me in English?"

"Hallmark cards versus birthday cards with bare-chested men."

That's when she launched the "loosen up" campaign that seemed to be bearing fruit judging from the grin Beau shot me over *Bull Durham*.

While we were talking, Darby hurtled past us on his new yellow bicycle. He's Myrtle's library nerd on call and works for hours down in the archives cataloging God knows what.

"The lad is certainly enjoying his new mode of conveyance," Beau said. "I do wish, however, that he would employ the attached signaling device."

He meant the bell, which would have helped enormously but I couldn't complain. Darby's two-wheeled hot rod status originated with one of my bright ideas.

It takes an hour to walk from the lair to The Valley's portal. I'm all for getting in your cardio, but by the third or fourth forced hike, I suggested to Tori that we bring our bikes downstairs.

When we did, Darby's eyes went round with amazement.

"Oh, please, Mistress," he pleaded, "may I have a horse with wheels for feet?"

After a couple of weeks of artful wheedling, Tori caved and drove over to Wally World. She came back with a kid's bike complete with a bell and streamers on the handlebars.

"Isn't that a girl's bike?" I asked under my breath.

"Technically," Tori replied, "but that's the one he wanted."

The one *he* wanted?

"Darby went with you?" I asked. "You took him into Wally World? Have you lost your mind?"

"Compared to most of the Walmartians, Darby looks completely normal," she said. "Besides, he was in invisible mode and I was wearing my Bluetooth, so it didn't look like I was talking to myself."

That made me feel better. "So why did he pick this one?"

"Because it's yellow," she said, smiling. "He said it's the color of the sun when it laughs."

That's Darby—a loveable blend of aged wisdom and youthful innocence. That first day, he rode his new bike in happy circles looking as excited as any kid on Christmas morning.

"Well, he's certainly got the hang of it already," I said.

"He does," Tori observed dryly, "but I'm not sure if that's a good thing or a bad thing."

Her skepticism was well-founded. The basement immediately became a potential hit-and-run zone.

Beau and I watched Darby careening by, the basket on his bike filled with books.

"Does he ever not work?" I asked Beau.

"He and I both appear to share nocturnal habits."

It had never occurred to me to ask before. "You don't need sleep?"

"No," he said, "that aspect of life was not returned to me."

"So what do you do down here at night besides read about baseball?"

"I have begun to keep a journal again," he said, "a kind of companionship denied to me in my post-mortem existence. You, on the other hand, are not quite so given to nocturnal wanderings. Is there something weighing on your mind, my dear? I would be quite happy to serve as a sounding board should you need one."

I think of Beau as a second father. I wanted to talk to him about the cup, the chessboard, and Myrtle, but I couldn't take the risk. We're in Myrtle's home. She can hear everything in the fairy mound.

"I'm fine," I said, smiling at Beau. "I just can't sleep."

"Well, then," he answered genially, "I shall keep you company until Morpheus chooses to grace you with his presence."

The Greek god of dreams didn't put in an appearance until 3 in the morning.

That's when I said goodnight to Beau and stumbled off to bed, shoving my cats—Zeke, Yule, Xavier, and Winston—out of the way to make room for myself on the queen-sized bed.

It was sometime after 9 o'clock the next morning when I stepped outside to find Chase photographing Fish Pike's body. Those six hours were the last decent sleep I would get for several days.

Chapter Six

All of that explained why I couldn't or wouldn't go to The Valley with Chase and Festus. After our talk on the old bus-stop bench, Tori and I went back to the store and got to work setting up the surveillance camera. We decided to concentrate on the chessboard since it displayed the highest level of activity.

The video feed went directly to Tori's laptop. She positioned me on a ladder to angle the camera at the board while she learned the controls to zoom and record. When everything was arranged to her satisfaction, Tori stretched out for a nap since she planned to stay up late watching the screen.

I desperately needed some normal time after being awake half the night, discovering Fish Pike's body, and quarreling with Chase. He and Festus weren't back yet—or if they were, Chase hadn't called me.

I went upstairs to zone out with Netflix. I fell asleep on the couch and was still there at 2 a.m. when furious knocking awakened me. I stumbled to the door and found Tori standing in her pajamas jumping up and down with excitement.

"What?" I said, rubbing the sleep out of my eyes. "What's wrong? What happened?"

"You have to come downstairs and see what I recorded," she said breathlessly. "You're not going to believe it."

Still half awake, I followed her downstairs and into her apartment. I struggled to focus on the laptop screen as she played the video. The reversed black and white night vision image started out showing nothing but the chessboard sitting on the table with all of the pieces arranged in their correct places. Then, something that looked like a pile of sticks settled in front of the picture and stayed there for several seconds. That woke me up.

"What the heck is that?" I asked.

"I have no idea," Tori said. "I've been staring at that damn board ever since I woke up from my nap. I was getting sleepy again, so I decided to take a shower. When I came back out and looked at the feed, that's what I saw."

She pointed at the laptop. The sticks were gone, replaced by the stationary image of the board—with all the major pieces moved aside and the pawns arranged in a pattern.

"Play it again," I said.

This time, I watched the whole thing closely. The strange bundle of sticks came down in front of the lens, stayed there for about two minutes, and then seemed to draw itself away to reveal the reconfigured chessboard. There was only one, inescapable conclusion. Someone or some *thing* watched us install the camera, waited for Tori's attention to be diverted, covered up the lens, moved the chess pieces, and then uncovered the camera.

That wasn't the work of a residual haunting.

We definitely had an uninvited guest no matter what Myrtle said.

After the third time through the video, Tori suggested we go out to the espresso bar and have a look around for ourselves.

I felt the hair on the back of my neck stand up. The reaction surprised me. You'd think after finding witchy powers and doing battle with an evil sorceress a gal might not be scared of what goes bump in the night.

You'd be wrong.

My anxiety DEFCON level hovered somewhere between "convict-with-a-hook campfire story" and "I am *so* out of here."

While I scrambled to come up with a plausible reason why we should lock the door and wait for the sun to come up, Tori gave me *the look*.

"I am not going out there by myself," she said, making it clear the subject was not up for debate.

Great. The "two cowards are braver than one" theory.

Which didn't stop me from saying, with great maturity, "Fine, but you're going first."

Tori leaves a night light plugged in beside her front door. A sea of distorted black shadows stretched between that weak pool of light and the unearthly glow of the streetlights at the front windows. The inventory and furnishings that looked innocent by light of day loomed ominously around us.

"What if that roach came back?" I hissed in Tori's ear, making her jump.

She hesitated for a fraction of a second before hissing back, "There's two of us. We can take a cockroach."

I wasn't so sure about that.

We crept along the wall, the floorboards creaking under our feet. The store is not a great location for a stealth op. If the bogeyman—or Jason with the hockey mask—was waiting for us in the espresso bar, they knew we were coming.

The darkness magnified the sound of Tori's hand brushing along the wall searching for the switch. When she found it and flooded the espresso bar with light, we saw nothing but the usual collection of tables and chairs.

No looming monsters, and even better, no cockroaches.

"Well, okay then," Tori said, "anti-climax?"

"I'm good with anti-climax," I said, glancing around nervously. "What are we looking for anyway?"

"How should I know?"

Feeling braver with the lights on, we walked over to the table and looked down at the chessboard. Other than the odd arrangement of the pieces, there was nothing strange about it. Even with my nerves on high alert, I couldn't help but admire the golden wood edging the squares and the elegant lines of the pieces.

The rest of the place looked completely undisturbed. Out of the corner of my eye, I noticed an open crossword puzzle book. The pencil lay angled across the page as if someone had just put it down and walked away.

Tori took out her phone and snapped a picture of the chessboard.

"That's a good idea," I said, "maybe we can figure out if there's a pattern to the way the pieces are being moved."

"Way ahead of you on that one, Jinksy," Tori said, handing me the phone.

I thumbed through about a week's worth of pictures. Each one showed a different arrangement of pawns. As I looked at them, an idea occurred to me.

"This is going to sound a little crazy," I said, "but do you think there's any chance the pawns are supposed to be music notes?"

"I wondered the same thing," Tori said.

Still holding the phone, I compared the picture on the screen with the current position of the chess pieces.

"Maybe we're too literal," I suggested. "If the ghost is trying to create music, the only pieces that look like notes are the pawns."

As bona fide band nerds, we can read music, but finding a

possible meeting point between chess notation and a musical score felt more like code breaking.

A chessboard is an 8 x 8 grid. The columns are labeled "a" through "h" from left to right. The rows are 1 to 8 from "bottom" to top. Since white moves first, the "bottom" is the white side of the board.

In music, you have five lines and four spaces. At least in treble clef, the lines going from the bottom to the top are E, G, B, D, F and the spaces are F, A, C, E.

Whoever designed the musical chessboard put a unique twist on both schemes. Our board has numbered rows, but the columns are marked C, D, E, F, G, A, B, C—the C scale.

When I noticed that detail for the first time, the use of the scale seemed like another clever way to incorporate music into the board's theme. The letters and numbers would never work to annotate chess moves, but maybe that wasn't their intended purpose.

We debated for a few minutes about how you could interpret the position of the pieces musically but drew a blank.

"Could they be chords?" Tori asked.

"I guess," I said, "but how can a single chord send a message? And if the pieces were supposed to be chords, wouldn't the sharps and flats be on the board too?"

The board's designer used the sharp sign for the rooks and the flat for the bishops. Our "ghost" had four of each to work with, but we never found those pieces on the board.

With no warning, Tori snapped her fingers. The sound echoed in the silent store. "Try your psychometry on the board right now!" she said. "If this is music, maybe you'll hear the melody."

"Uh, now?" I asked weakly.

"Can you think of a better time?"

"In the morning?"

"You are not serious!" Tori said. "You're afraid to touch this thing? What kind of badass witch are you?"

"The kind who was sound asleep in her bed and not thinking about ghosts until a crazy woman woke her up."

That got me *the look* again.

For the record, Tori learned *the look* from her mother. No one argues with Gemma.

"Okay," I said, reaching to lay both hands on the chessboard, "here goes nothing."

Except I didn't get *nothing*.

I found myself standing at the base of a cube, rooted in place under the sheer weight of the hellish dissonance rising around me. Rows of prison cells towered over my head. In each one, a trapped song strained to break rusty chains, their lyrics swirling into a mismatched cacophony of words and phrases. In the heart of it all, a single voice screamed to be released, undulating up and down the notes of a tortured minor scale. Clamping my hands over my ears, I struggled to form a single thought, "Get me out of here."

Tori heard me.

Her hands pulled mine away from the polished wood as her voice dragged me back toward our normal reality. "Jinx! It's over! Look at me!"

With effort, my eyes focused on her face.

"Are you okay?" she asked.

I nodded.

"What happened? What did you see?"

I tried to explain, but the words stumbled and fell out of my mouth in a confused babble. Off to my left, a door opened, and the sound of boot heels rapidly crossed the wood floor.

Beau.

"Miss Jinx," he said, scanning my face with anxious eyes, "what has happened?"

I tried to answer, opening and closing my mouth like a fish

out of water. Tears filled my eyes. I shook my head and Tori stepped in.

"Jinx tried to get a reading on the haunted chessboard," she explained. "She touched it, and then suddenly her voice was in my head, telling me to get her out of there."

"Jinx," Beau commanded quietly, "look at me."

I swiveled my head in his direction.

"You must calm yourself," he said. "You are quite safe here with Tori and me. Now breathe deeply and tell us what you saw."

Drawing in a shaky breath, I willed myself to settle down.

"Good," Beau prodded. "Now another."

On the third breath, he said, "Better?"

"Yes," I whispered. "I'm sorry."

Tori squeezed my hands. "You don't need to apologize. Whatever you saw in there must have scared the hell out of you. Can you tell us now?"

"I don't think it's just one ghost," I said. "It's like a prison in there. The whole chessboard is full of spirits. They . . . they're screaming."

Beau and Tori exchanged a look.

"What?" I said.

"Late this afternoon I asked Miss Tori if she knew why you were so troubled last evening," Beau said. "We shared a walk around the square during which she confessed to me her misapprehensions regarding Myrtle's handling of recent events."

"I'm sorry," Tori said, "but he's kind of an expert in the ghost department. I was going to tell you in the morning."

"No," I said, my voice still weak, "it's good he knows. There's no question now. She's lying about the chessboard."

"Do not be so hasty," Beau said. "Why does your mind immediately go to an accusation of untruth?"

"There's no way that a being as powerful as Myrtle

couldn't detect whatever is living in that thing," I said, looking at the board with a mixture of fear and horror.

"Why not?" Beau asked reasonably. "All things fade with the passage of time, Miss Jinx. Is it completely out of the realm of possibility that Myrtle in truth *cannot* detect what resides in the chess set?"

Tori said what I was thinking. "If that's true, then we have a much bigger problem on our hands."

"Perhaps until we have a better understanding of its significance, the chess set should be removed from exposure to the public," Beau suggested.

"Good idea," Tori said. "But what do we do with it?"

"Miss Jinx, do you have an appointment with Barnaby in the morning?" Beau asked.

"Not exactly," I said. "I'm taking my mom up to the Valley to see Aunt Fiona, but now that Fish has turned up dead on our doorstep, I'm planning to find Barnaby and get his take on all this."

Tori frowned. "Chase isn't back?"

"Your guess is as good as mine," I said.

"Well," Tori said, "okay then."

Beau had the good grace to ignore the entire exchange. "Perhaps," he said smoothly, "if Barnaby could examine the chess set, he might discover its true nature."

Tori nixed that plan fast.

"That's a bad idea," she said. "This thing has to be a magical artifact. You can't take it to the Valley. It's not safe."

After some back and forth, we decided to move the board into the storeroom for the time being. I'd fill Barnaby in on everything that had happened with the gameboard and we'd take his advice.

That's when the problem got a whole lot more complicated.

Tori tried to pick up the chessboard. It wouldn't budge. I

wasn't about to touch that thing again, so Beau offered to help. Even working together, they weren't able to lift the board. It wasn't going anywhere. They couldn't even pry the individual pieces loose.

"I fear," Beau said, "that we have made a tactical error."

"Huh?"

Beau put his finger to his lips and shook his head. He pointed toward Tori's apartment and motioned for us to follow. Once we were inside, Beau closed the door, put his ear against it for a minute, and then said softly, "We should not have had that conversation in the presence of the chessboard."

"Why not?" I asked.

Sometimes Tori catches on a lot faster than I do.

"Because," she said, "it was listening."

Chapter Seven

The sound of the door closing upstairs echoed through the empty store. The little witch waited, letting long moments pass until she felt secure enough to peel herself off the cup, breathe deeply, and reinflate. As always, the process disappointed her. Over and over again she tried to take in the least amount of air as possible, hoping to make the best of her situation and at least lose weight. Instead, parts of her body stayed stubbornly flat until she gave up and sucked in more air. It was just her rotten luck. Even living as a cursed illustration on the side of a coffee cup, she couldn't be thin.

Tori setting up that camera complicated things, especially now that there was a dead body to report. The little witch thought and thought about her problem, and came up with the plan of putting her broom over the lens long enough to move the chess pieces and send today's message. She even waited until she heard the shower come on in the micro apartment so she wouldn't get caught.

Most of the plan worked, but they were too smart. After all these weeks hiding in the store and watching them, she should have known. Part of her wanted to be discovered, to come right off the side of that cup and introduce herself. To say out loud for the first time, "My name is Glory Green, and I don't want to have to do this anymore."

Glory *Green*.

Her name gave that awful man the idea for her punishment.

How Glory wished she'd never seen his business card.

"Mr. I. Chesterfield, Antique Acquisitions. No request denied."

But that wasn't really her fault because Miss Shania Moonbeam gave Glory the card in the first place.

Glory relied on Miss Shania's psychic advice for years and thought she could confide in her. Glory told Miss Shania the truth. She didn't want to be a researcher at the state archives anymore.

Which was good, since that uppity Leroy Percy informed Glory that her job was "in transition," right along with the files.

Glory didn't care if "IT" was supposed to stand for "information technology."

When she went to school "i" and "t" spelled "it," and that's all Leroy Percy was, an "it"—and a suspicious "it" at that.

Glory didn't know what "World of Warcraft" was, but she didn't like the sound of the pastime one bit. Leroy was always talking about "missions" and killing people.

Well, Glory watched *Homeland*. She'd learned a thing or two from Carrie. Leroy was some kind of terrorist or something. He wanted to get rid of Glory because she knew where all the real records were, the ones printed on paper like they were supposed to be.

As far as Glory was concerned, Leroy Percy could just engineer the downfall of the government. Her taxes were too high anyway and nobody up in Washington, D.C. gave a flip about people like her. Glory had a bigger goal in mind. She was finally going after her dream—to follow in the footsteps of the King himself and take to the Vegas stage.

Glory wanted to be a singer like Elvis Presley.

That's why she confessed to Miss Shania because there was one teensy problem with her plan. Glory couldn't sing.

Miss Shania listened, nodding sympathetically, and said all Glory needed was a "talisman." Miss Shania knew a man, Mr. Irenaeus Chesterfield, who could get Glory a lock of Elvis's hair that would make her sing just like the King.

Very earnestly, Glory asked Miss Shania if she should trust a man named "Irene," so that was the first thing they had to get cleared up.

All the way to the shop, Glory practiced saying Mr. Chesterfield's name the right way. "Ear-ren-a-us."

It was an awfully silly name, but then Glory had a cousin named Little Bighorn Custer in honor of that general the Indians killed, so she wasn't one to judge.

Anyway, when she got to the shop, she said the name the right way and explained everything to Mr. Chesterfield.

She thought her heart would burst in her chest from excitement when he said he knew how to get the lock of hair, and that she should come back the next day.

Glory stayed up all that night dreaming dreams—and doing some worrying.

Sitting cross-legged on the floor of her retro-chic apartment that she'd created by pausing *Mad Men* episodes and taking notes on the decor, Glory leafed through her Elvis memorial scrapbooks. She hoped no one would expect her to do those karate moves. She did have a touch of sciatica from a failed attempt at Zumba, and she wasn't sure she had the hips for glittery jumpsuits.

But Glory had faith. All that would get worked out once she had her new voice.

People at work told her that she was too young to like "old" things, but Glory put them right in their place.

"The average age of an Elvis Facebook fan is 35," she said, countering her critics with cold, hard facts.

Of course, Glory didn't actually have a Facebook account, and she was only 33, but those were irrelevant details.

Besides, the 1960s weren't such a long time ago. Everyone then was so much more elegant than people were in the Eighties. Glory had done an extensive comparison of big hair from both decades. There was no doubt in her mind that women in the Sixties were *much* more expert in the use of hairspray.

Glory fell asleep that night watching *Frankie and Johnny*—the real one from 1966, with Elvis and Donna Douglas, not the other one with Al Pacino and Michelle Pfeiffer. Glory just *loved* Donna Douglas, whose signature role was Ellie Mae Clampett on *The Beverly Hillbillies*. It broke Glory's heart to think that same awful cancer took Donna Douglas *and* Patrick Swayze.

The next morning, Glory woke up bright and early and set out for Mr. Chesterfield's store with all the money from her annual bonus in cash in her pocket. He hadn't mentioned a price, but really, how much could one lock of hair cost?

In case it was expensive, Glory had taken the precaution of putting off going to the Dairy Queen to get her usual Wednesday night blizzard.

So imagine her shock when Mr. Chesterfield said he wanted $10,000.

Glory almost dropped dead right there at the counter.

That's when a kind of desperation came over her like she was watching her last chance to be something special disappear right in front of her eyes.

Without stopping to think what she was doing, she snatched up that envelope with the King's hair and dashed for the door. She would have made it too, but then she tripped over some big old ugly urn thing made of something called "alabaster."

As she lay there on the floor trying to get her breath, she saw Mr. Chesterfield looking at her with cold eyes. He put out one hand and all of a sudden Glory couldn't breathe. Then he said the oddest thing. "Glory *Green*, is it? Green, my dear, is the color of greed, and a most fitting shade for your punishment."

Everything around started to get bigger and bigger. Her skin began to crawl, and when Glory looked down, her pretty spring dress was gone. She was wearing some kind of awful black robe, and her hands had gone green.

Glory remembered how Mr. Chesterfield loomed over her as she begged and tried to apologize.

He laughed, a sound so hideous she scrambled backward until she ran into a cabinet with a glass front. That's when Glory saw herself. She looked like the wicked witch from *The Wizard of Oz*—and she knew how that story turned out.

"Are you going to throw water on me and make me melt?" she'd asked in a trembling voice.

It came out like the squeaking of a terrified mouse.

"Oh, no, my dear," Chesterfield said, reaching for her with his massive hand. He caught the back of her robe and dangled her in front of his face like a bug he'd plucked off the floor.

"I am going to put you someplace nice and safe until I have a use for you. Perhaps when you've had an opportunity to witness more of my dealings, you'll realize that offending me in even the slightest regard is not in your best interest."

He plastered her on the side of a coffee cup and set her up on a dusty shelf where she could see the whole store, and there she sat for a year, watching Mr. Chesterfield conduct his business, growing more terrified by the day.

Glory thought the man must be in league with the devil himself because Chesterfield could whisper strange words, move his hands and make things happen. He bought and sold artifacts with all kinds of powers, and he kept company with people who frightened Glory even more than Chesterfield himself.

Like that red-headed woman named Brenna Sinclair, who had wanted so much to get inside this store and hurt Jinx and Tori because of something their families did. Glory didn't really understand what that was all about, but she knew a blood feud when she saw one. Anger and jealousy filled that Brenna woman, and she wasn't going to let go until she ruined these people.

But it was because of Brenna that Mr. Chesterfield finally took Glory down off the shelf, wiping away the dust on her body and peeling her off the cup.

"Take deep breaths," he instructed, which she did, blowing herself right back up like a balloon.

"Very good," he said. "Now, are you prepared to be a good little witch?"

"What are you going to do to me?" Glory asked, her voice rough from a year of disuse.

"I have a job for you in the line of espionage," Chesterfield said, peering down at her malevolently, "and if you do exactly what I tell you to do, I might be persuaded to restore you to your former self and set you free. I trust I will not have to convince you to accept my instructions?"

Glory felt cold dread snake out through her veins, but she couldn't turn down a chance to win her freedom.

"No, sir, Mr. Chesterfield," she'd said dutifully. "I'll do anything you want."

What he wanted brought her to this store and put her in a position to kind of "meet" all these people even though they had no idea she was alive. And now she was in the most horrible fix.

Glory liked them all so much. The store felt more like a home than any place she had been since her Mama died.

Witch on First

True, Glory spent most of her time sitting up on a shelf, but the people Glory listened to now weren't scary; they were interesting and kind. Watching them showed her that good magic existed.

Which only made her feel worse, because she was taking orders from a very bad man.

What was she ever going to do?

Time and time again, Glory tried to work up the courage to step off the cup and introduce herself, but she'd never been able to do it. She had to send her reports to Mr. Chesterfield every day, or he would be furious. Now they were suspicious about the chessboard. Pretty soon, they'd probably catch her too.

Glory gulped as an awful idea came into her mind.

What if they squashed her like a bug or sent her levitating out the back door like that cockroach?

Glory would never survive outside at three inches tall. Something would eat her and . . . oh . . . she just could *not* think about that.

She had to be like her other hero, Scarlett O'Hara. Glory would have to think about all of that tomorrow. The middle of the night was the only time she could move around the store freely and she wasn't going to waste one minute of it worrying, especially if her days were numbered.

Climbing on her broom, Glory flew to the shelf by the front window where the old Philco radio sat. When she first came to the store, she spent three nights working to get the knobs to turn, but now Glory had the volume down as low as it would go and the dial set to pull in a classic rock n' roll station.

She threw her weight against the power knob, and sat down with her back to the speaker, dangling her legs over the edge of the shelf and absentmindedly swinging her feet back and forth.

As she gazed out over the deserted courthouse square, Elvis began to sing "Love Me Tender."

"Oh, Elvis," Glory whispered, "if you're out there listening, please tell me what to do, 'cause I'm sitting right here in Heartbreak Hotel, and I just don't know how to check out."

Chapter Eight

Great. Just freaking great. We couldn't talk freely in the store because Myrtle might be listening and now the damned chessboard was eavesdropping too. After we decided there was nothing more we could do that night, Tori and I went upstairs. She wasn't all that thrilled with the idea of sleeping downstairs, and I knew my cats would be demanding their breakfast in a couple of hours.

The boys were ecstatic to see "Aunt Tori" and happily settled on the couch with her in a big cuddle pile, which is where I had been sleeping until someone woke me up to go downstairs and play with *The Little Chessboard of Horrors*. In theory, Tori and I were both too wired to sleep, but five minutes after she sat down, she and the cats were snoring, and I was wide awake.

The day before when Tori first suggested that we might not be able to trust Myrtle, the idea bothered me so much I was up at midnight working off magical steam. I privately held out hope that there was a perfectly reasonable explanation for Myrtle's behavior. I had no idea what that reason might be, but denial isn't based on logic or facts.

Now Beau had raised the possibility that there might be something wrong with the aos si. That took me to such a deep level of worry I didn't know what to do with it. Myrtle trained the witches in our family. She's our protector, teacher, and friend. What would we do if . . .

My mind slammed on the brakes.

I got up to make tea, casting an annoyed look at my best friend and traitor tomcats on the couch. If I was up in the middle of the night worrying myself half to death, why should they be getting their beauty rest?

The more annoyed and worried I became, the more "innocent" noise I tried to make to get Tori to wake up and worry with me.

I banged the kettle on the stove, slammed the cabinet door, and clanked my spoon against the side of my cup.

Nothing.

For a brief moment of insanity, I considered using the can opener, which would have snapped the cats into instant consciousness, but I stopped myself.

Do things with cats once, and they think it's the new routine. Nothing was worth risking 3 a.m. becoming the new breakfast hour.

Instead, I took my tea and sat in the big wingback chair by the front window and watched the sun come up over the square. When the cats were ready to eat, I had already showered and dressed. I was on my second cup of coffee when Tori blinked into consciousness.

"Is there more of that?" she mumbled.

"There are more little plastic cups."

"Right. Plastic cup. Blue button. Coffee," she rattled off as she shuffled to the kitchen.

I heard the machine come to life and then Tori came back clutching a mug in both hands. "Why are you so awake?" she asked with a note of accusation in her voice.

"Oh, I don't know," I said sarcastically. "Maybe because I have to take my mother to The Valley to reunite with her older sister who faked her death—the aunt my Mom always called "crazy"—and while I'm there, I have to talk to Barnaby about the demonic chessboard, the body on our front sidewalk, and Chase *still* hasn't gotten in touch with me."

"Whoa," Tori said, "sorry I asked."

Sighing, I ran my hand through my hair. "I'm sorry I snapped. This is all getting to be too much."

"I hear you," Tori said. "Just go and handle it all. Take as long as you like. I've got things here to do."

"We really should be back by noon," I said. "There's a potluck at the Lodge tonight and Mom has to go with Dad. She's making the green bean thing with the onions."

Tori's face brightened. "Oh! Is she bringing some over for us?"

Grimacing, I said, "You know that casserole is funeral food?"

"All casseroles are funeral food," Tori said. "I wish she'd make the one with the chicken and potato chips again."

Clearly, both her brain and her stomach were kicking in.

"You going to be okay here today while I'm gone?" I asked.

"I'll be fine," she assured me. "I have Beau and Darby if I need any help."

"Okay," I said, standing up to head downstairs. "You coming?"

"Yeah," Tori replied, getting to her feet. "I'll bring the mug back."

We walked down together and went straight to the chessboard. The pieces were no longer arranged as they had been last night. Now all the men were lined up, ready to do battle. I started to say something and then thought better of it. Motioning Tori to follow me, we went into the storeroom.

"I don't want to talk in front of that thing," I said.

"Me either."

"Keep an eye on it, okay?"

"Don't you worry about that," she said. "I couldn't *not* watch that thing if I wanted to."

Scampering feet sounded on the shelf that runs along the back wall. Rodney emerged, stood up on his hind legs and gave us a good morning wave.

"Hey, Rodney," Tori said. "What's shaking?"

The sleek black and white rat trotted along the edge of the shelf, jumped effortlessly onto the back of the loveseat, and descended Tori's arm. He looked at her coffee cup and raised his whiskery eyebrows.

"You want some coffee?" Tori asked.

Rodney nodded his head vigorously.

"The last time I let you have coffee you ran on your wheel for four hours."

The rat fixed her with an appealing look.

"Okay, fine. But one rat-sized cup and no more," she said, opening the drawer of the end table and taking out a china cup from a doll's set. She carefully poured coffee from her cup into the tiny receptacle and set it on the table.

"It's not too hot to drink," she said, "but don't slurp."

I swear to you the look Rodney shot her said as plain as the world, "I do *not* slurp."

Tori read the expression as clearly as I did. "Fine, fine. You don't slurp."

Mollified, Rodney held his nose over the coffee, sniffing appreciatively, then began to lap up the dark liquid.

"I don't think that's good for him," I belatedly pointed out.

"It's probably not good for us either," Tori said, "but that doesn't stop us."

"Enabler."

"Guilty."

Leaving them with their coffee, I started for the basement. As I came around the corner from the storeroom, Mom walked in the back door. Instead of a "good morning," she started our day together with, "What have you learned about Fish Pike's murder?"

I called Mom the day before in between the covert conversation on the bus bench with Tori and setting up the surveillance camera. I told her about Fish and warned her to be extra careful. She still didn't know that Festus had been carrying a torch for her all these years, so I wasn't exactly forthcoming about the "werecats in love" angle of the whole situation.

She told me Dad was at the river trying out new equipment he'd bought at the convention in Houston, but promised to call Gemma to come over and stay with her just in case.

"We don't really know anything so far," I said, opening the door to the basement. "While you're talking to Aunt Fiona, I'm going to find Barnaby and discuss it with him."

Mom paused halfway over the threshold. "None of you have been to the Valley yet?"

As evenly as I could manage, I replied, "Chase went yesterday, but I don't know if he's back or not."

Her mother radar instantly surged to high alert. "Have the two of you had a fight?"

"It's more complicated than that," I hedged. "Can we please talk about this later?"

We were halfway down the stairs by this time and thankfully an unexpected savior intervened—Festus.

"Would you two dames get the lead out?" he groused. "I want to be back from the Valley before Chase realizes I'm gone."

Well, okay then, so that answered the question about channels of communication with my boyfriend, which ticked me off enough that I was sharper with Festus than I needed to be. "Who says you're going with us, hairball?"

"Norma Jean Hamilton!" Mom said, outraged. "You apologize to Festus this instant."

As any Southern child will tell you, when your mama uses your full name, you better start backpedaling fast.

"Sorry, Festus," I said. "I didn't get much sleep last night."

Fixing me with a beatific feline smirk, Festus said, "Apology accepted. Can we get going, please?"

Gritting my teeth at his smug satisfaction at having me over a barrel, I said, "May I ask why you need to go back to the Valley today?"

"Because yesterday that stuffed shirt son of mine wouldn't let me go to The Dirty Claw."

That did it. Mom could just have a fit. "I am not hauling your scruffy butt up to Shevington so you can get crocked in a werecat dive."

Mom started to pounce on me, but Festus held up one paw. "An understandable assumption, given my proclivities, Kelly," he said smoothly. "And may I say you look lovely today. That blouse compliments your eyes beautifully."

"Why, thank you, Festus," Mom said, smoothing the fabric with her hands. "How gallant of you."

"Yeah, that's him," I muttered.

Festus acted as if he hadn't heard a word. "To answer your rather direct question, Jinx, I want to go to The Dirty Claw to see if I can find out anything about Fish Pike's murder. Barnaby is in agreement that the killing could have a werecat angle due to the Pike family history."

Since there was no way that I was going to be able to ditch Festus, I retrieved the backpack with the special mesh compartment and unzipped it for him. As he stepped inside, I whispered, "Having fun?"

"Oh, yeah," Festus grinned. "The alley cat scores and the crowd goes wild."

Shouldering the backpack, we started walking toward the portal. Mom stoutly refused to risk her neck trying to "ride a bike at my age." She's 55, and hardly what I would call rickety, but I knew it was pointless to argue.

I spent most of the next hour listening to her and Festus hash over the sad tale of Jeremiah Pike's marriage to a human oddly interspersed with stories about the fishing convention. Since my mind was mainly on my growing irritation at Chase, it was just as well that the two of them were entertaining one another. I managed to get by with the occasional "uh-huh" or "really?" at appropriate moments.

Before I knew it, we were inside the city gate—where Mom stopped and asked me for the directions to Aunt Fiona's house. Surprised, I stalled. This was, after all, the first time she was going to see her sister since Fiona faked her death.

"The house is hard to find if you've never been here," I said. But Mom cut me off.

"I've been to Shevington before, dear."

Which only made sense, since both she and Gemma trained with Myrtle until they were teenagers.

That left me standing there awkwardly until I managed a lame, "Don't you want me to come with you?"

Mom stood her ground.

"No, dear," she said. "I'd like you to go to The Dirty Claw with Festus while Fiona and I talk."

Over my shoulder, I heard the *zwoosh* of a zipper opening. A yellow head appeared over my shoulder.

"Listen to your mother, dear," Festus purred sweetly.

"Old cat," I warned, "you are seriously pushing me."

"You can't let him go to The Dirty Claw alone," Mom said reasonably. "Left to his own devices, Festus will ask his questions, and then he'll tie one on."

To his credit, Festus shrugged and nodded, admitting that's exactly what he'd do.

"If that happens," Mom went on, "you'll have to explain to Chase why you let his father get roaring drunk, and since it would appear that the two of you aren't on the best of terms, that would be an added complication, now, wouldn't it?"

Mom logic. The bane of every daughter's existence.

Chapter Nine

Kelly smothered a smile as she briskly walked away from her daughter and Festus, making a point not to glance back over her shoulder. She knew she should feel guilty for being so happy to be back in The Valley after 37 years, especially with all the problems Jinx was facing, but Kelly couldn't help it.

Kelly raised her daughter in the immaculate house she shared with Jeff, but that three-bedroom ranch with the attached garage was also the place where her anxieties and insecurities took on a life of their own. From the labeled and dated plastic containers in the refrigerator to the spotless upholstery, Kelly crafted a cautious life.

But then Gemma looked at her that night in the basement and told her that if they wanted to defeat Brenna, it had to be like it was "in the old days." Kelly already felt the first vague stirrings of her long dormant magic, but in that moment the embers kindled to life. Kelly wanted the power that surged in her veins more than air, more than safety, more than fear.

Coming away from the battle with Brenna, Kelly remembered that being alive means getting splashed with mud every now and then. Trying to avoid the mess means you never get to play in the rain. Kelly wouldn't make that mistake again.

Her house was the home she made with her husband and daughter, but Shevington was a different kind of home—her magical home. How she'd longed to walk these streets again!

But even in her joy, Kelly felt regret, especially when a gang of happy children rushed past her clutching enchanted kites. The way the tails twitched and tugged, Kelly knew the kites wanted to reach the big meadow across from the field where the fairy guard drilled. There, the kites would take flight, dancing aloft in intricate patterns of their own making.

By lying to Jinx about her heritage, Kelly denied her daughter this part of her childhood; carefree play in a place where her magic could have been practiced with complete freedom.

Kelly and Gemma used to lie on their backs in that same meadow. They gazed up at the clouds, surrounded by singing butterflies, and dreamed of completing their training with Myrtle and Moira.

Gemma planned to be the first alchemist to find the fabled Philosopher's Stone, and Kelly privately hoped she would be the chosen one in Knasgowa's line and the next leader of Shevington.

Now, all these years later, Kelly marveled they'd ever been so young—so untouched by the harsher realities of life. A few days after Brenna's death, in a private moment, Kelly apologized to Myrtle for rejecting all this and for denying Jinx her birthright.

Myrtle, in her librarian guise, simply grasped Kelly's hand and said, "There are no accidents, Kelly. You have walked the path that was meant for you, and Jinx will do the same."

A new hope filled Kelly as she drank in Shevington's vibrant colors and brimming life. So many things seemed possible now, including one dearer to her heart than she could describe.

She'd asked Myrtle about that too, and the aos si counseled patience, but Myrtle hadn't said no. Had she?

The instant Jinx began to recite the directions to Fiona's cottage; Kelly knew where she was going—Endora Endicott's house. Endora and their mother, Kathleen Ryan, were lifelong friends. Kelly and Fiona spent hours in Endora's back garden learning about plants and herbs, stealing away from their lessons when no one was looking to go next door and feed tender green shoots to Stan's rabbits.

Stan.

An image of the sweet, eight-foot tall Sasquatch loomed fondly in Kelly's mind. She thrilled at the memory of the earth falling away beneath her as he swept her skyward in his strong arms before depositing her securely on one broad shoulder for a walk to the marketplace.

How had she ever taken the real magical moments of her youth for granted? How had she failed to appreciate the kindness and goodness of the people in Shevington?

Standing now at the cottage gate, lost in thought, the sound of a booming basso voice caught Kelly off guard.

"Little Kelly Ryan? What a lovely woman you've become."

Gasping in delight, her heart hammering against her ribs, Kelly turned and found herself staring straight at polished brass buttons on a tweed waistcoat. Craning her neck back, she looked up into a smiling, hairy face with a hint of silver at the temples.

Joyful tears filled her eyes. "Oh, Stan!" she breathed. "It is you!"

As she reached for a hug, gravity gave way once more. Stan lifted her three feet off the ground in a fierce but gentle hug, and she felt the rumble of his voice in her chest. "Welcome home, sweetheart."

Regaining her balance as the Sasquatch sat her down, Kelly said, "Thank you, Stan. I've missed The Valley so much."

"As did your sister," he said. "Are you coming to live with us too?"

Kelly shook her head. "I don't think Jeff is ready for that. He loves his fishing too much."

Stan frowned. "The fish in The Valley aren't challenging enough for him?"

"Oh, they're challenging enough alright," Kelly said, "he just never got used to them talking back and criticizing his bait choices."

"Well, that's the fun part of it for them," Stan said. "The bass even keep score, you know. So this is just a visit?"

"Yes," Kelly said, "I . . . uh . . . I'm here for the day to see Fiona. How is she?"

Seeming to understand that this was an important reunion, Stan laid a massive hand lightly on Kelly's shoulder. "Fiona's wonderful. I know she's going to be very happy to see you."

Kelly reached up and covered Stan's hand with her own. "Is she happy?"

"HAPPY?" Stan grinned. "When is Fiona not happy? She's planning on taking the Shevington Rose Cup away from Hester McElroy this year."

"Oh," Kelly said, wrinkling her nose, "I know what that means."

Stan nodded, as they both said, "Unicorn manure."

Kelly laughed, feeling some of the nervous tension drain from her body. "The rainbow kind?"

"Of course," Stan said. "Fiona has her standards."

"So she's home?"

"Yes," Stan said, digging a small roll of paper out of his

vest pocket and letting it unscroll toward the ground, "she asked me to pick up a few things for her at the market."

"That's my sister," Kelly laughed.

"Go around the back. I'll take my time getting these things so you two can talk. And whatever you're worried about, Kelly, don't be."

"Thank you, Stan."

He started to walk away but stopped when she called out to him. "Do you still raise rabbits?"

"I do," he said, "and when I come back, I'll introduce you to them."

Kelly watched as Stan covered the distance up the hill in great loping strides. Then, taking a deep breath to strengthen her resolve, she unlatched the gate and followed the cobblestone path around to the garden.

When Kelly stepped into the backyard, Fiona looked up from the table, a delicate china cup in one hand and a quill pen poised in the other. Without preamble, she said, "What were you thinking burying me in pink polyester?"

"It wasn't *you* we buried," Kelly said, walking over to stand by the table. "Your simulacrum spell was perfect."

"Of course, it was," Fiona said brightly. "I am a professional after all, but you still haven't answered my question about that hideous pants suit."

"You didn't have one decent thing in your closet. I couldn't put you away in blue jeans and a sweatshirt. What would people think?"

"That I looked like myself," Fiona said resolutely, "instead of a stuffed pink flamingo. Pink, Kelly? Honestly."

"I'm sorry," Kelly said, a knot rising in her throat. "For the pink polyester and for everything else. I know you and Myrtle were only protecting us. I shouldn't have blamed you."

Fiona put her cup down carefully, pushed her chair back, stood up and held her arms out to her sister. "Since I'm not really dead," she said magnanimously, "I forgive you for that hideous pants suit."

Laughing and crying all at the same time, Kelly stepped into the hug. "And the rest?"

"Oh, honey," Fiona said, holding her closer, "that awful man Ionescu didn't give us any choice. Now, here, wipe your eyes." She stepped back and offered Kelly a tissue that she plucked from the sleeve of her cardigan.

Kelly took the tissue with a wry expression. "You're turning into Grandma," she said, dabbing at her eyes. "She always kept tissues in her sweater."

"I wish I had one fraction of Granny's abilities," Fiona said, shooing her sister toward a second chair. "Let me get another cup so you can have some tea. You look like you need it. Shall I put anything in it?"

"No, thank you," Kelly said hastily, "I don't think I'm up for one of your potions just yet."

"Well, suit yourself," Fiona said, bustling toward the back door, "but it would do you a world of good."

She disappeared into the cottage, re-emerging shortly with the promised cup and a heaping plate of fresh cookies.

"If you won't take a potion," Fiona said, "maybe you'll be interested in one of these."

Kelly's eyes lit up. "Are those molasses cookies?"

"Well, of course, they are," Fiona said as if that was the silliest question she ever heard. "Anything else is a waste of time."

Kelly picked up one of the still-warm cookies, took a bite, and closed her eyes in happy appreciation. "I haven't had one of your molasses cookies in years."

Fiona let a moment of silence pass between them as she poured tea in Kelly's cup. Then she said quietly, "He likes them too."

When Kelly picked up the cup, her hand trembled. "Does he know who you are?"

Fiona shook her head. "No, we would never put him in danger like that. He knows me only as his Grandmother Endora's old friend."

"What does he do?"

"He works at the stables with Ellis Groomsby. Ellis says he's never seen anyone better with animals."

Kelly looked away, blinking back tears. "Just like his father."

"How are Jeff's fishing dogs?" Fiona asked mischievously.

In spite of herself, Kelly laughed. "You mean the lazy mutts that sleep on the bank with him? They're fine. All six of them."

"Six?" Fiona said with mock horror. "Good heavens! But then Jinx has four cats, so I suppose it runs in the family."

"Can't we tell her?" Kelly pleaded with sudden desperation. "Can't we tell them both? He's safe here. Jinx has her powers now. What can Ionescu do?"

"He's strigoi, Kelly," Fiona said, "and he cursed you. Those things don't wear off like nail polish, honey."

Kelly nodded numbly, casting her eyes down.

Scooting her chair around, Fiona reached for her sister's hands. "Look at me."

Kelly raised her head.

"Come help me plant my pansies?" Fiona asked. "I've always said when you don't know what else to do, play in the dirt."

"I wish it were that simple, Fi," Kelly whispered.

"Dirt is simple, dear," Fiona assured her, "that's why it always makes you feel better."

AS MOM WALKED OFF DOWN the street toward Aunt Fiona's, Festus hit me on the side of the head with his paw.

"Hey!" I yelped. "What was that for?"

"You're lollygagging," Festus said crossly. "And I'm thirsty."

"Lollygagging?" I grumbled. "Really, Festus? *Lollygagging*?"

"It's a word. Look it up," he said. "Are you going to start walking or do I have to cuff you on the other ear?"

Since he was seriously in need of a pedicure, I started walking.

"Now, when we get to the bar," he said, "I don't need any help from you. I'll do the talking. Keep your eyes open for anything unusual."

In a bar full of shifted werecats. Right. That would be a piece of cake.

As usual, The Dirty Claw was packed, but thankfully it was too early in the day for any of them to be thoroughly plastered. Festus vaulted over my shoulder intent on hitting the Red Dot table, but I grabbed him in mid-air.

"Slow down, hairball," I whispered. "You're supposed to be working here."

"I am working," he hissed back. "Like it would be normal for me to come in here and not head straight for the Red Dot table? Play along."

Okay, so I can be slow on the uptake.

"I'm serious, Festus," I barked crossly. "Don't make me scruff you."

"You. Wouldn't. *Dare*." Festus said, narrowing his eyes and putting his ears back.

No one else saw it, but I caught the approving gleam in those amber slits.

"Yes. I. Would." I said, narrowing my own eyes. "I promised Chase I wasn't going to let you get drunk again. We are going to sit at the bar like civilized patrons and have our Litter Box Lagers and nip nachos."

Laughter erupted from one of the booths by the window. "Hey, Festus!" Furl called out. "She's gonna have you wearing a cute little bell next."

Festus curled his lips back. "Knock it off, Furl, or I'll rip those puny flat ears of yours right off your head."

Merle, Earl, and Furl are Scottish Fold triplets. They work at the International Registry for Shapeshifters when they're not at The Dirty Claw.

Yeah, that's right, the IRS.

The Registry monitors all forms of shapeshifters, not just werecats, and makes sure there are no incidents with the humans. The werewolves get most of the bad press, but problems have died down since more of the wolves are opting to go vegan. Apparently, it's a cholesterol thing.

When I saw the triplets, I realized why we were in The Dirty Claw. If anyone knew about rumors in the werecat community, it would be Merle, Earl, and Furl. They're in the same Red Dot League with Festus, but none of them are serious players. Red Dot is a drinking game played on a pool table with a voice-activated laser pointer. Aloysius, a Cornish Rex, is the only Dirty Claw denizen who thinks it's possible to catch the Red Dot.

Hairless cats tend to be intense.

Anyway, for the rest of the gang, Red Dot is an excuse to slug losing shots of creamed whiskey. No one loses with more gusto than Festus.

Those were the only circumstances under which I'd seen Merle, Earl, and Furl, but I knew they did have an official and important capacity in the werecat community. Festus was being smart—very smart.

Manfred, the burly Canadian Lynx bartender, was on duty as usual. I caught his eye and called out our order before turning back to the triplets. "You guys mind if we sit with you?"

"Of course not," Earl said, jumping over the table and landing in between his brothers to make room for us.

"What are you two doing in Shevington this time of day?" Merle asked.

Depositing Festus in the seat by the window, I slid in beside him.

"My Mom is here visiting my Aunt Fiona," I said. "Festus tagged along. We're giving them time to talk in private."

Manfred appeared with one bottle, one bowl of lager, and a huge platter of nachos.

"Is that what I ordered?" I asked, eyeing the mountain of food.

"No," he said, "but with these three moochers sitting here, your chow would be gone in 10 seconds. It's on the house, by the way, with my thanks for keeping Festus away from the Red Dot table. He's on probation for another week."

"Will you just get over it?" Festus grumbled, lapping at his lager. "I said I was sorry already."

The triplets suddenly got interested in their food, and no one was talking.

"Okay," I said, "what am I missing here?"

"Zip it, Manfred," Festus warned.

The Lynx wiped his big paws with a bar rag, regarding Festus with twinkling eyes. "I'm not talking to you, McGregor. I'm conversing with the lady."

"Festus, what did you do?" I asked suspiciously.

"It was all a misunderstanding," Festus said, studiously examining the claws on his right paw. "I actually don't remember most of the details it was so insignificant."

"You don't remember most of the details because you were so drunk," Manfred said. "He was playing Red Dot when a couple of ligers came in, and Mr. Tough Guy here called them half-breeds."

I frowned. "What's a liger?"

"Half-lion, half tiger," Merle said helpfully. "Very few of them in the shifter community. All descended from one pride. It happened in the Sixties. You know. Free love and all that?"

I didn't know, and I didn't want to.

"So what happened?" I asked.

"What happened is that they were going to rip this old guy's head off," Manfred said. "They shifted. He shifted. The triplets shifted. Next thing I know, it's like freaking *Animal Planet* in here. I got tigers, panthers, cheetahs, a couple of jaguars. Everybody's name calling. They trashed the whole bar."

We all looked at Festus, expecting him to say something, but he suddenly decided his ears were in dire need of washing.

"Festus?" I prodded.

"Huh?" he said, pausing with one paw in mid-air. "What?"

"You started a cat fight in The Dirty Claw and you didn't tell anyone?"

"Oh, right," he said. "Like I'm gonna tell that uptight kid of mine. Mr. Law and Order. It was a discussion that got out of hand."

"He's banned from Red Dot for another week," Manfred said, "so I'd appreciate it if you'd keep an eye on him, Jinx."

"Not a problem."

"You are not the boss of me," Festus hissed.

"No," I said, "but if you don't settle down and behave yourself, I'm ratting you out to Chase."

Festus muttered something under his breath that I'm just as glad I didn't hear, and said, "Fine. Pass me a plate. I'm hungry."

After Manfred moved away, Festus said, "Now, boys, I want you to keep diving into that chow like the furry pigs you are and listen to a story about road kill."

The triplets exchanged glances. Furl said, "Do we have a problem?"

"You could say that," Festus said, wiping nip cheese off his whiskers. "We found Fish Pike dead on our sidewalk yesterday."

"Why didn't you inform the Registry?" Merle asked. "You know that's protocol."

"I'm informing the registry now, you moron," Festus said. "I'm not much of one for paperwork."

Earl made a clucking sound in his throat. "Play nice, boys," he said. "Tell us what's going on, Festus."

In between bites, Festus gave the brothers all the details. "So what do you think," he finished. "Transient or vengeful Pike relatives?"

I almost choked on my lager when Furl said gravely, "Neither. This isn't the first time we've heard about a killing with fake claws.

For the most part I'd been listening, but I couldn't stay silent any longer. "What are you talking about, Furl?"

"Two years ago in Seattle, we investigated a series of killings with the same kind of wounds Festus is describing," he said, lowering his voice and glancing around. "We never caught the guy, but he's a Fae hit man. I'm not saying somebody isn't sending you a message, but the killer's not your problem. It's his boss you need to find."

"And just how are we supposed to do that?" I asked.

"I don't know," Furl said, "but we have to turn this into the Registry officially."

"Can you give us a few hours?" Festus asked. "I need to run this by my kid, and Jinx here has to tell Barnaby."

"Yeah," Merle said, "we can do that."

We stayed long enough to finish the nachos and go through a second round of lager for appearances sake, then made our exit—theatrically. I stood up and interrupted the conversation and told Festus we really needed to get going.

He protested sourly and loudly.

"You're no fun," he declared as I literally stuffed him back in the mesh compartment while Merle, Earl, and Furl snickered.

"That might be true," I countered, "but I know you. You won't pull any of your stunts as long as my mother is around."

We said our good-byes and exited to a round of taunting questions about how Festus liked being domesticated.

"You know that act put a dent in my reputation," Festus grumbled.

"It was necessary," I said. "How are you going to get word back to Chase?"

"I'll get Fiona to place a call with her mirror," Festus said. "Think of it as the magical version of FaceTime."

We made straight for Aunt Fiona's tidy thatched-roof cottage. Laughter from the back garden drew us around to the side of the house. Pausing at the gate, I peered over the top, while Festus jumped down from the pack to look through the open space by the gatepost.

There they were; Mom and Aunt Fiona, giggling like school girls and planting flowers together. The reunited sisters looked so sweet, I actually choked up, and a couple of big tears rolled down my cheeks. Beside me, Festus let out with a choked gurgle of his own.

When I smiled down at him, he groused darkly, "What? You never heard a hairball before?"

"Right," I said. "You're a total mush ball when it comes to sentimentality, and you know it."

"I know," Festus said, jumping up on the gate and tripping the latch, "that we have work to do. Get the lead out."

With that, he made one of his perfect three-point landings, twitched his tail, and stalked toward mom and Aunt Fiona with a hearty, "Fiona! You get more beautiful every day!"

I followed, smiling at him fondly. Loveable old rascal.

Chapter Ten

Mom and Aunt Fiona looked up when the gate hinges creaked. My aunt stood, brushed the dirt off her gloves, and approached me with open arms.

"Jinx! Festus!" she called out. "Come play in the dirt with us!"

Nothing would have pleased me more. I think you have to be grown up to truly appreciate the uncomplicated pleasure of a good mud pie. Unfortunately, Furl's information about the Fae hit man made talking with Barnaby even more important.

"I can't, Aunt Fiona," I said. "I have to find Barnaby. Did Mom tell you what happened in Briar Hollow?"

"Good heavens, yes," Aunt Fiona said. "Old Fish Pike was several sandwiches shy of a picnic, honey. Lord only knows what he got himself into."

"He got himself into being dead, Fiona," Festus said, examining the holes in the flower bed. He opened his mouth, inhaled and backed away. "By the Great Cat! That reeks! Are you putting unicorn crap in there?"

"I am," Fiona said happily. "I shoveled it myself."

"Then count me out on the flower planting," he declared, sauntering over to a sun puddle and stretching luxuriantly. "My fur would smell for a month. I'll sit over here and keep you ladies company."

As we watched, Festus turned around three times, settled down and closed his eyes.

"Isn't keeping us company through closed eyelids an oxymoron?" Mom observed wryly.

Festus yawned. "I'm meditating, not sleeping."

"What about when the snoring starts?" I asked. "Are you going to tell us you'll be imitating a Zen chainsaw?"

"Adenoids," Festus retorted, but I saw his whiskers twitch with suppressed laughter.

Right. I did some research on that one. Cats don't have adenoids.

"Aren't you supposed to place a mirror-to-mirror call to Chase?" I asked.

Festus responded with something that sounded like "later" before the aforementioned snoring started.

Mom, Aunt Fiona and I exchanged bemused looks.

"How much Litterbox Lager did he have at The Dirty Claw?" Mom asked.

"Two or three," I answered. "Enough for him to go down for the count while I'm gone and not cause you all any trouble."

She looked at the sleeping ginger tom with loving tolerance. "Festus isn't any trouble. He likes to talk tough. He wouldn't hurt a fly. Unless that fly was trying to hurt one of us."

As I watched her face, I realized Mom was seeing the man under the fur. It occurred to me that Festus might not be the only one carting around an old crush, but I filed that thought away for future contemplation. You can only learn so much about your parents as real people before your brain goes into overload. I was already dangerously close to the red line.

I left the three of them in the garden and set out for the central square. Barnaby's office in the town hall sits next door to Hester McElroy's inn. The real heart of Shevington also resides in the square, the Mother Tree, a being older and wiser than Myrtle herself.

At the end of the block, I caught sight of a flock of six dragonlets circling in the air over the main gate. As I watched, they spread their wings and glided in for a landing in the one place they weren't supposed to be—inside the wall.

Great. They were probably looking for me.

I changed my course and picked up the pace. Maybe I could get there before they got themselves into any real trouble. Dragonlets are more curious by nature than cats, and they have a wicked sense of humor. Left to their own devices, mayhem will ensue.

The first day I came to Shevington the flock spontaneously attached themselves to me. Now, whenever I come to the Valley, the devoted creatures are never far away.

When the city's arched main entrance came into view, I beheld a scene that did not bode well for my winged friends. The dragonlets sat in a line on the cobblestones studiously ignoring a lecture being delivered by the Lord High Mayor himself.

Minreinth, the flock leader, spotted me instantly. He craned his head up and tilted it to look past Barnaby. A happy guttural cooing echoed off the stone walls as the dragonlet's eyes glowed gold with pleasure.

No matter what mischief the dragonlets manage to perpetrate, their sheer beauty always stops me short. Those shining orbs set against Minreinth's blue and purple iridescent scales created a breathtaking fairy tale image. The dragonlets aren't big; no larger than German Shepherds, but their size doesn't detract from their majesty.

Before I could say anything, Barnaby turned and saw me. "Thank heavens! Maybe you can reason with them."

I joined the assemblage and regarded the dragonlets, whose heads bobbed and weaved to welcome me.

"What did they do?"

"Tell her, Minreinth," Barnaby commanded.

Yes, I can understand them, and, no, I have no idea how.

The flock leader let out with a series of coos and chirps; all pitched at an exaggerated, reasonable tone and pace. He sounded like a kid trying to argue himself out of trouble.

That morning, Minreinth explained, Aspid "Ironweed" Istra, the fairy major in charge of the Brown Mountain Guard, invited the dragonlets to drill with his troops at dawn. Of course, they accepted in the interest of being good citizens of Shevington.

"Isn't that kind of dangerous?" I interrupted. "Fairies are tiny compared to you all."

Minreinth's eyes widened. He emitted a cautionary chirp emphasized with a warning shake of his head.

"Yeah, good point," I agreed, "I better not let Aspid hear me say that. A definite case of short guy syndrome."

Beside me, Barnaby coughed into his hand to disguise a chuckle.

I turned toward him. "What's the problem?" I asked. "Minreinth says they had fun, and no one got hurt."

"I'm sure they did have quite an enjoyable time," Barnaby agreed, "but the rule regarding flights over the city remains in force. The flock grew a bit enthusiastic with their aerial maneuvers and dived too close to the houses at that end of town. Mrs. Shinglebutter's cow was so frightened, the poor creature won't give milk."

Minreinth ducked his head and scraped his talons against the paving stones. His cohorts suddenly became incredibly interested in examining the archway over their heads.

"Save it, guys," I said. "Don't even try to sell the innocent act. Minreinth, apologize to the Mayor."

The dragonlet dipped his head lower and let out a mournful wail.

"Apology accepted," Barnaby said. "But if I may offer a suggestion? Mrs. Shinglebutter is quite fond of hollyhocks. Perhaps you and your flock could gather up a goodly number and drop them on her doorstep? The gesture will soothe her temper and save me from listening to another rant on the need for enhanced animal control measures."

The flock wagged their heads in agreement, rising immediately into the sky and heading off on their mission to pick flowers.

"Lovely creatures when you get to know them," Barnaby said, watching the dragonlets speed away. "Alas, some of our residents are still rather afraid of them, but I must say the dragonlets are thoroughly taken with you."

"Animals like me," I shrugged. "I thought it was just cats, but it looks like I have dragon mojo too."

"Dragonlet," he corrected me. "The larger species is another matter altogether."

I was willing to take his word on that one.

"In all fairness, Barnaby," I said, "they wouldn't have been flying over the city if Ironweed hadn't invited them."

"Oh, I am quite aware of Ironweed's hand in all of this," Barnaby said. "I will be speaking with him when the patrol comes in from Brown Mountain this evening. Now, were you looking for me?"

"Yes. I was headed for the town hall when I saw the flock coming in for a landing. I thought I better see what they were up to."

"Well," Barnaby said, gesturing down the High Street, "why don't you walk back to the square with me, and we can talk?"

As we fell into step beside one another, Barnaby said, in a neutral tone, "I was surprised when you didn't come with Chase and Festus yesterday to deliver the news about the discovery of Fish Pike's body."

Just the opening I needed.

"I know I should have been with them, but we have another situation Chase doesn't know about. I needed to help Tori with something, and now we need your help."

Barnaby stopped and turned toward me. "Does this have to do with Pike's murder?"

"I honestly don't know," I admitted. "I think there's . . . "

At the sound of approaching voices, I stopped and glanced over my shoulder. "Uh, can we go someplace private?"

Barnaby drew his brows together, perplexed by my request. "We closed a section of the upper wall for replanting," he said. "It won't reopen until this afternoon. We can go there."

I followed him a few yards down the street to a set of stone stairs barred by a chain. Barnaby undid the catch and held the barrier aside for me, fastening it again as I passed.

The top of the protective wall encircling the city houses lush elevated gardens that form a kind of promenade. Whenever Chase and I are in Shevington in the evening, we like to walk up there and find some secluded spot to . . . talk.

Barnaby and I emerged on a long straight section of the wall where newly mulched beds held a variety of gaily colored flowers.

"Please," Barnaby said, gesturing toward one of the ornate iron benches.

When we were settled, I took a deep breath and started talking. First, I described the discovery of Fish Pike's body from my point of view and ended by relating everything Furl told us at The Dirty Claw.

"Furl will be appraising the Registry?" Barnaby asked.

"Yes, but not for a few hours. Festus wanted to give Chase the information first, and I wanted to talk to you."

"Where is Festus now?"

"The last time I saw him, he was asleep in a sun puddle in Aunt Fiona's garden."

"Good," Barnaby said. "When we are done here, I will accompany you to your aunt's and have a word with him. But I think perhaps you have more to tell me?"

Oh, yeah. There was definitely more.

Barnaby didn't interrupt my account of Myrtle's actions, but his expression grew steadily more intent. At the mention of the chessboard, he stiffened, but still said nothing.

When I finished, Barnaby said, "Describe this chessboard to me."

"I can do better than that," I replied, taking my phone out of my pocket. "I'll show it to you."

That morning Tori suggested I make a brief video of the chess set.

To my surprise, Barnaby touched the phone's screen, paused the video, and expanded the image with his fingers. He must have seen the look on my face because he laughed.

"I told you that I make occasional forays into your world," he said. "From what I have been able to observe, it is no longer possible for people to function without one of these devices."

"Not really," I admitted.

"I find them highly useful," Barnaby said, going back to studying the screen.

"So is there something unusual about the chess board?"

"Perhaps," he said, "but before I offer an opinion one way or another, I want to discuss the matter with Moira."

He reached into the breast pocket of his coat and took out a polished block of quartz crystal. Placing my phone and the stone on the bench beside one another, Barnaby gently swept his hand over both. As I watched, the frames of the video floated up from the phone liked stacked playing cards and disappeared into the quartz.

"Whoa!" I said. "What is that thing?"

I've learned that wizards and alchemists aren't all that different from fishermen. They love to tell the story about "landing the big one." In a magical sense, their newest spell or experiment constitutes the catch of the day—and they always pretend to be humble about their accomplishments.

"This?" Barnaby asked, doing a lousy job of downplaying his enthusiasm. "A mere enchantment I designed after first encountering one of your 'smartphones,'"

"It doesn't look so 'mere' to me. That is seriously cool."

"Thank you," Barnaby said. "I was intrigued by the ability to capture and access information in such a compact, efficient form. I did make a few design improvements on the concept."

He was dying for me to ask, so I did. "Like what?"

"Oh, minor things," he said, trying to sound nonchalant. "I removed the need for a power source, created infinite memory, and made the stone self-aware."

Minor things? Apple would sell its soul for the battery life alone.

"What do you mean self-aware?"

"Allow me to demonstrate."

Addressing the crystal, he said, "Vicus, would you mind replaying that series of images you just collected?"

"It would be my pleasure, sir."

A beam of light emanated from the center of the quartz and my video began to play in midair like a hologram.

"Wow," I said. "Move over, Siri."

"Indeed," Barnaby grinned. "Vicus has a much more pleasant disposition than the spirit that animates the iPhone."

"Thank you, sir," Vicus answered.

The dang rock actually managed to sound embarrassed.

"You're quite welcome," Barnaby said. "That will be all for now."

The hologram shut off and Barnaby returned the stone to his pocket.

"After you and Moira look at the video do you think you'll be able to tell us what's going on with the chess set and explain Myrtle's weird behavior?" I asked.

Barnaby leaned against the bench and gazed over the wall toward the distant mountains. "I have known the aos si for centuries," he said thoughtfully. "The things you are telling me trouble me deeply. Myrtle should have known of Brenna Sinclair's presence. But that is not the most disturbing aspect of that series of events."

"It's not?"

"No. Myrtle never told Moira or myself about her inability to detect the sorceress. It is not like the aos si to fail to be forthcoming."

To my ears that was a fancy way to avoid using the word "lie," but I didn't say that. It was one thing for my faith in Myrtle to be shaken, but the implications of such a possibility for Barnaby were far greater.

"When are you planning to speak with Moira?" I asked.

"As soon as she and Myrtle return from the high valley."

"Oh," I said, "that's right. What are they doing, anyway? Something with seawater?"

"Yes. The merpeople have approached us about seeking sanctuary in the valley. Myrtle and Moira have an idea about creating a suitable habitat. They're surveying a potential location. When Myrtle returns to Briar Hollow, I will speak with Moira. She may have observed something unusual today with the aos si without realizing it."

"What do you want me to do?"

"Nothing for the present, but heed Colonel Longworth's

advice. Do not speak openly in the presence of that game board."

"That's it?"

My face must have betrayed my disappointment. Barnaby smiled at me kindly. "You were hoping I would have an instant answer for you, weren't you?"

I nodded, struggling to answer around the lump in my throat. "I don't want there to be something wrong with Myrtle, and I don't want Chase to be in danger."

"Nor does he want your life to be at peril. Did the two of you speak after he returned to Briar Hollow?"

I shook my head.

"Ah," he said. "I thought not. Chase was disturbed that you had quarreled, but he can also be quite stubborn when he thinks he is in the right."

Getting relationship advice from Barnaby hadn't been part of the plan. "I'm sorry," I said, wiping at my eyes. "This isn't something I should be bothering you about."

"You forget that I was married once," he said. "My wife had a rule. We did not allow the sun to go down on our anger. I understand why you didn't tell Chase about the events with the chessboard, especially after he discovered Pike's body, but I think you should tell him now, for both of your sakes."

I didn't really need anyone's permission to tell Chase anything, but Barnaby's words made me feel enormously better. "I will as soon as we get back."

"Excellent," Barnaby said. "Now, it's a beautiful day. I think we should take a few moments to enjoy it with a tonic that will set your mind right if only for the time being."

"Tonic?"

"Oh, yes," he intoned solemnly, standing and offering me his arm, "a magical elixir from Ethiopia—coffee."

Chapter Eleven

Cabin High in the Mountains

THE SOUND of the steel blades rhythmically sliding along the diamond grit arms of the sharpener calmed and focused his mind. A master craftsman cherishes his tools. Twenty strokes on each side of ten talons. Forty strokes per blade. Two hundred strokes per hand; four hundred for the full set. A mantra for razor precision.

The heavy gloves lay nearby on the makeshift table, newly cleaned with Pecard leather dressing. A master falconer taught him that trick. It would never do to leave bits of blood and meat in the seams and crevices of the gauntlets.

The bird man never discovered the real purpose of his student's meticulous curiosities or how the gloves came to be redesigned over and over again to fit around the steel exoskeletons. The private design process continued until the wrist braces held the deadly talons rigid and capable of savage blows.

His notebooks contained detailed, annotated drawings if fate ever forced him to build new instruments. He hoped that never happened. He shed blood and dispensed justice with his weapons. They were a part of his soul.

How many hours had he spent in innocent small town libraries studying weaponry in dusty tomes that never left the shelves? The Harlequin romances gadded about those towns dripping saccharin trails of true love and happy endings. His books spoke in the warm, crimson language of bloody realism.

Behind him, a floorboard creaked. The Strigoi might be stealthy creatures of the night, but he'd been listening to Ionescu's approach for five minutes.

"Why don't you just use your own claws?" his visitor asked.

There it was. The inevitable question.

Still counting strokes in his head, the man said, "I do not choose to get my claws dirty."

"So those things pretty all this up for you? Let you live with yourself?"

The voice was beside him now, so he looked up at the elegantly dressed lawyer standing incongruously in the cabin's dusty ruins.

"I have no difficulty living with myself."

"Ferguson, you are one cold-hearted son of a bitch," Anton Ionescu said flatly. "I admire that about you."

Ice blue eyes flicked away from the shining steel. "Coming from a creature like yourself, I take that as a compliment."

Ionescu flinched at the word "creature."

"Ah," Ferguson said, "you don't like to be reminded of your vampiric roots, do you, Anton?"

Ionescu's face hardened. "I'm not Count Dracula any more than you are the wolfman."

"But then neither one of us is human, are we? And this is a

most inhuman chore you've hired me to complete. I trust the manner in which I displayed Mr. Pike satisfied you?"

Had he been willing to admit it, Ionescu's stomach turned to acid at the thought of poor, crazy old Fish Pike slashed to ribbons and propped up like a macabre doll. But appearing to be weak with a psychopath-for-hire like Malcolm Ferguson was not a good idea.

"The whole town is talking about it," Anton replied. "The Hamilton woman was nowhere to be seen most of today. My sources say she didn't come out of the store, which means she went to the Valley."

Ferguson regarded his employer thoughtfully. "Why do you hate that woman so much? She's a thirty-year-old ex-waitress who dabbles in magic. How could she possibly be of any consequence to you?"

"She wasn't 'dabbling' when she dealt with Brenna Sinclair," Ionescu snapped. "Now that mother of hers is back on the scene. Apparently being deprived of her only son wasn't enough to teach Kelly Ryan a lesson. So now she gets to pay again by watching her daughter suffer and die. If I can get rid of the McGregors in the process, all the better."

Ferguson made a clucking sound in the back of his throat. "Anton, you *are* supposed to be reformed, you know."

"I am reformed," Ionescu said tightly. "We haven't fed on the life spirit of a human since Father Damian brought us here from Transylvania 265 years ago."

Curling his lips into a sardonic smile, Ferguson purred, "Ah, yes, the mother country, Transylvania. Are you quite sure the good father didn't round up Count Dracula with his unholy band of refugees?"

Ionescu took a step forward; his hands balled into fists. "Samuel Damian was a man of God, a scientist and a visionary. He cured us."

"Playing electrical games with Ben Franklin doesn't make

Damian a scientist," Ferguson sneered, "and housebreaking a pack of soul-sucking Strigoi doesn't mean he was a saint."

All the color drained from Ionescu's features, replaced with suppressed fury. "If you hate my kind so much, why did you take this job?"

"Because I hate Chase McGregor more," Ferguson said, his eyes shifting to amber slits as a rumbling growl rose from his throat. "Now, to what do I owe the pleasure of a visit from the King of the Gypsies?"

"We are not Romani," Ionescu said stiffly. "My people are Romanians."

"Your pedigree doesn't interest me."

"But *your* methods do interest me. What are you planning to do next?"

"Next?" Ferguson said, picking up one of the steel exoskeletons and running his thumb appraisingly along the edge of the longest talon. "Next, I intend to go for a walk in the moonlight."

AT THE DOOR of Moira's laboratory, Barnaby paused to delicately probe the interior with his senses. He felt Moira's warm, focused energy, and the less powerful, more chaotic essence of her assistant, Dewey, but not the ancient presence of the aos si.

Before Barnaby's knuckles could strike the heavy timbers, Moira called out, "Come in, Barnaby. There's no need to skulk on the doorstep."

He pushed the door open and stepped into the cavernous room. Glass-fronted display cabinets and overflowing bookcases. Moira's work table sat in the center buried by a wild riot of herbs, stones, and bottled potions. His eyes tracked to the raised dais under the picture windows where the Alchemist sat at her desk.

"Moira," he said, "I cannot remember the last time anyone accused me of skulking."

"That might be because you're quite bad at it," she said, handing a sheaf of papers to Dewey. The dwarf nodded curtly at Barnaby before lumbering out a side door muttering into his beard. Barnaby caught the words "glorified sardines" and "fish stench."

When the side door closed, Barnaby regarded Moira with a bemused expression. "What did you do to put Master Dewey in such a foul mood?"

Gesturing for him to join her, Moira said, "First I made him work with the merfolk representative all day. Now I've sent him off with a shopping list, which will require that he actually converse with people. Dewey has many virtues, but sociability isn't one of them."

"That can't be entirely true," Barnaby observed, sitting down across from her. "He and Darby get on famously."

"That is one of the great mysteries of friendship. Darby is the only living creature I know who can make Dewey laugh. Now, would you mind telling me what you're doing standing on my doorstep poking around with your powers like some nosey neighbor?"

Instead of answering her question, Barnaby took in the tired lines around her eyes and the weary set of her mouth. "You look exhausted."

Moira's expression gentled. "I am," she said, "but I think Myrtle and I have found the right combination of elements to make and sustain a saltwater environment in the upper valley. The dwarven engineers are going over our plans to dam the approaches to the deep meadow."

"Which is a most commendable feat, but did you remember to eat today?"

Moira frowned, her eyes shifting back and forth as if reviewing the last few hours. "Honestly, I don't remember."

"As I suspected," Barnaby replied, gesturing toward the surface of the table with his index finger. Two stacks of books obligingly moved over to make room for the large platter of cold beef slices, cheese, and fruit that materialized. With a second gesture, he added fresh bread, wine, and two goblets.

"Ah," Moira sighed appreciatively, "I do love a wizard who can cook."

Barnaby nodded toward the bottle, which uncorked itself, levitated, and neatly poured a measure of wine for them both. Moira beckoned the nearest goblet to come to her, plucking it delicately from thin air.

"To you, kind sir," she said, raising the glass and inclining her head toward Barnaby.

"And to you, fair maiden."

Moira eyed him wryly over the rim of her goblet. "I haven't been a maiden in several centuries, Barnaby."

"But you are undeniably fair," he responded gallantly.

In spite of herself, Moira chuckled. "You never stop until you make me laugh, do you?"

"Against the assault of laughter nothing can stand."

Reaching for a slice of cheese and a bit of apple, Moira said, "That sounds like a quotation."

"It is," Barnaby said, "from Mark Twain. A most pragmatic and good-natured human."

"Ah, one of your favorites, but somehow I don't think you're here to discuss 19th-century human literature."

Barnaby sighed. "You know me too well, and you are right. We have a rather more complicated subject to discuss."

"Which, I assume, is why you scanned the room before you entered?"

"Yes. I needed to make sure that you were alone."

Moira took a sip of her wine and gave him a long look. "Don't you mean to say that you wanted to make sure Myrtle wasn't here?"

Barnaby's brow furrowed. "Why do you say that?"

"Because you would have felt free to ask Dewey to leave if we needed to speak in private," the alchemist said. "You would not do that with the aos si, and since you know I spent the day with her, I can only conclude you wanted to avoid Myrtle."

He inclined his head in an acknowledging bow. "As always, you are too clever for me by half."

Reaching into his coat pocket, Barnaby removed the block of quartz and placed it on the table between them. "Vicus, would you be so good as to play the images you captured from the young lady's communication device?"

The stone came to life with a pale violet glow. "It would be my pleasure."

When the holographic image of the chessboard appeared, Moira leaned forward and studied it intently.

"That's not possible," she said finally.

Barnaby let out a long breath. "I hoped I was mistaken."

"Mistaken about the Liszt chess set?" Moira said incredulously. "We've been searching for this artifact since it disappeared in Europe at the end of the Second World War. Where is it?"

"Sitting on a table in Jinx's espresso bar in Briar Hollow."

"And the aos si didn't bring this to our attention?" Moira asked with raised eyebrows.

"According to Jinx," Barnaby said, "Myrtle not only did not bring it to our attention, she examined the chessboard and declared it to be of no consequence."

"How could the aos si have made a mistake of that magnitude?"

"That," said a quiet voice, "is perhaps the question we should all explore."

They both turned to find Myrtle standing at the door. She crossed the room to join them. "Barnaby, may I have a glass of wine?"

With a slight gesture, Barnaby materialized and filled a third goblet and offered it to Myrtle, who sat down in the empty chair. "To old friends," she said, raising the cup.

"Old friends," Moira agreed.

An awkward silence settled around them until Myrtle said,. "Now, now. Among us, there should be nothing but the truth. I did not tell you about the chessboard because I didn't detect its power, which, I think we can agree, is something of a problem. I assume Jinx raised other concerns with you?"

"She did," Barnaby said, "but out of genuine affection for you, aos si. The child is afraid."

"Jinx is not a child," Myrtle said. "She is a strong young woman, and growing stronger by the day. What did she tell you?"

Quietly and gravely, Barnaby related the details of his conversation with Jinx. When he finished, Myrtle said, "It would seem my errors are larger than I feared."

"You've been aware that something is wrong?" Moira asked.

The aos si smiled sadly. "Apparently, I am guilty of the sin of denial."

"Who among us," Barnaby said, "can claim we are not?"

Myrtle laughed, the bright lilt of the sound dissipating the tension in the room. "Gracious as ever, Barnaby, but Jinx is correct. I did not know that Brenna Sinclair had returned, and now I have missed an artifact of the significance of the Liszt chessboard. With a killer stalking the McGregors, my apparent deficits could be a serious liability."

"Then," Moira said, "we have to arrive at an answer for why those deficits are there in the first place."

"I am quite old."

Moira stood up, pushing her chair back from the desk. "So far as I know, Myrtle, dementia has never been an issue with the Tuatha Dé Danann."

"With due respect," Myrtle replied, "I am the last of my kind. How can we be sure my life's energy is not simply waning?"

"Before we come to any conclusions like that," Moira said briskly, "I need to examine you."

"And I," Barnaby said, "need to refresh my memory on the full details of the Liszt chessboard."

"You have a theory?" Moira asked.

"Possibly," Barnaby replied. "Brenna Sinclair was able to get one magical artifact into the store, the miner's lamp that opened the tunnel she used to break into the fairy mound. She may also have been responsible for the chessboard and perhaps other articles that are suppressing Myrtle's powers."

"A hopeful supposition," Myrtle said, "but Jinx, Gemma, and Kelly's powers are not affected."

"We don't know that," Barnaby said. "Jinx's powers have not yet been fully realized, and Gemma and Kelly are badly out of practice. They could be experiencing a dampening effect as well and not realize it."

"But Brenna arranged for the miner's lamp to be placed in the store after my failure to detect her presence," Myrtle said.

"Correct," Barnaby agreed, "but according to Jinx, the chessboard arrived before she first saw Brenna on the town square. The chessboard could be responsible for what you are experiencing."

"And its current behavior?" Moira asked.

"That," Barnaby said, "points to one rather inescapable conclusion. Brenna Sinclair was not working alone. Her accomplice is still attempting to infiltrate the fairy mound."

Chapter Twelve

While Moira examined Myrtle, Barnaby settled into the adjacent private study with a stack of leather-bound volumes containing the journals of a number of eminent Alchemists. Barnaby's personal knowledge of the Liszt chessboard began in 1935. In that year, a failed chicken farmer, Heinrich Himmler, became the head of the *Ahnenerbe*, Adolf Hitler's occult and treasure-hunting division.

Under the guise of researching the cultural and archaeological history of the Aryan race, Himmler set out to locate and seize some of the most esoteric and sinister artifacts to be found in the Fae world.

To counteract Himmler's activities, Moira, like many of the remaining alchemists, covertly joined the famous Monuments Men. The group, comprised of historians and museum curators, worked at the end of the war to recover and repatriate the priceless works of art plundered by the Nazis.

Using gentle enchantments of forgetfulness on their human colleagues, the alchemists reclaimed dangerous magical artifacts and secured them in Fae archives around the world, including the one that resided in the fairy mound in Briar Hollow.

The Liszt chessboard, however, eluded both detection and understanding. The board's status was, in some ways, more legendary than substantial, but the artifact was still widely regarded among Fae historians as both dark and dangerous.

Barnaby hoped to find something to trace the chessboard's journey from Franz Liszt to Himmler. Now that the board's current location was known, understanding its earlier travels might help them to guess who took the artifact at the end of the war—especially since that person was likely Brenna Sinclair's accomplice.

The first diary in the stack, a handsome oxblood book trimmed in gold, was entitled *The Journal of Gilbert Gulbranson - 1845-1885*. Holding his hand over the first page, Barnaby said simply, "*Loco Liszt*." The pages riffled obediently, settling on two entries from 1849:

OCTOBER 10, 1849 - When my old friend, the pianist, and composer, Franz Liszt, who serves as *Kapellmeister Extraordinaire* by appointment of the Grand Duchess Maria Pavlovna, learned I would be in Weimar, he dispatched an invitation for me to visit him in his quarters.

DURING OUR TIME together he played for me a new composition, *Après une Lecture du Dante: Fantasia quasi Sonata*, which he refers to simply as his *Dante Sonata*. I found the piece disturbing and of questionable origin. Liszt has made heavy use of the tritone, widely believed to be "the Devil's interval." The feverish pace of the music, especially the ending passage meant to depict the tri-headed devil from Dante's *Inferno*, unsettled my senses.

. . .

I FEAR THAT LISZT, in his desire for recognition of his musical genius, may have given in to the urge to barter for unnatural abilities. Like most humans, he does not realize that all such bargains come at a price well beyond the terms of the agreement. After the fashion of the ill-fated Dr. Faust, Liszt's desires may have outweighed his better judgment.

OCTOBER 31, 1849 - Dined with Liszt and made note of an odd chess set sitting in his study designed with a musical motif. I detected dark energy emanating from the board. I inquired of Liszt about its origin only to be informed that it was made for him by a "master craftsman" and has been a source of inspiration in the evolution of his music.

WHEN LISZT LEFT me temporarily alone in the room, I touched the board and was repelled to find therein imprisoned music. Is it possible Liszt, so renowned for his virtuosity at the keyboard is using this device not to enhance his own gifts, but to steal from his contemporaries?

TAKING Vicus from his coat pocket, Barnaby held the stone over the page. "Vicus, please copy this material."

The purple glow appeared briefly. "Your request is completed."

"Thank you." Reaching forward, Barnaby tapped the page and said softly, "*Procedo.*" The book settled on a new entry from September 1870:

. . .

I HAVE LEARNED that last month Liszt's daughter, Cosima, newly divorced from her husband, Hans von Bülow, has married Richard Wagner. My sources in Switzerland tell me that Liszt has gifted his friend and new son-in-law with the chess set I first saw in Weimar twenty-one years ago. Could this be the source of Wagner's increasingly controversial ideas and popular favor?

AS BARNABY CONTINUED to search the journal for references to the chess set, he followed Gulbranson's growing suspicions that first Liszt and then Wagner used the board to steal ideas from their rivals. The Alchemist attributed Liszt's more demonic compositions to the influence of the board, which he also believed could have exacerbated Wagner's rabid nationalism and anti-Semitism.

GULBRANSON WROTE his final entry mentioning the chess set in late February 1883:

WAGNER HAS DIED and the chess set has gone missing. What Salieri has wrought I fear may now be used for more sinister purposes, especially should the board be paired with a harp.

BARNABY FROWNED. Salieri? A harp?

Using his search spell, Barnaby examined the journal for additional references to Salieri and a harp, but with no results. Myrtle warned him that alchemists had a habit of keeping both a journal and a book of working notes. Unfortunately, Gulbranson's notebook was not in her possession.

"Vicus," Barnaby said, addressing the stone lying at his elbow, "when did Antonio Salieri live?"

"The composer Antonio Salieri was born August 8, 1759, and died May 7, 1825."

"Is there any connection between Franz Liszt and Antonio Salieri?"

"In 1820, Liszt received lessons in composition from Salieri.

"How old was Liszt at the time?"

"Nine years old. Liszt was a child prodigy."

A child prodigy who studied with one of the most ambitious and reputedly jealous composers of the 18th century.

"Interesting," Barnaby muttered.

"What is interesting?" Moira asked, coming into the room and joining him at the table.

"Hmm? Oh, an ambiguous reference," he said, "but first, tell me what you discovered with the aos si?"

Moira ran her hand through her dark hair, briefly resting the weight of her head against the palm. "The best way I can describe what is happening to her is that she is experiencing a sort of metaphysical aphasia. Just as it seems her powers are perfectly normal, a gap in understanding or perception appears. Many times she is not even aware that she is losing time. If she were a human, I would suggest she had suffered a cerebrovascular incident."

"You mean a stroke?"

"Yes," Moira said. "She exhibits a similar kind of confusion. I have no explanation for it, but when I applied a protection spell, the symptoms improved markedly. I think you may be correct that she has been exposed to something that has slowly drained her ability to focus. What have you found in the journals?"

When Barnaby finished explaining the results of his

research, he asked, "Do you have any idea what Gulbranson meant by 'paired with a harp?'"

"Possibly," Moira said, standing and moving to another shelf heavily laden with books. "I seem to recall reading something in the recollections of an alchemist living in Paris in the late 1700s about a miniature harp." She ran her finger along the spines until she found an ornately bound tome. "Yes, here we are, the notes of Claude Beaulieu."

Using the same search spell Barnaby employed Moira located the reference. "I have it, the Krumpholz Harp."

"Krumpholz?" Barnaby said. "Who on earth is Krumpholz?"

"The husband of Anne-Marie Steckler," Moira said, scanning the page. "Her father was a renowned instrument maker. She studied with the harpist Jean-Baptiste Krumpholz and later married him. Krumpholz nursed a passion for perfecting the design and musicality of the harp. It was rumored that he crafted a harp no more than six inches tall that possesses the ability to reproduce any music played in its presence. He supposedly used the tiny instrument to capture ideas for his own concertos and sonatas from other composers."

Barnaby nodded. "Which would make it a perfect companion for a chess set of similar abilities. Was this Krumpholz a wizard?"

"Not according to Beaulieu," Moira said. "Krumpholz was a human, but he was so attuned to the power of music, he discovered the magic that can be worked with it."

"What happened to him?"

"The poor man drowned himself in the Seine when his wife ran off with her lover," Moira said. "The harp is rumored to have later come into the possession of Antonio Salieri in Vienna who used it to further his own musical ambitions against rising stars like Mozart."

"Ah!" Barnaby said. "Now the pieces are starting to fall into place. Liszt studied with Salieri."

"And subsequently became the most technically brilliant pianist of the age."

"He left the chess set to his son in law, Richard Wagner," Barnaby added.

"Who was Adolf Hitler's favorite composer," Moira finished. "The last known location of the Listz chess board was in the hands of the Ahnenerbe."

"So, we have a full circle that connects the chess set and the harp, but how would they be used together?"

Moira placed the journal back on the shelf and returned to her seat. "Jinx says the pawns are arranged in different configurations every day?"

"Yes, and no one ever plays a game on the board."

"They wouldn't," Moira replied thoughtfully, "it would repel users as a means of self-protection if it is charged with a mission."

"What mission?"

"I think the chessboard is being used as a kind of transmitter," Moira said. "The pieces form the message, which must be sent to the harp for decoding. The Nazis may have been interested in the pairing of these two artifacts for their ability to unobtrusively gather and disseminate information."

"But did the Nazis have the harp?"

"Not that I am aware of. It was not on the list of items that the alchemists working with the Monument Men were charged with recovering and containing."

Barnaby digested that information for a minute and then asked, "Would the board be capable of arranging the elements of a message unaided?"

"I don't think so," Moira said. "From what little we know about it, the pieces must be manipulated."

"Then we are left with three questions," Barnaby said,

holding up his hand and ticking the points off on his fingers. "Is the board affecting Myrtle? Who sends the messages? Who receives them?"

"Five questions."

"Five?"

"How is Fish Pike's murder connected," she said, "and how do we shut down that chess set?"

Chapter Thirteen

When Mom, Festus and I came out of the city gate, the dragonlets appeared to act as our escort. As we walked, Mom chattered happily, regaling us with light-hearted stories about Aunt Fiona and her "projects." By silent agreement, Festus and I let her set the tone of the conversation. We both knew we had to jump right back into getting answers about Fish Pike's murder once we were home again. We welcomed the distraction.

When we reached the portal, Mom insisted on using her magic to open the gateway, saying she needed all the practice she could get. She went through first, but I paused to deliver one more mini-lecture to the dragonlets about flying too close to the houses in Shevington. They promised to be good. Halfway through the opening, I looked back to see Minreinth watching me closely.

"What is it?" I asked.

The dragonlet danced forward until he stood just on the other side of the portal. Turning his head to the side to fix me with one of his amber eyes, he let out a series of worried chirps.

"You can't come with me," I told him. "There are plenty of people on this side who have my back."

The dragonlet made a whining sound.

"I'm sorry," I said, "but there are no dragonlets in my world. If you came with me, you'd be the one in danger. I'll be back. You have my promise."

Minreinth nodded, but I could tell he didn't like it. The door closed behind me. I stood looking at the blank wall for several seconds. The dragonlets had never been reluctant for me to leave The Valley before. Were they getting attached to me, or did they know something the rest of us didn't?

"What was that all about?" Mom asked.

I shrugged. "Separation anxiety, I guess. They don't usually act that way."

"I'm having separation anxiety too," Festus groused from his mesh compartment. "For my food bowl and a glass of creamed whiskey."

"Don't get your fur in a twist. You know it takes an hour to walk back to the lair."

"From where I'm sitting," he grumbled, "you're doing more standing than walking."

"Fine, fine," I said, "we're moving. Why don't you finish your nap?"

That was code for "stuff a sock in it," which I couldn't say with Mom standing there.

I heard something over my shoulder about "expiring from hunger," but we hadn't gone more than a few steps until light snores replaced his grumbling. Mom and I continued our conversation about Aunt Fiona and her life in Shevington until we saw the lights of the lair and Chase's tall, lean figure waiting for us.

"Now, Norma Jean," Mom said, dropping her voice, "whatever you two argued about, you fix things with that man before this nonsense goes on any longer."

Wincing at the use of my full name, I said, "It wasn't an argument, it was more of a disagreement."

"Over what?"

"He was doing that whole caveman needing to protect the little woman thing."

Mom sighed. "And you did the whole I'm a powerful witch, I can take care of myself *thing* in response, didn't you?"

I hate it when the parental units are smart.

"How did you know that?"

"Because I had the same argument with your father . . . several times."

"Wait a minute," I said, "you told me Dad doesn't know about your magic."

Mom made a sort of dismissive gesture with her hand. "I may not have been entirely forthcoming about all that," she said. "It's a long story that we don't have time for right now, but your father doesn't know I've come back into the possession of my powers."

Sensing a theme in the works, I said, "Which I assume also means you haven't told him about my powers either?"

"Not exactly."

"Oh, come on, Mom! That's like saying someone is 'kinda' pregnant," I protested. "If Dad knows about magic, then he needs to know about us both."

We were almost in earshot of the lair, and I could tell Mom really didn't want to continue the conversation. "I know, I know," she said, "but it's complicated."

"Cop-out answer there, Mom, or what?"

"I'll tell you about it later," she hissed. "Now be nice to Chase and fix things."

That left me with nothing to do but mutter an obligatory "yes ma'am," before putting a genuine smile on my face for Chase and greeting him with, "Hey, you! What are you doing here?"

To my immense relief, Chase reached to give me a hug and a kiss, actions that woke Festus up immediately.

"Could you two get a room or something?" the old cat groused, extending a lone claw and unzipping his compartment. "Bend down so I don't break a leg getting out of this thing."

Obediently I went down on one knee. Festus jumped clear of the backpack, shook out his fur, and looked up at his son. "Hello, boy. You do anything productive today or did you spend the whole morning mooning about making up with your girlfriend?"

"Wow," Chase said, looking at me with wide eyes. "Has he been this sweet all day?" Turning toward mom, he added, "Hi, Kelly. Sorry you've had to endure Dad's bad mood."

"Festus is never cross with me," she said loyally. "He's just hungry and thirsty."

Chase looked down at his father. "I suppose water would be out of the question?"

"Don't be ridiculous," Festus said. "Why would any sane person put water in Scotch?"

Sighing, Chase said, "Duly noted." He moved to the liquor cabinet and poured a dram of single malt into a silver bowl, which he placed on the hearth.

"Now we're making some progress," Festus said. "What do I have to do to get a meal around here?"

"Darby!" I called.

The brownie instantly appeared beside me. "Yes, Mistress?"

"Any chance we can all get some lunch?"

Before he could answer, Chase said, "Actually, I was hoping I might steal you away for lunch and take you for a gourmet meal."

Before I could answer, Mom chimed in with, "What a

lovely idea! You two run along. Festus and I will keep each other company."

Exchanging a bemused look with Chase, I said, "A gourmet meal of pizza?"

"Of course," he said, brightening, "today's lunch special is that pineapple monstrosity you love."

He was taking the easy banter between us as a good sign, so I turned the smile up a few notches when I answered. "Says the man who can eat his weight in disgusting pepperoni."

"Felines," he informed me archly, "are carnivores. We need meat."

From the direction of the hearth, Festus said, "A point this feline has been trying to make for more than an hour."

Laughing, I turned back to Darby. "Do you mind fixing lunch for Festus and my mother?"

"I would be most happy to, Mistress," Darby answered cheerfully. "I can prepare anything they like."

Honestly, I don't know if Darby has some kind of kitchen hidden in the lair or if all of his "cooking" is pure magic, I just know our grocery bill has gone down since he's been around and we're eating better than ever.

As Chase and I headed upstairs, I heard Festus ordering a steak and Mom asking if Darby could manage cottage cheese with fresh fruit—proof that opposites attract.

Tori must have heard us coming because she stepped out from behind the counter in the espresso bar to great us.

"Hey," I said, "how is everything?"

"Quiet," she said in a low voice. "Nothing out of the ordinary."

Chase swiveled his head between the two of us. "Is there something going on here I don't know about?"

Ignoring the questions, I said to Tori, "I'm going to fill Chase in over lunch, and I had that conversation with Barnaby we talked about."

Chase likes to be ignored about as much as his father does.

"Fill me in about what? What conversation?"

Tori turned the same deaf ear to his questions and said to me, "Okay. I think that's a good idea. How long will we have to wait for an answer?"

This time, the note of consternation in Chase's voice ratcheted up a notch or two. "Are we even having the same conversation any more?"

I held up my hand in the universal sign for " hold on," and answered Tori. "I don't think it will be long. Maybe even later today."

Before Chase could express more of his growing impatience, I turned to him and said, "Okay. We can go to lunch now."

"If lunch will get me some straight answers," he grumped, "lead off."

He was still frowning when we walked out the front door of the shop. "What the heck was that all about?" he asked. "I expected one of you to start talking in code about dogs barking at night."

"Not here," I said firmly and headed across the street without another word. Normally we would have gone around the square on the sidewalk, but I was in no mood for the long route today. I cut straight across the courthouse lawn.

Chase caught up with me a few strides past the Confederate monument. "Are we far enough away from the store now for you to give me a clue about what's going on?"

"You know the mystery musical chessboard?"

"Sure," he said, "the one Tori thinks is haunted."

"That's the one," I replied, "but it's not haunted. I think 'possessed' might be a better word."

That was enough to make Chase stop in his tracks. "Possessed is a very serious word, Jinx. What makes you say such a thing?"

We were standing across the street from the Stone Hearth pizzeria. "Let's go inside and order," I said. "The story was complicated enough before I talked to Barnaby. Now it's a real doozy."

"You'd be surprised how many conversations with Barnaby turn out that way," Chase said ruefully.

He held the door of the restaurant open for me. Pete, the owner, greeted us. He didn't seem to find it at all unusual when Chase asked for one of the private booths in the back. It was common knowledge around Briar Hollow that Chase and I were becoming an item. Pete obviously assumed we wanted to be alone—which we did, but not for the reason he thought.

When we were settled with big glasses of ice tea, and Pete was off to the kitchen with our order, Chase said, "Now, talk to me about this possession business."

"Why does that word bother you so much?"

"There is dark magic in the world, honey," he said, "far darker than anything Brenna Sinclair could dish out. Possession is serious business."

"I think I figured that out when I tried my psychometry on the chessboard," I said, describing my vision of the board's hellish interior prison and watching as Chase's expression grew even more clouded.

Finally, I couldn't take it anymore. "You're scaring me with that look on your face."

"From what you're telling me, we should all be scared of that thing," he replied. "What did Barnaby say about all this?"

"That," I said with a sigh, "is where things start to get complicated. I think he knows something about the chessboard, but he wouldn't tell me until he talked to Moira. That's the conversation I was talking to Tori about. Barnaby said he'd get back to me just as soon as he and Moira talked."

"Okay," Chase said, "that's good. Nobody knows more about magical artifacts than Moira unless it's Myrtle so . . . .."

He stopped and looked at me.

"Okaaaaaay," he said warily, "I know that expression. There's more, isn't there?"

I nodded and launched into a long recitation about our suspicions regarding Myrtle's behavior. Chase didn't say anything, but when I finally ran out of steam, he took a long drink of his tea like he wished there was something stronger in the glass. Then he said, with complete conviction, "The aos si would not lie to you knowingly."

"I don't want to think she would, but how can you be so sure?"

"Because I know her. Her behavior has to be tied to that damned chess set in some way."

"I could use a dose of that faith."

Chase considered my words and then said, "Why don't we go get some for you?"

"Where?" I laughed. "The Faith Store?"

My wisecrack made us both laugh, which was something we really needed to do. The last lingering tension between us dissipated and Chase reached across the table and caught hold of my hand. "I'm sorry I made it sound like I don't think you can take care of yourself."

"And I'm sorry I went all 'I am woman hear me roar' on you," I admitted. "A lot of that was rattled nerves over finding Fish out front and not wanting to give you more to deal with by telling you about Myrtle."

"That's okay," he smiled. "Water under the bridge."

I can tell you exactly what I thought at that moment. *"If Chase and I never had disagreements more serious than this one, life was going to be easy."*

File that one away under "Tempting Fate." You'll see why by the time this story is done.

"So," I said, "what's this business about getting me some insta-faith?"

"What I had in mind," he answered, "was a trip out to the waterfall tonight. It's still a full moon, you know."

Knasgowa.

Why didn't I think about that?

My ancestor's spirit dwells near an enchanted pond. The night I met her, she told me to talk with her any time. I hadn't been back since but Chase was right. I needed the advice of the founder of our line.

"That's a really good idea."

"I do get them occasionally," he said, adding firmly, "and I'm coming with you."

Chase cut the protest that rose to my lips short.

"Don't even. I'll go in panther form and hang back at the edge of the clearing, but I'm going, and that's that."

Since we had just made up, and I really didn't like the idea of wandering around the woods with a killer on the loose, I gave in.

"Okay. I won't argue."

Then something occurred to me.

"You realize you've never shifted around me," I said.

Chase grew still, studying me with eyes that betrayed a flicker of doubt. "How do you feel about that?"

"Well," I said reasonably, "it's not like I haven't seen you as a panther before."

"You didn't know it was me.

"Oh," I said, "I think I did. No one else looks at me the way you do."

Chase colored. "You're nice to look at."

Reaching back across the table, I caught hold of his hand again. "Thank you, and it doesn't bother me at all. We need to get you over being afraid of that."

"We do, huh?"

"Yeah, we do."

"Okay then," he said, "it's a deal. Leave at sunset?"

"Sunset it is."

We made a point of talking about anything but "business" for the rest of the meal. When we were ready to leave, it took several tries to get Pete's attention. He seemed completely preoccupied with a text conversation on his phone.

When we finally paid the bill, we decided to make our usual circuit of the square before we went back to the shop. We hadn't gone a block when Chase received a text message of his own.

"Well," he said, squinting at the screen, "I'll be damned."

"What?" I asked, on high alert for more trouble coming our way.

"It's from Furl," Chase said. "He and his brothers are coming to Briar Hollow tonight. He wants to talk to us about the hit man."

"Do we still have time to go to the waterfall?"

"Yes. They won't be here until late. It looks like we're going to have an interesting evening."

Right. Because things had been so boring up to that point.

Chapter Fourteen

We saw the Sheriff's car pull up in front of the shop when we were about halfway around the square. John Johnson spotted us too, and waited with crossed arms until we joined him.

"Thought I'd come by and tell you what we know so far," he said, "and maybe drink a cup of that fancy ex-press-o stuff while I'm here."

Smothering a laugh at his exaggerated pronunciation, I said, "Hi, John. I'll make the espresso myself if we can talk in Chase's shop instead of mine."

"How come?" Johnson asked.

For a fraction of a second Evil Jinx, who sits on my shoulder some days wanted to say, "So our possessed chessboard won't hear what you say and send messages back to the mothership," but I caught myself.

Instead, I smiled and said, "My customers have bat ears. Anything you tell us will be all over town before you get back to the station."

Johnson chuckled. "Yeah, reckon you're right about that. We'll go in the cobbler shop."

"I'll be right back with coffee," I said. "Chase? Vanilla latte?"

"Please," Chase said. "And if there are any of those bear claws left . . ."

"Bear claws?" Johnson said, his face lighting up.

"Coffee and artery-clogging pastries coming right at you," I laughed, opening the door to the store.

As I walked past the seating area, I noticed our usual afternoon regulars at their favorite tables. Mrs. Larson, a retired schoolteacher, had her head buried in a cozy mystery and two old men were absorbed in a game of checkers. The musical chess board sat untouched in its usual place. I knew it was my imagination, but I could have sworn I saw an evil, glowing aura hovering around the damn thing.

Tori was behind the counter. When I joined her, she asked, "Where's Chase?"

"Next door in his shop with the Sheriff, who is getting ready to fill us in on what he knows about Fish Pike as soon as I get back over there with coffee and bear claws."

"Well," she said, "I know who gets the pastries. I hope John's wife doesn't find out we're helping him sabotage his diet."

"Actually, it was Chase who asked for them," I said. "How he can put pastries on top of all the pepperoni pizza he just ate is beyond me."

"Vanilla latte for him?" Tori asked, moving toward the machine.

"Yep," I said. "Double espresso for the Sheriff, and a cappuccino for me. I'll get the bear claws . . . oh, and we're going to have company tonight."

"Company?" she said. "Who?"

"The triplets."

She stopped in mid-coffee grind. "Here? In fur coats?"

"Yes, here, and I have no idea how they will be dressed.

"This," she said, going back to the espresso machine, "ought to be interesting."

"That's what Chase said."

"Great minds," Tori quipped.

She finished making the drinks, snapped lids on the cups, and secured them in a cardboard carry tray, which she held out to me with the firm admonition. "Go get the scoop. Come back and tell me *everything*."

"Always," I said, wedging the paper bag in between the cups before I took the tray and headed for the door.

When I came in the cobbler shop, Chase stood up to help, handing Johnson his espresso and setting our drinks on the counter. "Let me grab a roll of paper towels for the pastries," he said, ducking into his work area.

I might have wondered how Chase could eat a bear claw after a big lunch, but that didn't stop me from bringing one for myself too. The three of us settled on the benches that form an L-shape in the waiting area. Chase and I watched Johnson gnaw through his first pastry. I brought two for the Sheriff in deference to his diet-deprived status.

"Jinx," he said, washing down a mouthful and wiping the crumbs off his chin, "you may have just saved my life. I love my wife, but what kind of woman sends her husband to work with a salad that has tofu in it? What the hell is tofu anyway?"

"John, that's one of the great mysteries of the modern world," I assured him.

"Well, I am not into mystery meat, especially when it's not meat at all," he declared defiantly.

Privately, I wondered if that was how he talked to his wife, or if he ate what she put in front of him without complaint. My money was on option number two.

"You wanted to tell us something about Fish?" Chase prodded.

In between bites, Johnson filled us in on the investigation to date. As we suspected, Fish was killed with what the Sheriff called a "weapon with fixed multiple blades," but the old man had, as Festus suspected, died of a slit throat.

"That was the only lucky break the poor old bastard got," Johnson said.

Grimacing at the imagery, Chase asked, "How do you figure that was a break?"

"Probably didn't take him more than a couple of minutes to bleed out. All the really terrible damage was done later."

Johnson was right. Fish caught a break.

"Do you have any clues about the murderer?" Chase asked.

"Not the kind where we can go out and arrest somebody and honest to God, I don't think we ever will. Looks like to me Fish got mixed up with something kinky online."

I was swallowing a mouthful of coffee, and the conjunction of the words "Fish" and "kinky" sent me into a paroxysm of choking. Chase had the good sense to get my cup to safety before he started patting me on the back.

First rule of rescue: save the coffee.

When I could breathe again, and I'd wiped enough of the tears out of my eyes to see the Sheriff with some degree of clarity, I croaked, "Kinky? What on earth are you talking about?"

Johnson flushed. "Maybe I should just tell Chase this part."

Oh, for God's sake.

"Maybe," I said, "you should just quit beating around the bush and talk."

Johnson shot me a wary look. "Sorry," he said. I don't like to talk about things that are potentially sexual."

"John," Chase said, "at Fish's age, you're not seriously suggesting that sex had anything to do with his death, are you?"

Reddening even more, Johnson said, "Well, not the normal

kind anyway. I think Fish may have had himself one of those fetishes."

"A fetish?" I said incredulously. "For what?"

"Mountain lions," Johnson said. "When we opened up his house, everything looked pretty much the way Martha Louise left it except for this one room that was padlocked at the back of the house."

"And?"

"Damnedest thing I've ever seen. The whole place was plastered with pictures of mountain lions. He had this big ole map of Briar Hollow and all the surrounding counties up on the wall with red push pins in it and lines of yarn run between them. The whole thing was covered in sticky notes."

I didn't dare look at Chase, who asked calmly, "What did the notes say?"

"Crazy stuff," Johnson said, shaking his head. "A lot of nonsense about portals to some hidden valley and parallel streams of time. I knew Fish was nuts, but I didn't know he was that bad. He had an old computer hooked up to the Internet. My deputy knows about that technology stuff. Fish was talking to a lot of other nutjobs about paranormal crap. Werewolves and sh. . . . stuff like that. Near as we can figure, Fish got it in his head he could turn into a mountain lion. There was a notebook filled with rambling entries about mountain lions mating with humans."

Chase took a drink of his latte and made a show of shaking his head. "That's really sad. You think maybe he started having some dementia after Martha Louise died?"

Dementia. Good angle. Certainly more believable than Principal Snyder on *Buffy the Vampire Slayer* blaming everything on street gangs tanked on PCP.

I waded in. "That breaks my heart!" I said, making my face crumple to the point of tears. "Dementia is a terrible disease.

Fish was all alone. Someone must have taken advantage of his diminished capacity."

"Maybe it was dementia," Johnson said as if the idea hadn't occurred to him. "He wasn't drinking or doing drugs, but he was talking to another crazy guy online who had that same idea about turning into a mountain lion. My money's on crazy Internet guy showing up with some kind of fake claws or something and killing Fish. We found a username on one of those discussion boards we think is probably the killer. Looks like he was somewhere in the Seattle area."

Alarm bells started going off in my head.

"What was the username?" Chase asked.

Johnson reached into his hip pocket and took out a notebook permanently bent into a banana curve. He flipped through a few pages filled with scrawled handwriting and then said, "Jeremiad. Whatever the hell that means."

"It means a long, mournful complaint," I said softly, "a lamentation or a list of woes."

"Huh," Johnson said, unclipping a pen from his shirt pocket and adding the definition to his notes. "Well, there you go. Somebody with a grudge looking to work it out on a crazy old man. The whole thing is God awful."

"It is," Chase agreed. "Did it look like a robbery too?"

"Nope," Johnson said. "There wasn't a drop of blood in the place. Looks like Fish went willingly with the killer. We still haven't found the actual crime scene, but I imagine this nut job is long gone. I think he propped Fish up down here for show. The bench outside your shop is the only one on this side of the square, and this is the road straight out of town. The note must have been a reference to the mountain lion thing, kinda the killer's way of saying, 'Look what I did.' We'll poke around a few more days, but like as not all of this will go straight to the Feds and right into a cold case file."

Which we couldn't risk happening. The Registry might

have looked into the Seattle killings, but human law enforcement had to have been involved as well.

Johnson lingered a few minutes longer before heading back to the station. As the door closed behind him, I said, "Chase, are you thinking what I'm thinking?"

"That the username 'Jeremiad' is awfully close to the name Jeremiah?"

I so wanted that similarity to be a figment of my imagination.

"Do you think the hit man is one of the Pikes?"

"I think there's a good chance."

"But if the killer is another werecat, why the fake claws? That doesn't make sense."

"No, it doesn't, but we have a more immediate problem."

"The mountain lion room."

"Exactly," he said, blowing out a long breath. "We have to get in there and make sure that nothing falls into the hands of the authorities that could lead them to the Valley or . . . "

That's when the lightbulb switched on in my head.

"Or that implicates you," I finished. "Oh my God, Chase. This could be a frame job in the works. What if somebody figures out the symbol on the dagger is from your family crest?"

"Honestly, honey," he said, "I don't think John's that smart, but we don't want somebody smarter having any reason to start asking more complex questions. I don't think we have a choice. When the triplets get here tonight, we have to perpetrate a little cat burglary."

That turned out to be a literal statement.

Chapter Fifteen

Thanks to what my father calls "that damned made-up daylight savings time," leaving at "sunset" meant Chase loaded my bike in the back of the Prius around 8:15. We reached the trailhead at dusk with a full silver moon rising over the mountains. On my last visit to the waterfall, Knasgowa's spirit told me not to fear the five-mile ride through the woods. She assured me my magic would protect me. I believed her. It also didn't hurt that my hypervigilant mountain lion boyfriend would be loping along beside me.

We parked the car in a clearing off to one side of the small parking lot in recognition of the prominent "No Cars After Dark" signs. Chase lifted my bike out of the trunk. While I checked the tires and tested the headlamp for the third time, he took off his shoes and belt, depositing them neatly on the backseat. I suspect if I hadn't been standing there he would have stripped before he shifted. Instead, he looked at me and asked, "Are you sure you're ready for this?"

"I'm sure. Go ahead."

In bad horror movies when a werewolf shifts, the process looks contorted and painful. The makeup and special effects people must love the challenge of creating the gruesome transition. Fictional lycanthropy however, is a disease or a curse depending on how the author sets up the story. Real shapeshifters have inherent magic. They are born to live a dual existence.

For werecats, the shift begins with a shimmer at the top of the head that slowly pushes the human form toward the ground. Werecats have two size options, large and small. I've never seen Chase as a house cat, I only know that he's a Russian Blue.

In a matter of seconds I went from looking at a six-foot tall man to admiring a massive tawny mountain lion. When the shift finished, Chase stepped out of the puddle of discarded clothing and looked at me expectantly.

"How are you doing with this?" he asked. His voice sounded deeper, more gravelly, but it was definitely Chase.

As much as I hate to confess this, I said exactly what I felt, "I'm resisting the urge to pet you."

Something between a purr and a laugh rumbled up from Chase's chest. "Don't let me stop you."

I knelt beside him and laid my hand on his head. Chase closed his eyes and leaned into the touch. Honestly, I didn't know what to say. I wanted to tell him he was magnificent, but the words stuck in my throat. Instead, we sat quietly for a moment or two, enjoying the sounds of the night and the unexpected closeness in our opposing forms. I needed Chase to know I accepted him completely. I'd been careful not to allow myself to have any emotional expectations about being with him when he shifted, so I was both surprised and pleased by the feeling that washed over me—an incredible sense of peaceful warmth.

Chase finally broke the mood, saying regretfully, "We have to get started for the waterfall if we're to get back to the store and talk to the triplets."

Reluctantly I stood and climbed on my bike. "Do you want me to go slow?"

"No. Pedal at your regular speed. I won't be far away, I promise."

With that, he melted into the woods. I switched on my headlamp and pushed off down the trail.

Riding a bike creates a wonderful sensation of freedom. My enhanced perception of the surrounding forest filled me with an exhilarating awareness of my growing powers. I sensed Chase moving through deep undergrowth off to my right. As he negotiated the darkness, a silent pathway cleared before him. The night-dwelling creatures stilled and drew inward. To them, Chase was an alpha predator, a thing to be feared.

When the path opened into the clearing at the bridge that spans the pond, only the sound of the waterfall broke the quiet. Chase stopped at the edge of the woods and watched me as I parked the bike and descended to the water's edge. The moon cast a long shining path across the water.

"Grandmother?" I called. "Are you here?"

"I am here, granddaughter," Knasgowa answered—and she was—sitting on the flat boulder amid a cluster or rocks directly across from the waterfall.

In whatever realm where she now resides, my ancestral mother appears ageless. She wears the simple blue gingham dress of a pioneer woman with her long, black hair parted in the middle and done up in a bun. Her rich, brown skin is smooth and flawless, and her smile gentle and kind.

When I sat beside her, she reached to embrace me. Unlike Beau, who in spectral form can manage only the cool suggestion of contact, Knasgowa's touch feels warm and strong.

"You are troubled. Tell me."

The recitation I gave her was different from the way I'd spoken with Barnaby. With Knasgowa, my fears and insecurities tumbled out. The words gushed forth in a confused torrent that perfectly mirrored my desperate need to tell her everything. Through it all, my grandmother held my hand, absently stroking my knuckles with her thumb, her eyes never leaving mine.

The entire recitation fell somewhere between a panic attack and a meltdown.

Honestly, people, think about what I'd been through over the last few days.

A dead man on the doorstep on Sunday, a demonic chessboard on Monday, and right in the middle of it all, doubting my mentor, and having a fight with Chase.

Sitting in the moonlight in the middle of the woods talking to my several-times-great-grandmother was the most normal thing I'd done since taking the trash out the previous Thursday. I really, really, *really* wanted her to fix everything.

Knasgowa listened until I ran out of breath. Then she patted the back of my hand and said, "You must focus your mind. You are not even aware of the thing that really frightens you."

"I'm not?"

She laughed gently. "No, you are not. What you fear most, child is not the presence of a murderer in your midst or this chessboard with its unknown intent. The son of the McGregors is here with you tonight, lying at the edge of the trees, so your disagreement with him is forgotten. What you fear, Jinx, is the passing of the one you know as Myrtle and what that means for the responsibility you must assume for your own life and powers. Your fear, granddaughter, is the fear of every young person. You must face the prospect of taking your first steps on the journey to becoming an elder."

Did she have to use the word "*elder?*"

The instant that thought crossed my mind, Knasgowa laughed outright. "Elder does not mean old, Jinx. It means wise and in complete possession of your abilities. In your mind, in that safe inner space where you make careful plans that keep you secure, you had thought many years would pass in this apprenticeship with the aos si. They may still. That is not knowledge I possess. But like your friend, Colonel Longworth, I, too, know that all living things change with the passage of time. You must prepare your heart and mind for the possibility that Myrtle must now embark on the next portion of her own long journey in this existence."

"I don't want her to die," I blurted out.

"Oh, child," Knasgowa said softly, "I am not so much speaking of dying as becoming. Myrtle is an ancient being beyond our understanding. I know well the power that resides within her. That cannot die, but it can change form. Remember that the winter rain freezes against the earth to sleep until spring when it melts and fills the rivers. Life demands such cycles of us all. Fear is born of resistance to what is and must be. You cannot help the aos si, nor can you discover the answer to the old man's death or the reason this game board sits in your store until you become the mistress of your own fears."

"What if I'm not ready?"

"You would not have reached this point in your life if you were not ready," she said. Then, turning toward the treeline, she called out, "Son of McGregor, I would speak with you."

Obediently, Chase emerged from the shadows and padded over. He stood before my grandmother, bowed his head and said something in a language I didn't recognize but guessed was Cherokee. Knasgowas answered him in English.

"Your family's debt to me has been repaid countless times these many years since Degataga's death. Callum McGregor's sin is not your own. This trouble that has come to your doorstep stems from the fruit of a different tree. Look to the descendants of Jeremiah Pike for your answers."

Chase raised his head. "Do you know the killer's identity?" he asked.

"No. I only know that he is one who hates what he is and hates you for what you have."

"Can you tell us how to find out who he is?" I said.

"The killer will come to you in a way that will make you confront your fears and surpass the strength of your mothers. I am sorry, granddaughter, that is all I can tell you. I love you, child. Come to me again. Do not let your trust falter in those who have never done you harm. There are reasons that secrets must often be held close in silence."

With that, she was gone.

If you've never dealt with your ancestors, let me give you a word of advice.

Don't expect straight answers, and don't be surprised when they still manage to comfort you even when what they just told you makes absolutely no sense.

"Any idea what that was supposed to mean?" Chase asked.

"None, but it's starting to sound like this Fae hit man is also a Pike."

"One who kills with fake claws because he hates being a werecat," Chase said. "It's not much to go on, but it's something. We need to get back to the shop and talk to Merle, Earl, and Furl about this."

We needed a change of subject, and the triplets names—or at least one of them—had been bugging me since the day I met them.

"Is his name really Furl?"

Chase grinned. "His name is Ferlin."

He looked at me like I ought to be instantly getting the joke, which I wasn't.

"Sorry to be slow," I said, "but what's funny about that?"

"Ferlin. Like Ferlin Husky."

I still didn't get it.

"Wasn't he some old country singer?" I asked, searching my memory from the days when The Nashville Network constantly played on our living room TV. "Was he that guy with the pompadour and the rhinestones?"

"No, that was Porter Waggoner. Ferlin Husky didn't do sequins. The triplets mother was raised in Nashville. She was a Grand Ole Opry groupie and named the boys after her favorite country and western stars."

The light was starting to dawn. "Merle Haggard?"

"Right."

I wracked my brain. "The guy with the banjo?"

"Earl Scruggs, and Ferlin Husky."

"Him I still don't get," I admitted.

"*A Fallen Star?*" Chase said. "*Wings of a Dove?*"

For the first time in our relationship, he sounded like a guy in his 80s.

"I get the gist," I said. "So people shorten 'Ferlin' to 'Furl' so the names will rhyme, right?"

"Wrong. When Furl was little, he was indignant that he was the only brother named after a dog, so he changed his own name."

I frowned, "Named after a . . ."

Oh! He thought his mother named him after a Siberian Husky.

"*Seriously?*"

"Seriously," Chase nodded, adding solemnly. "It's a cat thing."

That did it. I cracked up.

Between my grandmother being wise and loving, and Chase telling me that ridiculous story, I was relaxed and enjoyed the ride back to the car. The clue Knasgowa gave us wasn't much, but it was something. She told me I shouldn't lose faith in Myrtle. At least I thought that's what she said.

But then we got back to the car—where we found Chase's

clothes neatly folded on the trunk and the upholstery ripped to shreds.

There was a note.

"When the cat's away, the mice will play."

Hit man or not, this guy was starting to get on my nerves.

Chapter Sixteen

The evening made for an emotional rollercoaster. Knasgowa's words comforted me, but looking back, her warning about the killer carried ominous foreshadowing. The lighthearted exchange over Furl's name gave us a brief respite which the discovery of the shredded upholstery destroyed.

For the record, the thing about the seats pissed me off. You don't want to mess with a girl and her hybrid.

I fumed about the upholstery for the first mile or so back to town. Chase clearly couldn't believe what he was hearing. Finally, he couldn't take it anymore. Banging the steering wheel with both hands, he said, "Jinx, the seats can be fixed! This guy is *watching* us."

"Really, Chase?" I asked sarcastically. "You think?"

He opened his mouth to bark back, then caught himself, and clamped his jaws tightly shut.

We drove another mile in complete silence before I said, "I'm sorry. My nerves are as shredded as these seats."

"Mine too," he said. "makes me crazy to think he was out

there with us and I didn't know it. It makes me feel like I'm not doing my . . . "

"If you say 'job' you will not like my reaction."

Chase pursed his lips but had the good sense to rethink his next words.

"Let me rephrase that. If this guy is a werecat, I should have been able to sense his presence."

"How?"

"Werecats have heightened senses. I didn't hear or see anything out of the ordinary tonight. He must have been fairly close to the trailhead when we parked."

"Not necessarily," I said. "You were watching the rearview mirror all the way out here. Do you think we were followed?"

Chase shook his head. "No. The road was empty, and nobody drove by while we were getting ready to go into the woods."

"Then the killer must have known where we were going and waited until he thought we were away from the car."

He considered my words. "That's one theory, but he also could have been watching us from a distance, some place high up with a good pair of binoculars."

"So, the real question is: How did he know we were coming out here tonight?"

Chase frowned. "I assumed it had something to do with that damned chessboard."

"Maybe, but we've been super careful not to say anything in front of it."

"But you told Tori we were coming out here, didn't you?"

"Yes," I said, "but we were downstairs in the lair. Chase, there's really only one place that you and I talked about the waterfall, and that was at Pete's over lunch."

Paling visibly, Chase said, "That could mean the killer was in the pizza place with us."

He knew where I was going with my line of thinking, but he didn't want to come with me.

"No one was sitting near us," I said. "The only person we talked to or who came near us was Pete."

Chase shook his head. "There's no way Pete is on our list of possibles. He's not Fae, and he's not a shifter."

"But he was preoccupied texting someone as we were leaving the restaurant."

"That could be a coincidence," Chase said. "I've known Pete for years. He's a good guy."

By this time, Chase was guiding the car through the town square. I decided to drop the subject, but that didn't stop me from looking across the courthouse lawn toward the pizzeria and wondering.

Chase wanted a more definitive answer. "You think so too, right?" he pressed. "About Pete?"

"Hmm?" I said absently, snapping out of my reverie. "Yeah, of course, Pete's a good guy."

There's just one problem. Magic can do bad things to good guys.

Chase parked the Prius in the alley, and we walked into a dimly lit, deserted first floor.

I looked at Chase and shrugged. He pointed toward the basement door and raised his eyebrows. I nodded but held up my hand indicating we should wait a minute. I stepped closer toward the seating area and strained to look at the chessboard. All the pieces sat in proper order. I glanced at my watch and made a mental note of the time, 10:30.

Nodding at Chase, I opened the door to the basement and started down. He almost careened into me when I stopped dead in my tracks.

Twelve people and a rat sat grouped around the fire waiting for us: Tori, Beau, Festus, Myrtle, Moira, Barnaby, Aunt Fiona, Mom, Gemma, Merle, Earl, Furl, and Rodney.

"This," Chase muttered, "can *not* be good."

As we negotiated the last few steps, I silently agreed.

The only member of the magical family not present was our fellow witch, Amity Prescott. She was out of town at an art dealer's convention in Atlanta. We did, however, have a congregation of three alchemists, five werecats, one corporeal ghost, three witches, the aos si, a brownie, and a super smart rodent.

Festus lounged on the hearth as his usual ginger cat self, but the three young men sitting with him could only be the triplets. I'd know those jovial, round faces and bright eyes with or without the striped fur and curled ears.

As I held my hand out to the first of them, I said questioningly, "Hello. . . ?"

"Earl," he answered, taking my hand and giving it a bouncy shake.

I made a mental note: *Earl - cowlick.*

Merle was next. *Nerdy glasses.*

And finally, Furl. *Star Wars wristwatch.*

After we finished the introductions, I hugged Mom and asked, "What are you doing here?"

"I have no idea," she replied. "Myrtle sent a message to both Gemma and me asking us to come over tonight."

Clearly this was some sort of summit conference, which likely meant things were even worse than we thought.

Chase claimed a chair near the hearth as if unconsciously seeking werecat solidarity with Festus and the triplets. I took the last remaining place between Beau and my mother. No sooner had I settled down than Rodney hopped over Beau's lap, hit my forearm, and ran up to position himself on my shoulder.

We waited until the silence stretched past the point of comfort.

Finally, Myrtle seized the proverbial bull by the horns.

"Barnaby and Moira have shared your concerns with me," she said.

Oh, great.

Had I mistaken a family intervention for a summit conference?

Myrtle caught the look of uncertainty on my face. "You were right to go to him."

I let go of the breath I hadn't even realized I was holding. Everyone else seemed to relax as well.

"I do have to ask, however," Myrtle continued, "why didn't you speak with me directly?"

She sounded hurt, which made my face color with instant shame.

Tori and I exchanged a guilty glance. I was hoping Tori would answer the question, but she told me in unspoken but no uncertain terms that I was the one up at bat.

Swallowing, I admitted the truth. "We thought you were lying to us."

This time Myrtle, for all her wisdom, appeared to be perplexed. "Why would you think I would lie to you?"

The question, so innocently put by a being of her age and experience, made me feel even worse.

I didn't have a good answer, and Tori's expression told me she didn't either. I did the best I could.

"I'm sorry, Myrtle. You've always had all the answers."

"And when I didn't, you decided that I must be lying?"

Now both Mom and Gemma were fixing us with their custom versions of *the look*, and Tori and I were blushing redder by the minute.

"Answer her, Norma Jean," Mom commanded.

Barnaby came to my rescue.

"It is a human failing," he said kindly. "It is not entirely Jinx's or Tori's fault. They were raised in a world where mistrust in one's fellow man is quite common."

Aunt Fiona cleared her throat. "Actually, we're all to blame."

Every head in the room swiveled toward her.

"Don't look at me like that," Aunt Fiona said stoutly. "If you'll stop and think, you'll know I'm right. We've been feeding these girls half truths from the beginning. We thought we were protecting them and not piling too much on them all at once. Good intentions or not, that is lying."

Barnaby sighed. "Fiona is right. We've asked you to trust us, but we haven't always given you a reason to do so."

Until that moment, Myrtle had been with us in her librarian "look."

Without warning, a gentle wave of golden light washed over her. As she assumed her true form, regret etched her beautiful features.

"Fiona is right," Myrtle said sadly, "and my crime is greater than any sin of omission. I knew something was wrong when Brenna Sinclair returned to Briar Hollow undetected, but I refused to admit the truth. I attributed my failure to the absence of her powers, but now there is the matter of the chessboard. I feel nothing unusual in the store even now, but I am not correct, am I, Moira?"

The alchemist laid a hand on the aos si's arm. "No, my dear, old friend, you are not correct. I feel the chessboard and something else above us, something smaller and more confused, but definitely magical."

"As do I," Barnaby said.

"If I may?" Beau said.

"Of course, Colonel Longworth. What is it?" Barnaby said.

"Have you determined the origins of the chess set?"

"We have," Barnaby answered. "It is a magical artifact called the Liszt chessboard, so named because it is believed to have been crafted as part of a dark deal made by the composer Franz Liszt. In exchange for an innocuous device that allowed him to capture musical ideas from his contemporaries, Liszt employed the devil's chord in many of his major compositions."

Whoa, whoa, whoa, *whoa*!

"The devil *devil*?" I croaked. "You all said there is no devil. There's lying and then there's lying, and if you've been . . ."

Moira held up her hand and stopped me.

"In the sense of a Christian dichotomy pitting absolute good against absolute evil, there is no entity called the devil, Lucifer, Beelzebub, or any of the other names ascribed to him," she assured me. "The dark wizard Mephistopheles, however, was quite real."

While I was still trying to slow down my racing thoughts, Beau said, "Fascinating. The demon to whom Dr. Faust bartered his soul was Fae?"

"Yes," Moira said, "but one utterly without principle."

"Hold on," Tori said. "Who is Dr. Faust?"

Moira nodded at Beau. "If you will, Colonel?"

"Dr. Faust," Beau explained, "is the central character in a play of the same name written by Johann Wolfgang von Goethe and published in several versions early in the 19th century. I read it during a tour of Europe several years before the conflict you call the Civil War. As I understand it, the motif of a man bartering with the devil for ultimate knowledge is common in German mythology. Herr Liszt apparently made a similar bargain to enhance his musical abilities."

"He did," Barnaby said, "and to dubiously earn his reputation as one of the greatest pianists of his age."

"How do you know all this?" Gemma asked.

"The alchemical diaries," Moira said. "An alchemist who was a friend and contemporary of Liszt's had his suspicions about the chessboard. We believe it may have been paired with a secondary artifact, a miniature harp, that is being used at a distance to receive and translate messages."

Tori was following all of this a lot better than I was. "The pawns are arranged in a code? That message gets sent to the harp and its owner for translation?"

"We believe that to be the case," Barnaby said.

Chase leaned forward in his chair. "I don't suppose you know who sent the chessboard to Jinx and Tori?"

"We do not," Barnaby said. "But we do know the chessboard was last seen in the hands of Hitler's treasure-hunting institute, the Ahnenerbe, at the end of World War II."

That was the last straw.

"You are *not* serious!" I exclaimed. "Nazis? Next you're going to tell me the Ark of the Covenant is the real deal."

"Actually, the Nazi interest in . . ." Barnaby started.

"*STOP!*" I ordered.

The Lord High Mayor of Shevington blinked at me in obvious incomprehension. "I'm sorry?"

"I think what the girl is saying," Festus supplied helpfully, "is that dealing with the devil and Nazis in the same conversation is more of a hairball than she's ready to toss."

"*Thank* you!" I said fervently. "What he said."

A trill of laughter rippled through the triplets.

"And what the heck do you three think is so funny?" I asked crossly.

"Jinx," Earl said, "you've seen too many Indiana Jones movies. None of these artifacts is what Hollywood has made of them. Try to think of it all in modern terms. The chessboard is like a hidden electronic bug. It runs on magic, not on microchips."

That actually did help. I took a deep breath.

"Okay," I said, "fine. Let's go with the 'someone has bugged our place' line of thinking and stop all this evil-Nazi-devil talk. What do we do to take out the surveillance system?"

Still looking confused at my reaction, Barnaby said, "We don't want to take it out."

"And why would that be?"

"Because we need to know who put it here and why."

He said it like the answer was so obvious that I was painfully slow for not getting it immediately.

Which I probably was.

But can you see how these magical family conversations tend to go?

I swear to God I'm going to start demanding somebody type up an agenda so I can prepare for the bombshells the Fae tend to drop without a thought.

"We do have a somewhat larger problem than the matter of the chessboard," Moira ventured delicately.

"Which is?" I asked.

"Helping Myrtle."

That would be the moment when I instantly felt three inches tall.

Chapter Seventeen

"Myrtle," I said, "I'm sorry for doubting you, and for not instantly asking what we can do to help."

The aos si smiled at me with warmth and affection. "We have asked so much of you these past few months," she answered. "You have overcome your fears time and time again. I think we are all remiss for not saying more often and with greater feeling how proud we are of you, Jinx, and of you, Tori. Your reactions to the things we tell you are perfectly understandable and, well, frankly, thoroughly amusing at times."

I looked at the familiar sparkle in her eyes and couldn't suppress a sudden giggle. That was all Myrtle needed to start laughing as well. Our mirth proved to be contagious, moving around the assemblage in a wave of snorts and guffaws.

"The ark of the covenant," Merle gasped, tears of merriment streaming down his face. "Now that one was a *classic*!"

Wiping my own streaming eyes, I said, "I am *so* glad you all find me entertaining."

"Well, dear," Mom snickered, "you always have been given to overreaction."

"And where," I asked archly, "do you suppose I got that from?"

It was Mom's turn to look innocent. "From your father?"

"The only time my father overreacts is when he's got a big fish on his trot line."

"Oh, there was that time a grasshopper got down his shorts . . . " she said.

"Stop," I begged, doubling over laughing again, "please, I can't take it."

It took a few minutes before we composed ourselves. It might have been a mild instance of group hysteria, but the shared merriment erased all the awkwardness in the room and re-forged the team—which was good because the game plan was about to get more complicated.

Chase regained his focus first. "Moira, is there a way to help Myrtle?"

"We hope so," Moira said. "Obviously, artifacts were smuggled into the store by Brenna Sinclair and her associates. Barnaby and I believe there may be something here that is specifically damping Myrtle's powers."

Gemma beat me to the most obvious flaw in that scenario. "Then why haven't the rest of us been affected?"

"I am not like the rest of you," Myrtle said. "My magic derives from older, more elemental roots. There may be a substance here that directly counters the forces from which I was born."

Tori snapped her fingers. "Kryptonite!" she exclaimed. "Of course!"

Myrtle frowned. "I'm sorry?"

Earl jumped in. "Kryptonite," he said enthusiastically. "From the Superman comic books. Kryptonite robbed the Man of Steel of his powers. I loved those comic books when I was a kitten."

"Uh, for the record, Earl," Tori asked, "when did you get your first Superman comic book?"

He thought for a minute and said, "Sometime around 1937."

"Do you still have it?"

"Yeah, I have all of them. Why?"

"Oh, nothing," she said *but we need to have a talk when this is all over.*

I sensed an eBay conversation in the works.

Ignoring her daughter's entrepreneurial side, Gemma looked at Moira thoughtfully. "Are we talking about the unity of opposites?"

"Very good," Moira nodded approvingly. "Your alchemical training is returning to you quickly. Tori has intuitively grasped the concept, albeit in a unique context. Gemma, you may recall that it was Anaximander who first posited the idea that every element has an exact opposite or is, in some way, connected to an opposite. His student, Anaximenes, suggested that rather than a war of these substances, a continuum of change exists."

Even though they were talking way over my head, I followed the basic premise. They believed an object or substance in the store that canceled Myrtle out. Any *Trekkie* would catch on immediately: matter and antimatter.

"Whatever you choose to call the substance or the item," Barnaby said, "we need to locate it, and determine the nature of the second magical signature upstairs that Moira and I both feel."

Chase cleared his throat. "Actually, we have three things we need to do."

He quickly outlined our conversation with Sheriff Johnson, finishing with a description of Fish Pike's hidden room.

Furl hardly let Chase finish before he declared, "We have to see that room."

"I agree," Chase said, "but we can't risk getting on the Sheriff's radar. Right now, he doesn't think we're involved in Fish Pike's murder. I'd like to keep it that way."

Festus sat up and stretched. "You thinking what I'm thinking, boy?"

Chase nodded. "Cat burglary."

"Hot damn!" Merle said, pumping his fist. "Count me in!"

"Ditto," Earl grinned, "Let's hit the alley, boys."

This was starting to sound too much like one of those "hold my beer and watch this" kind of conversations.

"Slow down," I said. "What are you guys talking about doing?"

Festus regarded me with that same "slow child" look Barnaby gave me earlier. "The lads are going to get furry, and we're going to break into Fish Pike's house."

"And do what exactly?" Tori asked.

"Evaluate the material and get rid of anything damaging," Furl said. "It's part of our job at the Registry. Clean up and obfuscation."

"Huh?" I asked.

"Cover up," Tori said. "They go in and sanitize the scene."

"And you can do that and not get caught?" I asked.

"Really, Jinx?" Furl sniffed indignantly. "We *are* professionals."

After some bantering back and forth, we came up with three plans, one more unorthodox than the others. We were going to send a rat to do a wizard's job.

Everyone agreed we couldn't give the chessboard more information about our activities. Barnaby found no reference in the historical record to indicate the chess set was animate. In other words, the pieces didn't move themselves. It seemed likely that the second magical presence composed and activated the transmissions. None of us could go looking for that agent, but Rodney could.

"Are you sure you're up for this?" I asked the rat, who sat balanced on my knee, upright on his hind legs, regarding me with bright, expectant eyes.

Rodney nodded enthusiastically.

"You understand what we want you to do?"

He pointed upstairs and mimed nosing around. Then, his inner drama rat took over and we were treated to a rodent pantomime wherein Rodney wrestled a bad guy into a choke hold emerging victorious with fist upraised.

"Okay, Double O Seven," I said, "you got the search part right. But If you find something, don't bite off more than you can chew. Come get us. Promise?"

Rodney held up one paw in the Boy Scout salute.

"Do you mean that?"

His eyes went round, and he put one paw over his heart as if I had wounded him deeply.

"Okay, okay, fine," I said. "But be careful."

We all watched as Rodney jumped off my knee and took the steps in leaping bounds. He wasn't big enough to open the door, but he had one of his own, neatly gnawed behind the shelving unit that sat to the right of the basement entrance.

Next, Merle, Earl, and Furl discreetly stepped into the stacks to shift. They trotted back as their usual Scottish Fold selves. After some initial protest, Chase agreed to stay behind and join in the artifact scavenger. Festus, as the senior werecat present, would lead the stealth op.

"Dad," Chase said, looking pleadingly down at his father, "please don't cause any more trouble. We've got enough on our hands. Just get in there, assess the situation, and get out."

Festus let out with a sound something between a sigh and a hiss. "I was pulling off cat burglar operations before you were born, boy. Have some faith in your old man's discretion."

Faith in Festus' discretion? Yeah. That's how desperate we were.

The rest of us split into teams chosen by Moira based on complementary abilities: Mom and Gemma, Barnaby and Chase, Beau and Aunt Fiona. Tori was with me.

Myrtle, Moira, and Darby remained in the lair to continue their research on the chessboard and to examine anything we found.

"Barnaby," Beau asked, "can you give us any direction to guide our search?"

"Those of us who are practitioners should use our senses to read the power signatures of what we may encounter in the collection," "What Tori is calling 'kryptonite' may most directly affect Myrtle, but it should also register as unusual to us."

"Unusual how?" Gemma asked.

Moira spoke up. "The 'flavor,' if you will, of the energy should be caustic. It should touch your own magic with a kind of bitterness. Do you understand?"

Gemma nodded. "It's an antagonist. It should feel like it's pushing against us."

"Correct. If you locate anything that gives you that sensation, contact us here."

"How?" I asked.

"Why not just use our phones?" Tori suggested.

"I don't think the signal is strong enough down here," I said, pulling my phone out of my pocket and staring at a lone, pathetic bar.

Moira didn't look up from the stack of books she'd sent Darby into the shelves to retrieve. She raised her hand and spoke a few words in Latin. "Try now," she said.

Five bars.

"Can you do anything about getting us free unlimited data?" Tori asked.

Moira waved her hand again.

I cocked an eyebrow at Tori.

"What?" she asked. "We might need to stream video or something. I was being proactive."

As we headed off into the stacks, Tori said, "So, Jinksy, do we have the slightest idea how we're going to do this?"

"Nope," I said.

"Ah. So it's business as usual. Good to know."

That began three days of searching. The moms phoned home and told the dads they were staying over because we needed extra help taking inventory, which was only a semi-lie. Chase put a closed sign on the front door of the cobbler shop, but Tori and I were forced to keep our place running because of the chessboard. During regular business hours, pretended everything was perfectly normal. We wouldn't rush into the basement when the last customer was out the front door.

The situation would have been maddening, but it lasted only a day.

On the second night, Rodney caught a rat of his own.

Chapter Eighteen

The triplets followed Festus through the darkened streets. After a couple of blocks, Furl moved up beside him. "I thought you had trouble getting around on your bad leg."

Cutting Furl a look out of the corner of his eye, Festus said. "It comes and goes according to need."

"Uh-huh. is that like selective deafness?"

"Something like that. I'm retired. I only do things that interest me. This interests me."

"We're not gonna let this guy get to Jinx."

Keeping his eyes on the road ahead, Festus said, "I'm not worried about Jinx. I'm more concerned that boy of mine is going to do something stupid trying to protect her."

At the edge of town, Festus halted the group in the shadows across the street from a simple white cottage showing significant signs of neglect. No lights burned in any of the windows. The cats darted across the pitted asphalt and slipped through the slats of the white picket fence into the tall neglected grass.

Skirting the building, they made their way around to the back yard.

"You're up, Merle," Festus whispered.

Silently Merle jumped onto the back porch and examined the screen. He extended a single claw and made a careful cut along the wooden frame. When the opening was large enough, he worked his paw inside and flipped the simple hook and eye latch.

"Earl, a paw here?" he hissed.

When his brother joined him on the back steps, Merle said, "Hold the screen open so I can get a look at this lock."

Standing on his hind legs, Merle leaned in close to the hardware.

"How does it look?" Furl asked.

"Stock hardware," Merle said, running his paw over the surface. "Seriously old. Piece of cake."

Using his mouth, Merle extracted a long pick from a sleeve strapped to his front leg. The tool slid easily into the lock. Merle twisted his head side to side humming to himself contemplatively. Within a second or two, the lock clicked sharply. Replacing the tool in its case, Merle said, "Right side, Earl."

Earl stood up on his hind legs as well. Together the brothers rotated the doorknob and shoved against the door. It opened easily.

Looking over his shoulder, Merle said, "We're in."

After Festus and Furl slipped inside, Earl threw his weight against the door and closed it quietly, just in time to hear Festus swear, "Bastet's whiskers!"

"What?" Earl asked.

"It smells worse than a litter box in here," Festus said. "How do humans live like this?"

Merle nodded toward the counters piled high with stacks of dirty dishes and open cans of pork and beans. "I'd say this human didn't care. Doesn't look like Pike was much for housekeeping."

Festus shook his head. "I knew Fish was never the same after Martha Louise died, but I didn't know it was this bad. Of course, he wasn't exactly firing on all cylinders when she was alive. Come on, let's find that room. The Sheriff told Chase it's at the back of the house."

The cats stepped into a short hallway with scarred wood floors.

Earl stuck his head in the first door on the right. "Got a bathroom here. Pretty sure the cure for something is growing in the tub."

"Closet on this side," Merle said, "or a moth sanctuary depending on how precise you want to be."

Farther down the hall, Festus called out, "Boys, I think that's the one."

Three heads turned to follow his gaze to a door outfitted with a hasp that now stood open, a thick padlock dangling from the ring hook screwed into the frame. Festus went in first and let out a low whistle.

"Hey," Earl said, "how did you do that? Cats can't whistle."

"I've had more than 100 years to practice," Festus said absently. "Get your head in the game and look at this joint."

"Oh, crap," Merle said, spotting the huge map plastered on one wall. "Those pins are all the entrances to Shevington from the human realm. Even the ones that are secret."

Furl jumped up on the desk to get a better look. "Not just Shevington. There's the Raleigh portal and the one in Asheville."

He glanced down at his feet and backed up to read what he was standing on. These are reports of investigations on the Brown Mountain Lights."

"I've got reports on shapeshifter incidents all over the United States," Earl said, using his paws to dig through papers on the work table. "All kinds, not just werecats—and there's stuff here on the killings in Seattle."

"What the hell was Pike doing?" Merle asked.

Festus sighed. "In his head, he was trying to find his way home to the Valley. I tried to make him understand about the taboo, the shunning from the werecat community, but clearly, I never got through to him. The last time we talked, he told me he knew if I'd take him to the Valley, he'd be able to shift."

"Poor old coot," Furl said. "It wasn't his fault Jeremiah chose to take up . . . "

The words died in his throat, his whiskers twitching uncertainly. "Aw, geez, Festus, I'm sorry. I didn't mean anything about Chase and Jinx."

"I know," Festus said. "Don't worry about it. They're young. They're not thinking about the consequences—like what we're standing here looking at."

"We can't let the humans keep this stuff," Earl said. "They've seen too much already."

"No," Festus said, "we may have caught a break on that one. The Sheriff told Chase they hadn't processed this room because they wanted the Feds to see it intact. There aren't any pictures because the department's digital camera crapped out. Sometimes living in a poor-ass county has its advantages."

"This is an awful lot of stuff," Furl said, lifting one hind leg to scratch his ear. "I think there's only one thing we can do."

Merle flicked his tail. "Aw, man. Do we have to call those wild animals?"

Furl sighed. "We do. They're masters at making destruction look natural. We need them."

Earl groaned. "God. Don't tell them that. You know how easy they get the swelled head."

"Okay, can it, all of you," Furl said. "We don't have a choice. I'm placing the call. Make room."

As the others backed away, Furl stared into the space in the center of the room. A low, rumbling purr began to emanate from deep in his chest. The tip of his tail flicked rhythmically until a ball of light formed in front of him. After a few seconds, the sphere flattened into a cloud and cleared to transparency. Bright eyes twinkling in the depths of an ebony mask peered out at him over a sharp snout and button nose.

"Furl! Brother! How's the fur hanging, man?" the raccoon asked merrily. "You got a job for my wrecking crew? We've been working on some wicked new techniques."

"Hey, Rube," Furl said. "We've got a Class 1 security breach at this location. One room, but I need it to look like your boys broke in and trashed the place. It's a whole house job. Full shredder effect on documents and pictures."

"*Suh-wheet!*" Rube grinned, revealing a mouth full of sharp, white teeth. "Brother, we are on the case. Oh, man, this is gonna be a blast! Let me pull the boys out of the bar and catch a portal to the local sewer system. Be at your coordinates in thirty."

When Rube broke the connection, Merle said, "Do they *always* have to come through the sewers?"

"The sewers are like raccoon highways," Festus said. "You ought to see the database of nationwide diagrams they maintain."

"And you know this how?" Furl asked, cocking an eyewhisker at the old ginger cat.

"I may have gotten drunk with them a few times," Festus answered complacently, licking one front paw with studied nonchalance.

"Festus!" Earl gasped. "You've been to a raccoon bar? Do you have *any* standards?"

"Don't be so self-righteous, Earl," Festus snapped. "Those mangy critters make primo home brew. You think they're that crazy naturally? Not a chance. We're talking serious chemical help. Now if you're done questioning my morals, we've got half an hour before Rube and his team get here. Can we get some work done and case this joint, or would you rather keep lecturing me?"

"Fine, fine," Earl said, "but I can just imagine what Chase would say."

Festus put his ears down. "What you should imagine is what I'll do to you if you say one word to him."

"Gentlemen," Furl said, "enough. Spread out. Let's see what else is here."

Half an hour later, the sound of rapidly scampering feet from the kitchen brought all four cats back into the hall where they came face to face with a pack of six burly raccoons.

"Festus!" Rube said, moving forward and cuffing Festus in the whiskers. "Look at you, old man, all on the case like the suits here. You going straight on us?"

Festus returned the smack. "Don't be counting me out any time soon, you stinking gutter rat. This your best team? Looks like a bunch of sewer scum to me."

The raccoons broke into chattering laughter.

"You know my boys are the masters of mayhem," Rube enthused. "Leon there is our raccoon crap specialist. He can let it fly on command. Booger can gnaw through anything, and Marty has claws of steel. We will take this place down to the studs if you need us to."

"Nothing quite that drastic," Furl said. "Let me show you the real target."

Rube waddled after Furl and let out his own version of a whistle when he saw the secret room.

"Damn," he said, "whose house is this? Those are all the approaches to The Valley."

"Sorry, Rube," Furl said, "this is a need-to-know situation."

"Yeah, I hear you, brother. No worries," Rube said. "I'm not into this cloak-and-dagger stuff anyway. I'm all about destruction." Then he added somberly, "You guys may want to go out back and wait until we're done. Sometimes we get enthusiastic and don't watch out for bystanders. Don't want any collateral damage."

"Noted," Furl said. "We'll wait until you're ready for us to inspect the work."

As the cats headed through the kitchen, Rube cracked his knuckles and turned to his crew. "Okay, boys, let's burn this joint to the ground."

Furl hissed over his shoulder, "Nix on the fire, Rube."

"Don't get your tail in a twist. It's a metaphor, man," Rube called out. "You cats are always so damned literal."

"Which is a good thing when you're dealing with raccoons," Furl grumbled as he and Festus headed down the stairs. "Did you smell the breath on those guys? What the hell have they been drinking? Kerosene?"

"I wouldn't strike a match and find out," Festus said.

Two hours later, Rube emerged from the back door pulling shreds of fabric out of his claws. "Okay. I think we're done. Work of freaking art if I do say so myself. Go see for yourself."

Furl and Festus started forward, but Merle and Earl stayed in place. "You guys coming?" Furl asked.

"No way," Merle said. "I can smell the coon crap from here. I'll take your word on the quality control."

"Me too," Earl said. "You know I have a delicate stomach. I've already barfed three times today, so I'm not looking to do it again."

"Suit yourself," Furl said, heading for the door.

"So he's still the barfinator, huh?" Festus asked, limping beside him.

"Totally," Furl said. "He's one of those texture cats. Feed him chunky and up it comes."

"Lighten up on him," Festus said. "I've always been a pâté man, myself. Just cause you and Merle can eat everything in sight doesn't mean we're all that way."

"Says the man who can plow through his weight in nip nachos," Furl said.

"Nip is good for the digestio. . . "

The sight of the interior of the house rendered Festus speechless.

"Holy hairball," he finally managed. "This place looks like an earthquake *and* a tornado hit it."

"Aw, thanks, Festus," Rube said, trying to look humble and failing. "We put some signature moves on the place. I did the cabinets personally."

Festus looked at the cabinet doors. They were all hanging at odd angles, the contents of the shelves spilled out on the counters and down into heaps on the floor. "Spreading the flour and mixing it in with the sorghum was a nice touch," he said appreciatively.

"I thought so," Rube said clinically. "Marty worked a similar routine with feather pillows and vapor rub in the bedroom. We trashed all the living room furniture and dug up most of the carpet. Got into the coat closet for good measure."

"And the target room?" Furl asked.

"Now that," Rube said, waddling down the hall, "is a work worthy of a grand master. Gotta admit I took a few pictures for our portfolio."

"I told you this was a Class 1 security matter," Furl said. "No photos."

"Post demo, man. Totally post after it was all toast," Rube assured him. "No before pics."

"Fine," Furl said, "but I'll need to clear those before you share them."

"Absolutely, brother," Rube said earnestly. "Wouldn't dream of breaching protocol."

At the door, Festus and Furl were met with a sea of ripped paper and liberal deposits of coon by-products. The stench was so powerful, even Festus took a step backwards.

"Laid it on a little thick, didn't you?" he said, stifling a cough.

"Didn't want the humans to get it in their heads to try to put any of it back together," Rube said proudly. "They're not gonna want to touch any of that stuff now. We good?"

"We're good," Furl said. "Excellent work as always. I'll transfer your payment as soon as I get to The Registry in the morning."

"No sweat, man," Rube said. "We know you're good for it. Any objections to us hitting a few hen houses on the way out of town? We're craving eggs."

"I can't tell you what to do on your own time," Furl said, "just remember, you're in shotgun territory."

"Got it," Rube said. "Catch you cats on the Flipside. Come on, boys. Let's roll."

Festus and Furl watched as the raccoons lumbered down the hall and out the kitchen door.

"Would you just look at the size of the backsides on those guys?" Furl said.

"You taken a look at your own gut lately?" Festus asked.

"That's just fur," Furl said defensively. "I have very thick fur."

"Keep telling yourself that," Festus snorted. "Come on, let's get the boys and get home. Our job is done here. I want to get back and help out in the basement. I've got a bad feeling about all this."

Furl stopped. "You're still hung up on Kelly, aren't you? You want to get back and make sure she's safe."

Festus scowled at him. "She's my charge, Furl. You know that."

"Come on, Festus," Furl said, "it's just you and me here. We've known each other too long to play games with each other. Do you think this hit man has something to do with what happened before Jinx was born?"

Festus sighed. "I hope not, but I'm afraid it might. Fiona told me Kelly asked about the boy."

Furl's eyes went wide. "Oh, not good."

"Not good at all," Festus agreed. "If this hit man just has it out for McGregors that's one thing, but he wasn't after McGregors in Seattle. He's a claw for hire, which means the real bad guy is the one signing his paychecks."

Chapter Nineteen

We spent the rest of the night in the basement. Since Tori and I had to work the next day, we grabbed a couple of hours sleep on the cots that appeared in the shadows under the stairs. At dawn, we awakened to the smell of fresh coffee and a hot breakfast prepared by Darby, only to find a fully-organized command center in the lair.

During the night, it became obvious to Barnaby and Moira that the archives were too huge for a row-by-row search. When Tori and I headed upstairs to open the store, they were huddled over a collection of grimoires working on a focused scanning incantation. Mom and Gemma would be testing versions of the spell for them throughout the day. Beau was immersed in research duty with Myrtle, which left Chase and Aunt Fiona to conduct spot checks in the stacks at their direction.

Festus and the triplets, still in cat form, snored in a fur pile on one of the other cots. They'd come trotting in before Tori and I crashed, totally full of themselves over the success of their operation. Sheriff John Johnson was in for a nasty surprise when he returned to the Pike house, but Furl assured me there was ample and aromatic evidence to pin the whole caper on marauding raccoons. I couldn't imagine that half a dozen coons could be capable of the kind of destruction the triplets described—until I did a Google image search.

After we ate, Tori and I went upstairs. We made casual small talk, determined that the chessboard wouldn't learn anything interesting from us. It rankled that we couldn't work with the others, but our presence in the store was an important diversion. Thankfully, we enjoyed an unusually busy morning, which helped to keep my mind off of the ongoing search. Rodney was nowhere to be seen, but I knew he was there somewhere, hiding and watching. I found a package of his favorite treats ripped open in the storeroom, so the little guy was not only holed up but also well provisioned.

At noon, Tori said, "We need more take-out cups."

"Okay," I said, looking at her oddly. The extra take-out cups were in a carton in the storage closet at the back of the shop. Right where she put them.

"They're in the basement," she said with slightly exaggerated emphasis. "Downstairs. Would you mind getting them for me?"

Oh!

"Sure," I said, trying not to sound lame, "but there are a lot of boxes down there. Where did you put them?"

"I really don't remember," she answered. "You may have to hunt for them. Take your time. If you need help, holler."

She was as curious as I was to know what was going on down there. The manufactured errand created an opportunity for me to get a report.

Everyone was pretty much where I'd left them, except the werecats were awake, and the triplets were back in human form. Beau, Moira, and Myrtle had books and papers spread on every available surface in the lair. Beau looked like he was completely in his element. After all, he was an old soldier, and we were coordinating a campaign of sorts.

"How's it going?" I asked.

Moira rubbed her eyes. "Slowly. Barnaby is in the stacks with Kelly and Gemma testing the scanning incantation. It should be ready for you and Tori to try when you close the shop for the day."

"Have you found anything so far that shouldn't be here?"

"Yes and no," Moira said. "We have located some items that are not in the inventory of the collection."

That sounded promising. "Like what?"

"Nothing that would affect Myrtle, although I'm afraid Chase took quite a tongue lashing from the Skatert-Somobranka."

"The what?"

"The most ill-tempered tablecloth you can imagine," Chase said, walking into the lair and setting an armful of objects on the table. "These don't have inventory tags. I thought you should check them out."

He turned toward me and leaned in for a kiss, which I deflected and converted to a hug. "Everything okay?" he whispered in my ear.

"Too much of an audience," I whispered back.

Straightening up, I said in my regular voice, "Tell me about this Scattered Sambuco."

Chase chuckled. "Skatert-Somobranka. It's a Russian artifact that magically produces a feast when it's laid out. Fold it up, and the cloth cleans everything up for you."

"Now that," I said, "is a keeper."

"Not really. Unbeknownst to me, the thing is sentient and has a real hang-up about respect. I apparently offended it and was presented with three dozen rotten eggs for my troubles, complete with a thorough chewing out. How was I supposed to know the tablecloth was sick of cooking and officially retired?"

"You make it sound like a bitchy overworked housewife," I said.

"That's exactly what it is," he shuddered. "Trust me on this one. Stay away from Aisle 632, Section B, Shelf 42. It's the one with the stench."

"Got it," I laughed. "Anything else?"

Beau spoke up. "This, I am afraid," he said, pointing to something on a side table. I looked closer and recoiled in horror. The artifact looked like a mummified hand with a candlewick sticking out of each finger.

"Please tell me that thing is made of wax," I said.

"It is not," Beau said with evident distaste, "but according to Moira, this particular specimen is a forgery, which I have now confirmed by reviewing the recipe contained in Volume 2 of the *Compendium Maleficarum*, circa 1608."

"A *recipe*?" I said. "For a human hand candle?"

"Yes," Moira said distractedly, "to create a proper Hand of Glory one must have the *left* hand of a hanged murderer. That is a right hand."

Man, I *hate* it when that happens.

"So what does it do?" I asked.

"This one does nothing," Moira said. "A functional Hand of Glory has the ability to unlock doors and to freeze individuals in their place. According to our records, this one was acquired to stop a spate of scams attached to its repeated sale. Beyond that, it is purely decorative in nature."

Decorative? Uh, *no*.

Beau correctly interpreted my reaction and said helpfully, "It's on the list of things to be returned to their proper shelves."

Dang straight.

Myrtle was seated in one of the wingback chairs by the fire with a large book open in her lap. I went over and sat down on the hearth. "How are you?"

She closed the volume, holding it in her lap lightly with the long, elegant fingers I so admired. "Better since Moira covered me with a protection spell," she said. "All I can really do at the moment is peruse our inventory records and act as a Fae . . . " A frown creased her features before she looked at me appealingly. "A mechanical device used for the detection of radiation."

"Geiger counter,"

Myrtle sighed. "I should know that. I danced with Hans Geiger in Berlin before the Second World War."

"I didn't realize you'd been back to Europe," I said, trying to get her mind off the memory lapse.

She smiled. "My curiosity has always been both my blessing and my curse. I have visited many times and many places in human disguise."

"Who were you when you danced with Hans Geiger?"

The golden glow washed over her and I found myself looking at a flapper version of Myrtle, complete with bangs and heavy eye make-up. "Did you do the Charleston?" I grinned.

"Not with Hans," Myrtle said, transforming back to her golden self. "He was a bit of a stick-in-the mud, but in the night clubs of Berlin? Well, that was a different matter."

On an impulse, I reached over and took her hand. "We're going to find an answer."

Myrtle folded her hand over mine. "The only answer any of us have, Jinx, is to work with what the Fates give us. I have no say if Clotho decides to cut the thread."

"I'm sorry," I said, "I don't know what you mean."

"There are three Fates, the sisters, Lachesis, Atropos, and Clotho, the youngest. They spin the story of our lives. Clotho's thread is that of longevity."

"You're not done with your longevity."

Myrtle smiled again and squeezed my hand. "You should get back upstairs. I'll see you this evening."

I went, but I didn't want to. Tori was wiping down the tables in the now empty espresso bar when I closed the basement door.

"So," she said, "did you find the cups?"

Her eyes asked a different question, and mine gave a different answer, but what I said aloud was, "Yeah, lots of them."

Unfortunately, she had to wait for the rest of the day to get the real answers, and some of them did have to do with cups.

You know how little old ladies save butter tubs and jelly jars?

Turns out we have a whole collection of "lost" chalices.

It would appear that in the world of magical paraphernalia, when in doubt, enchant a freaking cup.

When we finally did get back downstairs, Tori took one look at the display piled up on the third work table that appeared in the lair and dubbed them all the "Dixie Cup Collection."

"This really could be the scene from the Indiana Jones movie when he has to figure out which one is the Holy Grail," Tori said, examining the tags on the cups. "The Chalice of St. Drogo. Who the heck is St. Drogo?"

"Drogo is the patron saint of repulsive people," Aunt Fiona said brightly.

"Really?" Tori said.

"Well, actually," Fiona explained, "he's an all-purpose saint. He's also supposed to protect people with hernias, sheep, and coffee shop owners."

I stared at my aunt. "And you know this how?"

"Oh," she said, "I'm a three-time champion in the Shevington Metaphysical Trivia League. You all should join. We have great potlucks."

"*Okkkaaayyy* then," Tori said. "So unless ugly, herniated, sheep-raising coffee shop owners can help Myrtle, I'm guessing we don't need Drogo."

"You do own a coffee shop," Aunt Fiona said.

We chose to ignore her.

"It's a shame we don't have the actual Holy Grail," Tori said. "That's supposed to be able to cure anything."

Moira put down her pen. "You are misinterpreting the legend. The Holy Grail isn't an object, it is the spiritual quest that each living soul takes in this life. The literature of the 12th century objectified the Grail to make the concept more comprehensible for the uneducated. The name of the Grail knight, Percival, means "piercing the vale," describing the path we all take between the light and the dark."

While she was speaking, Mom and Gemma walked into the lair, their arms laden with boxes and something that looked distinctly like Aladdin's lamp. Mom started humming a tune that sounded vaguely familiar, so I asked her about it.

"Oh," she said, "when Moira talks about the Grail legends I always think about this old song the Carter family sang. My grandmother loved it. It's called *Lonesome Valley*."

"What are the words?" I asked.

Mom sang it for us in her clear, sweet contralto. "*You gotta walk that lonesome valley, you gotta walk it for yourself, ain't nobody here gonna walk it for you, you gotta walk it for yourself.*"

"Well," Tori said, "that's certainly cheerful."

Myrtle, who was still sitting in her chair by the fireplace, said, "The words are realistic. We must each negotiate our journey alone."

The group in the lair grew quiet. "You're not alone, Myrtle," I said. "We're all here for you."

"Which I appreciate, dear Jinx," she said, "but we must be prepared. There may be no artifact affecting me."

I looked at Moira. "What is she talking about?"

"It is my personal opinion that Myrtle is being somewhat fatalistic," she said, "but it is possible that her energy may be in transition to another form."

"What does that mean?" I asked in a strangled voice.

"Energy does not dissipate, Jinx," Myrtle said, "but it can change form. That may be what's happening to me. I think you must prepare yourself for that."

"You're not changing or transitioning, or whatever the heck you want to call it," I said heatedly. "We are going to find something, and you're going to be fine."

With that, I turned on my heel and marched off into the stacks without looking back. When Mom found me, I was sitting huddled against a shelf, crying. She sat down with me and pulled me into her arms. I'd like to tell you she said something profound, but honestly? She cried with me. None of us wanted Myrtle to go away, and giving up wasn't an option.

I said a prayer while I sat there sobbing on my mother's shoulder. "Please God, help us find something."

With some help from a rat, I got an answer.

Chapter Twenty

Rodney sat on a high shelf above the espresso bar staring at the chess set. His assignment was to search for the unusual. Nothing he might investigate could be stranger than that game board. Last night he found the pawns rearranged. Sometime around dawn, he looked away, or maybe he dozed off. When he looked back the pieces were properly aligned. A major clue to their current problems lay in that board and he was determined to unravel its mysteries.

The night before, he kept close to the baseboard when he went into the storeroom for supplies. Rats don't have cheek pouches like chipmunks so Rodney retrieved a cranberry granola bar and carried the stick in his mouth to the outpost he scouted earlier in the day. He slipped covertly behind the front counter, organized between the display cases under the front windows, and scaled the magazine rack by the front door.

From there he crept from one shelf to the next, positioning himself behind a stack of dish towels that served as both a blind and a temporary resting spot.

All day long he watched the humans come and go in the

espresso bar. They were a strange species, so intent on doing things that made them unhappy. Rodney listened for more than an hour as two old men argued over a newspaper article about a Congressional scandal. In Rodney's experience human newspapers were good for only one thing—to be chewed up for bedding.

Rodney watched Tori operate the espresso machine enjoying the clouds of steam and the aroma of the rich, dark brew. He wished he could hop down to the counter and ask for a cup of coffee, but he couldn't give his position away. Although he didn't mind when Tori cooed at him and scratched the bridge of his nose, Rodney had made it clear to her early in their relationship that he possessed an active intelligence.

When she left her laptop open one day, Rodney looked up "how smart are rats" and left the search results on the screen. When she saw the article, she looked at Rodney and asked, "Are you trying to tell me something?"

He nodded.

"You understand me when I talk to you, don't you?" she asked.

He nodded again.

"Okay, little dude," she said cheerfully, "no more talking down to you."

Since then, they'd become fast friends watching movies in her apartment at night, and spending time with the others in the lair. Breaking his leg the night of the fight with Brenna Sinclair hadn't been fun, but Rodney clearly demonstrated his desire to be part of the action.

He believed his human friends had given him this mission in part because he'd proven his courage in facing the evil sorceress. As these thoughts were running through his mind that evening after the shop closed, Rodney heard a coffee cup rattle on the shelf behind the bar.

As he watched, a tiny witch peeled off a mug, hopped on her broom, and flew directly to the chessboard. There, she began to laboriously arrange the pieces, struggling with the ones that were taller than herself. His sharp ears picked up the sound of her gasping breaths. Rodney assessed his options. He couldn't catch the witch on the table and given Jinx's experiences with the board he didn't want to try.

He opted to run along the edge of the shelf and position himself for a single leap onto the counter while the witch's back was turned.

When he landed, Rodney, quickly ducked behind the pastry cabinet and sprang over the top of the microwave to get to the shelf where the now empty cup sat. Shrinking into the shadows behind the bottles of flavored syrup, he waited.

Minutes passed, and then he heard three sharp taps. Peeking out, Rodney watched as each of the pawns on the board levitated and settled back in place. The little witch flew to the basement door and hovered, clearly trying to listen to what was going on downstairs. Apparently, she couldn't hear anything, because she turned in mid-air and started back for her shelf.

When she landed beside her cup and stepped off the broom, Rodney came out from the shadows and squeaked to get her attention. The move worked entirely too well. The witch shrieked in horror, raised the broom like a weapon, and swung it at him, yelling, "Go away you filthy rat! Leave me alone!"

Ignoring the slur regarding his personal hygiene, Rodney advanced on the figure, trying to keep an open expression on his face. For his troubles, she whacked him in the snout with her broom. That was entirely too much. He did, after all, have a right to defend himself. Glancing around, he spotted a carton of wooden stirring sticks.

Grabbing one, Rodney struck an en garde pose, holding

the makeshift sword in one paw and gesturing at the witch with the other to come at him.

Taken aback, the witch swung wildly. Rodney parried neatly and knocked the broom out of her hand. With a perfect lunge, he pinned his opponent to the ground.

A look of sheer terror contorted the witch's green features. She tried to back away, but the shelf was too slick and smooth for her failing hands to get any traction.

"Don't eat me," she whispered in a trembling voice.

Rodney put down the stir stick and smiled at her, but the sight of his perfect white teeth only made the witch shriek again. They had a definite communication problem. There was only one thing to do—take her to the lair and let the humans deal with her.

Trying not to look menacing, Rodney moved toward the witch. As gently as possible, he used his forepaws to push her down on the shelf and roll her over. Then, he picked her up by the collar of her black dress, and making sure not to hit her head on anything, he started toward the basement.

"Put me *DOWN!*" she screamed. "Put me *DOWN!*"

Her protests died off into choked gurgles when he approached the edge of the shelf and gathered himself for the leap onto the counter. It was trickier with the extra weight, but Rodney made a perfect landing, repeating the maneuver to reach the floor. The witch went slack in his mouth, which made it much easier to carry her through the door and down the steps to the work table in the lair.

Jinx and Tori were both seated at the table having sandwiches. They looked up when he appeared at the edge of the table.

"Rodney," Tori said, "what on earth are you carrying?"

Trotting to the edge of her plate, he gently put the witch down, nudging the crumpled figure with his paw. She came awake with a start, jumping to her feet and looking around in panic. The vibrant emerald of her face washed out to the color of a pea when she saw Tori and Jinx peering down at her.

"I told you there was something weird about that cup," Tori said triumphantly. "There's our resident spy, the cup witch."

"I am not the '*cup witch*,'" the figure protested indignantly, stamping her foot. "My name is Glory Green. I would appreciate it if you'd keep that disgusting beast from eating me."

Tori looked at Rodney. "Why on earth does she think you're going to eat her?"

Rodney shrugged. Turning to the witch, he bowed and offered her his paw.

"What's he doing?" Glory asked suspiciously.

"He's trying to be your friend," Tori said. "It might help if you'd quit calling him names."

"He showed me his teeth before," Glory said suspiciously.

"That's called a smile," Jinx said. "He isn't going to hurt you, and neither are we. We do need you to answer some questions though."

"What are you doing?" Tori said out of the corner of her mouth. "She's supposed to be one of the big bads."

"Tori," Jinx replied, "look at her. She's three inches tall."

"I can hear you, you know," Glory said, smoothing the folds of her black robes. She then took a few steps towards Rodney. Even though her hand trembled, she took his paw and shook it. "Pleased to meet you, Rodney. Don't you *ever* pick me up and jump off a shelf with me again."

Rodney held up one paw in promise.

"Okay," Glory said, "then I guess you're alright. I'm sorry I called you a disgusting beast."

She looked up at Jinx and Tori. "I didn't want to do any of this," she said earnestly, "but I can't tell you why I'm here."

"Why not?" Jinx asked.

"If I tell you anything," she said, "Mr. Chesterfield will never make me big again."

Then, realizing what she'd done, Glory burst into tears.

Chapter Twenty-One

It's a toss up what wound up being stranger; the artifacts we found during the scavenger hunt or the discovery of our miniature spy. Tori and I didn't need our magical elders to confirm for us that while Glory might have been moving the chess pieces, she posed no other threat. She did, however, need to quit crying and start talking.

We tried to give her a tissue, but given her size, we might as well have handed her a tarp.

When Moira and Barnaby walked into the lair, Tori was tearing off tiny pieces of Kleenex and offering them to the wailing mini-witch while I attempted soothing talk. None of it worked. Glory's crying jag showed no sign of slowing down, especially after Moira retrieved a magnifying glass from the roll top desk to get a better look.

"Stop that!" Glory wailed. "I'm not a bug with a pin stuck in me. Oh! You're going to stick a pin in me, aren't you? It's because I'm green, isn't it?"

Moira hastily put the magnifying glass down as a new wave of shrieking started up.

Barnaby backed off toward the fireplace and motioned for

Moira to follow. "We're not going to get anywhere with her in this excitable condition. Perhaps you could reverse the magic Chesterfield used to create her?"

"Hmm," Moira said, "she does appear to be fully human, but without knowing the exact spell, I cannot reverse it."

Little or not, Glory had excellent hearing.

"Of course I'm human!" she sobbed. "All I wanted was a lock of Elvis's hair and a career in Vegas and instead I'm going to look like an Apple Sour Jolly Rancher forever!"

Barnaby frowned at me. "Do you have the slightest idea what she's talking about?"

"It's a bright green hard candy."

Holding out her thumb and forefinger to take a rough estimate of Glory's size, Tori observed clinically, "She's really more like a cocktail pickle."

That touched off a fresh wave of hysteria.

"Not helpful, Tori," I hissed.

"Look at her and tell me she doesn't remind you of one of those little cornichons," Tori whispered back.

From our years waiting tables at Tom's Cafe, I knew what she was talking about. For the uninitiated, a cornichon looks like a mini gherkin, and Glory did indeed resemble one.

That's when I got an idea. Cornichons made me think of gherkins, which made me think of dill pickles.

"Moira," I said, "if you can't reverse the spell, can you at least make her a little bigger?"

"I'm not sure," Moira said, "it depends on how Chesterfield miniaturized her." She approached Glory cautiously. "Excuse me," Moira said politely. "Excuse me! Did Chesterfield make you drink anything?"

Glory sniffled and shook her head. Hiccuping slightly, she said, "He said something in a foreign language that made me feel funny, and then I shrunk up like cotton in the hot water cycle."

"Uh, yes, well, of course," Moira said uncertainly. "Thank you." To Barnaby, she added, "No potion, just an incantation. I believe this is more in your line of expertise."

"My pleasure," he said.

He held his hand over Glory, who shrank away.

"Now, now," he said gently. "This will not hurt you. *Amplifico!*"

A shower of what looked like glitter rained down over Glory, who instantly grew to the size of an action figure. She was not only bigger but to our immense relief, she stopped crying. Unfortunately, she continued screeching.

"Quick! Get a ruler!" she demanded. When none of us moved, she stamped her foot, "Now!"

"Geez," Tori muttered, "bossy much?"

She went to the desk and came back with a wooden ruler stamped with the words "Briar Hollow Funeral Parlor: Let Us Measure You for a Custom Casket."

"We're in an ancient fairy mound surrounded by priceless magical artifacts, and *that's* the only ruler you could find?" I asked.

"Something tells me it's a leftover 'treasure' of Aunt Fiona's," Tori shrugged.

"I don't care what it is," Glory said impatiently. "How tall am I?"

This was taking the short-person syndrome to a whole new level.

Tori directed Glory to stand up straight so she could take a measurement.

Eleven and a half inches.

"Oh, praise the little baby Jesus!" Glory exclaimed when she heard the number. "I'm exactly the size of a Barbie doll! I can finally get some new clothes! Do you think I could wear anything from the Jackie Kennedy Barbie collection?"

I had my doubts, but since the last thing we needed was

any more crying, I murmured something about how we'd try. That launched Glory into a recitation of all the things her new size would allow her do, which could have gone on all night if Barnaby hadn't cleared his throat and cut her off.

"While I'm sure the potential of your new condition excites you, Miss . . . "

"Green," she said, "Glory Green."

For a minute I thought Barnaby was going to laugh, but he managed to hold it together. "Miss Green," he continued, "would you be so good as to explain your connection to Irenaeus Chesterfield?"

"Connection?" Glory said angrily. "That awful man imprisoned me on that cup and made me spy on these girls."

She turned back toward Tori and me. "After the first few days I didn't want to do any such thing," she said earnestly. "You are both just the nicest young ladies in the world. Your mamas raised you up right even if you are real witches. I don't think the Southern Baptist Convention would approve of you, but only because they don't know that you're good Christians. You are good Christians, aren't you?"

I nodded numbly, and Tori pointed out the obvious, "You're a witch too, Glory."

"In appearance only," Glory said. "I'm an involuntary witch, so that doesn't count, and I can't do anything but put myself on the side of the cup and then peel myself back off again and fly around on my broom. But now I won't fit on the cup or the broom, so that means that unless you have a magic travel mug or a whisk broom, I can't really do anything anymore."

A magic *whisk* broom?

"Uh, I think you're safe," I assured her.

"There you go," Glory said triumphantly. "So I'm really just a little person with a skin condition. But anyway, where was

I? Oh! Well, I just knew after the first or second day sitting up there on that shelf that you all weren't in league with the forces of evil, but that Mr. Chesterfield is the devil himself. I swear to you I wouldn't be one bit surprised if he has horns and a tail!"

In case you haven't caught on, Glory can be exhausting, but if you let her talk, she'll tell you everything you want to know and a whole lot you don't. It took the better part of an hour, with endless rabbit trails veering off the subject, but she ultimately told us the entire story about how her deal with Irenaeus Chesterfield to buy a lock of Elvis Presley's hair went badly awry.

She confirmed his alliance with Brenna Sinclair and described in excruciating detail her arrival by special courier on our doorstep. "Those uppity delivery services are *not* worth the money," she said. "I had bruises for a week after getting bounced around inside that box, tissue paper or not. Mr. Chesterfield should have used UPS like the rest of us."

"Miss Green," Barnaby said, "do you think Chesterfield was behind the murder of the man found on the sidewalk here at the store?"

Glory shook her head. "I don't think so. They did hire that old man to break in and put something down here in the basement. I guess Mr. Chesterfield might have killed him to keep him from telling you all about that, but wouldn't he have done that right away?"

"Indeed he would have," Barnaby said.

Out of nowhere, Festus jumped up on the table. "Where'd the talking dill pickle come from?"

To our utter astonishment, Glory marched forward and smacked him solidly on the nose. "Bad kitty!" she said sternly. "Bad kitty!"

"You are *not* serious," Festus growled, narrowing his eyes and curling back his lips. "I'll show you 'bad kitty.'"

"Dad, stop!" Chase ordered, joining the group standing around the table.

"The munchkin punched me in the nose," Festus said indignantly. "I'm just supposed to put up with that?"

"Lighten up, Festus," Tori said. "Glory is having a bad day."

"Oh, but I'm not!" Glory trilled happily. "I've *tripled* in size minus half an inch. I don't have to be on the cup any more, and I can go *shopping* again. Can I go shopping now, please?"

Seizing the opportunity to get Glory occupied doing anything but talking, I said, "Tori, why don't you and Glory get on Amazon and order some clothes in her size."

Tori glared at me, but she held her hand out to Glory, who happily deposited herself on Tori's palm. They went over to one of the secondary work tables, and Tori fired up her laptop.

"Good heavens," Barnaby said in a low voice, "that woman is utterly exhausting. I cannot imagine what she would be like at full size."

"She must be what you've been seeing flying around upstairs," Chase said.

We went over everything Glory had told us for him and Festus, who was still rubbing his nose with his paw and looking grumpy. "I might have known this would all go back to that Creavit scum Chesterfield," he said darkly. "You should have taken that guy out when you had the chance, Barnaby."

"I do not disagree," Barnaby said tightly, "but at the time, I believed I was acting on my principles."

"You were," Moira said, "but Chesterfield abused those principles badly."

"So what do you think?" I asked. "Did Chesterfield hire the hit man to kill Fish Pike?"

"Possibly," Barnaby said, "but now that we are aware of his involvement in all of this, I do believe it is even more likely that there is something in this basement dampening Myrtle's powers. For the time being, our efforts are best spent continuing the search."

We continued all right, unearthing Leonardo da Vinci's lost manuscripts, which contained all his notes on the Fae, including several wine-drinking sessions with Brenna Sinclair. There's a good reason why only about a fifth of his papers are known to have "survived." The guy was a major magic groupie. Think mosh pit level obsession.

Mom and Gemma turned up the missing end of the Bayeux Tapestry.

Never heard of it? Don't feel bad. I thought it was one of Aunt Fiona's abandoned needlepoint projects until Myrtle explained the 10-foot long piece of cloth should have completed the 230-foot piece considered to be the world's most recognized tapestry, which dates from 1092.

Whatever they used for mothballs in the 11th century worked.

Anyway, the end of the tapestry had to be cut from the original because the imagery showed shapeshifters, wizards, and other magical creatures in attendance at the crowning of William the Conqueror.

We could have hosted the world's most lucrative garage sale, but nothing we unearthed seemed to affect Myrtle in the slightest until the third night. That evening, first Moira, and then Barnaby, turned sharply and looked into the stacks.

"Do you feel it?" Moira asked.

Barnaby nodded. "An object of great power, approaching with some velocity."

At that moment, Merle, Earl, and Furl burst out of the archives batting a jet black ball in front of them in a wild game of feline hockey. With one last resounding smack of his paw, Furl sent the ball careening into the lair where it slowed and rolled to a gentle stop in front of the fire.

Everyone froze except Moira, who drew her wand. Myrtle, who was seated at the table, went catatonic.

"Where did you find that?" Barnaby asked, cautiously approaching the ebony sphere.

"All the way at the back of the north section of the archives," Merle said. "Earl spotted it and took a swipe at it. He has an obsession with stuff that rolls."

Earl shrugged. "It's a cat thing. Anyway, the instant my paw touched it, there was like this blue energy wave that rippled off the thing and then we could feel the artifact's power, so we brought it in."

"You didn't think to warn us?" Moira asked. "That was incredibly reckless."

Barnaby bent to study the object. "It must have been shielded," he said to Moira, "but how did they get through?"

"They are in their shifted form," she replied. "Their native magic must have disrupted the shield sufficiently to shatter it."

"Is it what I think it is?" Barnaby asked.

Moira nodded. "Yes, that is the Orb of Thoth."

As usual, I was out of the metaphysical trivia loop.

"And he was?" I asked.

"An Egyptian Fae revered in the ancient world as a god," Gemma answered. "He was believed to be the scribe of the underworld, the maintainer of the universe, the developer of science, and the master of magic."

Oh. *Him.*

"Thoth was the Egyptian equivalent of an Alchemist," Moira said. "Legend has it that Thoth fashioned an orb from a meteorite that damaged the step pyramid at Saqqara during its construction sometime around 2630 B.C. The artifact has long been considered apocryphal since no astrological records record the descent of any such meteorite."

"How can you be sure this is the orb?" I asked.

"Look closely on the surface that is turned toward the fire."

The flames highlighted an Egyptian hieroglyph. The body of a man with the head of a long-billed bird.

"What is it?" I asked.

"Thoth," she said. "That is his sigil, his mark of power."

Great. Signed, sealed, and delivered. Now, it was time to mark the thing 'return to sender.'

"How do we get rid of it?" I asked.

Moira shook her head. "According to the story, Thoth used the flames of the Otherworld to create sufficient heat to melt the metal and fashion the sphere. The material retains both the icy cold of deep space and the burning heat of the earth's core. Thoth forged the orb as a symbol of the balance which must be maintained between good and evil. It is an alchemical creation of phenomenal skill and genius, second only to the Philosopher's Stone. It must not be destroyed."

"Wrong answer, Moira," I said. "Look at what it's doing to Myrtle."

Moira turned to Myrtle, who sat frozen in her seat at the table, pen poised over the page of her notebook. When Moira touched her arm, Myrtle looked up and smiled, but there was no recognition in her eyes. Moira spoke softly to her in Gaelic and Myrtle responded in the same language.

"What did she say?" I asked.

Moira's eyes welled with tears. "She told me that she is lost and asked if I could help her to find her way home."

Chapter Twenty-Two

"If we don't have good information about what makes this orb tick," I said, "then I have to use my psychometry. We have to find the off switch."

Mom started shaking her head before the words were even out of my mouth. "You can't do that. It's too dangerous. This thing comes from outer space, for heaven's sake."

For a minute I thought Chase was going to take her side, but then his eyes met mine, and he nodded imperceptibly. If my incredibly over-protective werecat boyfriend could get onboard with the plan, so could my mother.

"I'm sorry, Mom. This isn't your call to make. It really isn't anyone's call to make but mine. I don't work for any of you, do I?"

After a minute or two of restless shuffling from the group, Barnaby said firmly, "You do not. Free will is one of the most cherished of all Fae principles."

Now, let's pause for a reality check here. To be honest, we all kind of *do* work for Barnaby. After all, he is the founding Fae father in our merry band, but Barnaby was making it clear he didn't intend to pull rank, which amounted to a stamp of approval. After that, there wasn't much the others could say. Plus, Barnaby's confidence in me bolstered my resolve.

Honestly? I was scared to death to touch the Egyptian Magic Eight Ball from Planet X. There was no way in hell I was going to admit that, though, and I couldn't see any other option.

Instead, my voice fairly rang with determination when I said, "Then let's do this thing."

Moira said quietly, "I believe it would be safer if Myrtle were in Shevington when you examine the object. We have no idea how your connection with the orb might affect her."

"We can handle that," Furl volunteered. "I want to go over the file on the deaths in Seattle last year anyway. It would be our honor to escort the aos si to the Valley. Just give us a minute to change."

The triplets gathered up their folded clothing and disappeared into the stacks, re-emerging in a few minutes as humans —and well-pressed ones at that. While they were in feline form, Darby did their laundry.

Furl approached Myrtle, who was still sitting at the table with a dreamy expression on her face. He bowed low from the waist. "Dear lady, would you care to take a walk with us?"

Myrtle smiled at him. "Are we going some place nice?"

"We are. A beautiful valley filled with flowers."

Her next question brought tears to my eyes. "Will I know anyone there?"

I bent down beside her chair. "Myrtle, you may not remember them right this minute, but you know everyone in the Valley, and they all love you. The boys will take good care of you."

She gave me the same vacant, but radiant smile. "If you say it's alright, then I'll go."

The complacent absence of all thought and purpose stood in complete contrast to Myrtle's usual vibrant wit and intellect.

The change in her broke my heart at the same time that it frightened me deeply.

Myrtle stood and accepted the arm Furl offered to her. We watched in silence until the four of them were out of earshot. I turned to Moira. "Will she be better in the Valley?"

"Yes," Moira said. "The greater the distance she attains from the orb, the more her mind will clear."

For the next hour, we all puttered around the lair waiting for Moira and Barnaby to detect the portal's activation. As soon as Myrtle was safely through to the other side, we began.

The Orb of Thoth lay against the hearth where it landed when the triplets rolled it out of the stacks. Moira picked it up carefully with both hands. "What do you feel?" Barnaby asked.

"It weighs more than its size would suggest," she said, "and there is definite power, but I am experiencing no negative effects."

She carried the sphere to the work table. Surprisingly, it sat perfectly still. Either the table was incredibly level, or the orb knew something was up.

I pulled back a chair and sat down. Tori positioned herself beside me.

"Okay," I told her, "if I get into trouble in there, pull me out."

"Don't worry," she assured me. "Just call out like you did with the chessboard. I'll hear you."

From across the table, Mom tried one last time to get me to reconsider. "Jinx, please. You're not ready for this."

All my life, Mom had fed me variations of that same sentiment. As a grown woman and with a better understanding of what my mother lived through, I understand the sources of her hypervigilance. Over the past few weeks however, I'd watched a new confidence replace her usual trepidations. I wasn't about to let her—or myself—backslide.

"Stop it, Mom," I said firmly. "If you keep waiting to be

ready, that's all you'll do, wait. Myrtle needs our help now. I've spent hours practicing my psychometry. I can do this, and I trust Tori completely if anything goes wrong. If you can't watch this, maybe you better go upstairs."

Her lower lip trembled, but then Gemma put a hand on her back. Mom turned and looked at her best friend. "She's not you, Kell," Gemma said softly, "and Tori's not me. Myrtle was right when she told you they have to walk their own path. It's our job to support them, not to get in their way."

Tears brimmed in Mom's eyes, but she nodded—a short, jerky, thoroughly unhappy nod, but a nod all the same.

Turning back to me and swallowing hard, she said, "Okay."

Softening, I said, "Don't worry. I'll be fine."

Using the techniques Myrtle taught me, I drew in several deep breaths and stilled my mind, creating an empty space for another awareness to enter. Unlike my encounter with the chessboard where I'd foolishly gone in unprepared, I took my time. When I felt ready, I laid both hands on the shining curved surface.

The cold struck me first, not like an icy wind but as something solid and real. Currents of torrid heat snaked through the frigid atmosphere. You're probably waiting to hear that it all looked like the interior of an Egyptian pyramid from some mummy movie. Sorry. I walked through bare rooms with walls as black as the stone itself. Some unseen force guided me in ever-tightening circles toward the center of the sphere. When I reached it, a man was waiting for me.

"Are you Thoth?" I asked.

"I am a representation of the one called by that name in your reality. You may refer to me as you please. Why are you here, witch?"

Okay, so introductions weren't necessary.

"The orb is harming my friend, the aos si."

With an unreadable expression and a flat voice, Thoth said, "You seek to destroy this place."

"Not if I don't have to. I want to help my friend."

"Do you know why the orb was created?"

I really wasn't in the mood to play 20 metaphysical questions, but it didn't look like I had much choice.

"I've been told it was made to balance the forces of good and evil."

"This is a place of opposites, conceived as an experiment to mix in harmony the forces of heat and cold, light and dark. The material from which the sphere is forged was made in the depths of the universe in the unmovable blast that set in motion the momentum of all that is. Your philosophers would call it a product of the First Cause."

"Isn't that just another name for God?"

For an instant, a flicker of a smile threatened to mar his impassive features. "Man has made many gods, but there is only one universal force. That is the First Cause."

"Okay," I said, "the orb is really, really old. So is my friend, and this thing is killing her."

"No," Thoth corrected, "it is killing her powers."

"Same difference."

"You cannot reconcile in your mind the very opposites from which this was conceived. That is your limitation. The one you call Myrtle has always been known to you as a source of great power. Your mind cannot conceive of her in a diminished state."

So, he did know what was going on.

"I love Myrtle no matter what her state."

"But you prefer that she be at her full capacity to counter your fears and insecurities. The opposite of fear is valor. Do you have valor, witch?"

When it doubt, bluff.

"Try me."

It didn't work.

"Bravado is not valor, but it is a step in the correct direction. To help your friend, you will be called upon to summon bravery that at the moment you do not dream you possess. Your answers do not lie with me, but I have a request of you."

Oh, perfect. *"I can't help you lady, but how about you do something for me?"*

"What is it?"

"Hide this orb where no one can find it. It was appropriated by the wizard named Chesterfield and has long languished in his possession. He used it for a minor purpose, as a weapon, not as an object of evolved contemplation. He must not be given an opportunity to reconsider his understanding."

"I'm the one who doesn't understand," I admitted.

"That is of no matter." Thoth said. "Your Alchemist comprehends. She is correct when she says that removing this material from the proximity of the spirit known as the aos si will alleviate the damage done to her. But that is not the greatest concern."

"It's the greatest concern to me," I said.

"You must broaden and deepen your concerns, witch, if you are to fulfill your purpose. Mark my words, Irenaeus Chesterfield must not recover the orb. Should he ever come to understand its true potential, all will be lost."

Before I could ask anything else, widening eddies began to churn around me. I plunged into a morass of searing temperatures that alternately froze and burned my body as I fought to stay upright. This time, the current pushed me away from the center toward the shell of the sphere until I found myself flattened against a black wall, straining to get out.

"Tori!" I called. "Now!"

Suddenly I was in two places: inside the orb and sitting at the table in the lair. I felt Tori's hands resting on mine and unconsciously reached for our shared power. A wave of blue energy engulfed us both, giving me the strength to pull away. We sat there for several seconds, staring into each other's eyes. I realized the physical connection allowed Tori to see and hear everything I'd experienced. As the light around us dissipated, she said, "Do you have any idea what the hell that guy was talking about?"

"What guy?" Mom said worriedly.

"Jinx?" Chase asked, cautiously laying a hand on my shoulder. "Are you okay?"

"Moira?" I said shakily.

"I am here," the Alchemist answered, stepping into my line of sight. "What is it?"

"We have to get this Orb as far away from Myrtle as we can, and we can't ever let Chesterfield get his hands on it again."

Chapter Twenty-Three

Barnaby and Moira made me recount every nuance of my exchange with Thoth. I described the interior of the sphere in detail and tried to remember the exact words the entity used. When I finished, Tori said, "Now, wait a minute. Is this guy actually *living* in there?"

Moira shook her head. "I don't think that is the case. It sounds as if Thoth bound a portion of his essence to the sphere, perhaps even at the time of his death."

Tori frowned. "I don't get it."

Opting for language I knew she would get, I said, "Princess Leia. Hologram. R2D2."

"Oh!" Tori said. "Why didn't you just say so?"

It was Moira's turn to look utterly confused. "I have no idea what the two of you are talking about."

I couldn't resist. "Now you know how *we* feel most of the time."

Moira laughed. "Fair enough, but I will correct one point. I do not think what you encountered in the sphere is a hologram. I am familiar with that aspect of human technology. A hologram is a projection of recorded data. The being you encountered is more than that."

"More how?"

"He is, I believe, a guardian consciousness for the artifact. Judging from your report of the verbal exchange, the Thoth that resides in the orb not only reacted to you and correctly extrapolated from your statements, but he injected observations of his own. While the artifact itself is not sentient per se, it does contain an element with awareness."

"And it's been listening to us," Gemma added.

"Yes," Moira said, "which led to the two recommendations Thoth offered: remove Myrtle from the proximity of the sphere and remove the sphere itself from the reach of Irenaeus Chesterfield."

As simple as those two things might be, they gave us a great deal of information. The orb did cause Myrtle's odd behavior, which gave us the hope that she could be returned to her usual self and we now had confirmation that Chesterfield was behind Brenna's attack. But, did he hire the hitman who killed Fish Pike? We had to deal with that problem, but finding some place to stash the orb took priority.

"Where can we put the artifact so Chesterfield can't find it?" Mom asked.

Barnaby offered a startling and brilliant solution. Since the merfolk wanted sanctuary in the Valley and their ambassadors were already on site, Barnaby wanted to ask them to carry the orb into the coldest depths of the ocean.

"The material from which the sphere has been crafted should be impervious to the extreme conditions," he said. "Should we need to retrieve the orb, the merfolk can easily return it to us. They are so reclusive by nature, it has taken them several hundred years to even suggest forging a relationship with Shevington."

"You don't think Chesterfield can get to them?" Chase asked.

"Unlikely. The merfolk are motivated by strict ethics. Remember that their world has suffered significant damage from the activities of humankind. Watching the pollution of the waters they love has made the merfolk completely opposed to altering the workings of any natural system. Magic is such a system. As a Creavit, Chesterfield goes against the natural magical order."

I could understand the merfolk's position, but something bothered me. "If the merfolk are against altering natural systems, why are they agreeing to the creation of a saltwater environment in the high valley?"

"They are desperate," Barnaby answered. "Their seas are filling with plastic and garbage. Their coral beds are dying. The merfolk want nothing more than a place to live at peace with nature. Man is making it impossible for them to do that in the oceans they have inhabited for eons. We can offer them an alternative."

"Where are you going to suggest they hide the orb?" I asked.

"I will leave that to their discretion," he said, "but the ocean depths should be more than sufficient for our purposes."

I still wasn't sure. "How deep are we talking?"

Tori reached for her iPad and typed a search phrase. "Holy crap," she said as she scanned the screen. "The Marianas Trench is 6.8 miles down."

"Other than returning the orb to the void of space from whence it came," Barnaby said, "I can think of no more remote location on earth than the deep ocean where we can place the artifact for safekeeping."

You have to admire Barnaby. The man thinks big.

Moira agreed that the plan was a good one, but said she would need to discuss the terms with the merfolk ambassador back in the Valley. Taking the sphere there would place Myrtle in its path again, which none of us wanted to do.

"What if we found a temporary hiding place?" Chase asked. "When Myrtle comes back here, we can take the orb to the Valley through one of the portals in the mountains."

Barnaby agreed that would work, which is when Beau volunteered his obelisk in the cemetery. "My ghostly friends in the graveyard will guard the obelisk and apprise us of any activity in its vicinity. It should only be a matter of hours before the orb can be transported to the Valley."

While Myrtle and Barnaby returned to Shevington to conduct the negotiations, Beau and I would stay near the cemetery in case we needed to get in fast to protect the orb. Glory would send her usual report to Chesterfield, minus any reference to the discovery of the orb. The message would make it seem as if everything was status quo in the shop.

Glory was proving to be a flamboyant and interesting addition to the team. After Barnaby enlarged her to 11.5 inches, she swore complete devotion to our cause and promised to do anything she could to help us. She also supplied a highly useful piece of information.

The chessboard could not hear what we were doing. It could only extract information from people who played a game with its pieces. All the reports sent to Chesterfield that reflected our conversations came directly from her.

Now that Glory understood we needed her to act as a double agent, she embraced the role enthusiastically. Tori ordered the Barbie clothes Glory requested from Amazon. The new wardrobe delighted her thoroughly. She happily ditched the black witch's robes and currently sported a jaunty red pantsuit. No one had the heart to tell her she looked like the Grinch in a Santa suit.

With the plan in place, the moms asked if they could go

home. "I don't even want to think what Scrap has done to my kitchen," Gemma said.

"Jeff's not much better," Mom lamented, "but at least he's been at the river most of the last three days."

"Do you think it's safe for them to go home?" I asked Chase. "The killer is still out there, and we know he's watching us."

Chase chewed his lip. "Can you put in an appearance and come back here tonight? This guy seems to prefer to work at night."

"I think we're all ignoring a salient point here," Gemma said. "The killer has been making attacks on the periphery of your world to scare you. Did it ever occur to you that Scrap and Jeff could be in danger as well? They are Jinx and Tori's fathers, in case you've forgotten."

Damn.

I never thought of the dads in relation to magical affairs.

"We can protect ourselves, honey," Mom said soothingly. "Remember what you said about choices? This is our choice. We need to go home."

After promising to check in via text every hour on the hour, Mom and Gemma headed out. Barnaby and Moira left for the Valley. Tori and I went upstairs to the store and were surprised to find out it was 3 o'clock in the afternoon. After spending three days in the basement, we'd lost all sense of time. I ripped pages off the wall calendar behind the counter and realized it was Friday.

"I better go upstairs and make nice with the cats for a couple of hours," I said. "Darby's been looking after them for me, but they're still going to be mad at me."

Tori yawned. "Good idea. I need a nap in my own bed. What time are you and Beau heading out to the cemetery?"

"We want to get there after dark, so probably around 7:30 or 8."

"Don't forget to set an alarm on your phone," she said, stumbling off to her micro apartment.

As expected, I was greeted by accusing looks and feline indignation. After a long ear-scratching session, I took a shower only to come out and find all four of the cats lined up in the doorway glaring at me. "Look, I'm sorry. Major *stuff* has been going on. It's not like you've been neglected. You love Darby. He *cooks* for you for heaven's sake!"

Starting with Winston and working down to Zeke, each cat did an abrupt about-face, gave me the tail, and stalked off.

"The four of you are worse than Festus," I called after them.

Which isn't true, because at least my four can't talk. Thank God for small favors.

I was dressed and making a sandwich in the kitchen when I heard furious pounding on the back door downstairs.

"Now what?" I mumbled, going to peer out the window. To my shock, I saw my father standing on the back step beating on the door with his fist.

By the time I rushed downstairs, Tori had already let him in and was trying to get him to calm down.

"Dad!" I said. "What on earth is wrong?"

My Dad isn't a big man. He stands under six feet tall. His hair is brown, like mine, and I have him to thank for my reddish highlights. Normally, he's easy-going and genial. "Hurry" for him is glacially slow by anyone else's standards. Now, for the first time in my life, I could only describe him as frantic, and it scared the hell out of me.

"Is your mother here?" he demanded breathlessly, taking hold of both of my arms and almost shaking me.

"No," I said, glancing at the clock, "she left almost three hours ago. Why?"

"Damn it, Jinx," he said, "I know she left three hours ago. She sent me a text message. When she didn't come to the house, I thought I'd drive over here and find out why your inventory is taking so long. I spotted Gemma's car on the side of the road. There wasn't a sign of either one of them and . . ."

His voice broke. My blood went cold.

"And what, Dad?" I said in a harsh whisper.

"All the seats in the car were ripped to shreds."

I looked at Tori, whose face had gone white. "Tori . . ." I started.

"Don't," she said, stopping me. "Mom wouldn't let him take Kelly without a fight. Same way I wouldn't let him take you. We just have to figure out how to get them back. Together."

Dad dropped my arms and stepped back. "Oh God," he said. "You know everything, don't you? You have your powers. You're witches."

My jaw dropped.

"You know about magic?" I gasped.

"Of course I know about the damned stuff," he said miserably. "I lost my only son because of magic."

That one pretty much knocked the wind out of me.

"I had a brother?" I whispered.

"No," Dad said in an anguished voice, "you *have* a brother. We had to send him to the Valley because the father of those girls who died in the car accident cursed your mother. The boy doesn't know anything about us. His name is Connor."

The world started to reel around me. I think I might have actually dropped to the floor if Tori hadn't put her arm around my waist to steady me.

"Calm down, Jeff," she ordered. "You're not making any sense. If we're going to find Mom and Kelly, we need some straight answers. You're scaring Jinx half to death."

"Don't tell me I'm the one not making sense," Dad said. "*This* doesn't make sense."

He pulled a crumpled sheet of paper out of his shirt pocket and held it out. Tori took the wadded mass and smoothed it flat.

Cats have nine lives. Humans don't. Ready to lose two? Midnight. The mouth of the pass. Tick tock. Tick tock.

Chapter Twenty-Four

Boyfriend-father introductions are iffy at best. When you have to explain to your father that his wife has been kidnapped because you're dating a werecat, things can go south fast. Just as dad started to bristle and get up in Chase's face, Festus ambled into the lair.

"Hey, Jeff," he said conversationally, jumping up on the hearth and stretching in front of the fire. "Sounds like you're still the same blowhard you always were."

I watched in amazement as my normally non-confrontational father turned almost purple with rage. "Festus McGregor, turn your smart ass human and say that to me."

"If I didn't have better manners than to get naked in front of the ladies," Festus purred amiably, "I'd be more than happy to kick your ass again."

Again?

"Dad," Chase said, "stop helping."

My father turned to me. "Of all the guys in the world, did you *have* to take up with Festus McGregor's son?"

Apparently, I inherited my temper from dad, and at that

moment it flared. That phrase "take up with" did not sit well with me.

"For your information," I snapped, "I didn't know Chase's father was an alley cat or that I was a witch because nobody in my life ever thought enough of me to tell me the damned truth!"

"Hey!" Festus cried indignantly. "Who are you calling an alley cat?"

At the same time, Dad, Chase, and I all wheeled around to the ginger tomcat and said, "Shut up!"

Holding up one paw as if to push us back, Festus said, "Geez, did you three miss your worming this month? What's all the commotion about, anyway?"

"What it's about," Dad said, "is that Kelly and Gemma have been kidnapped."

Festus' ears went flat. He glared at Dad and me. "You two zip it," he commanded. Then turning to Chase, he added, "Boy, talk to me."

Chase gave Festus a terse description of the condition of Gemma's car and the contents of the note. Festus listened, flicking his tail angrily. "So, he wants us in the pass. That can only mean he's looking to get into the Valley."

If Chase had been in feline form, I have no doubt his tail would have been lashing back and forth as well.

"He can look all he wants to," he said. "I have had enough. This guy is going down tonight."

"Agreed," Festus said. "How do we do it?"

"Hold on," I interrupted. "Shouldn't we contact Barnaby and Moira and get their input?"

At that suggestion, Dad threw up his hands. "Barnaby and Moira? Them too? Hail, hail, the gang's all here!"

"Deal with it," I said. "Oh, and by the way, Aunt Fiona's alive."

He plopped sullenly into one of the chairs. "Of course, she is. Where is the old bat?"

"Dad, *really!*" I said in exasperation. "You're not the only one here who's worried. Aunt Fiona went back to the Valley early this morning, and she is *not* an old bat."

He passed a tired hand over his eyes. "I'm sorry, Norma Jean. I shouldn't have said that. Look, I really don't care if you have to drag the Mother Tree herself through the portal. Find Kelly and Gemma and get them home safe."

The portal? The Mother Tree? There was only one way he could know about those things.

"You've been to Shevington?" I asked, feeling every bit as astonished as I sounded.

"Many times. Barnaby and I used to fly fish together. Catch and release. Damned trout up there critique everything you throw at them."

Dear God. When this was all over, I was going to have to have a *long* talk with the parents. Enough already with the edited family history.

Beau had listened to all of this in silence. As I watched, he went over and sat down beside my father. Dad looked at him with a puzzled expression. "Who are you again?"

"Colonel Beauregard T. Longworth, late of the Army of Northern Virginia."

Dad thought about that for a minute. "Ghost?"

"Newly corporeal thanks to a magical artifact."

"Lucky break."

"Quite," Beau agreed. Then he added, "Sir, I was once a married man, and I can well appreciate the torment you must be feeling. I do not fully comprehend the personal sacrifices you have made in association with the magical community, but please accept my assurances that your daughter is a practitioner of considerable skill and genuinely pure intent. Jinx will find a way to rescue her mother unharmed."

Tears brimmed in my father's eyes. "How long have you been dead, sir?"

"Since 1864."

"Do you still miss your wife?"

Beau nodded. "Deeply,"

"Mine's been missing three hours," Dad said, his voice breaking, "and I can't breathe."

Festus got up and walked over to sit beside Beau. When he spoke to my father, there wasn't a hint of sarcasm in his voice. "Jeff, I'm going with Chase to the pass tonight. If you don't believe anything else, believe that I will lay down my life if that's what it takes to get Kelly home."

"I do believe that Festus," Dad said, "but I'm coming too."

Chase opened his mouth to speak, but I shook my head. Festus had this one.

"You can't do that, Jeff," Festus said quietly. "You're the only human in the bunch. The werecat who has Kelly and Gemma will sense that. You go up there with us, and you're instantly our Achilles heel. I don't take any pleasure saying this, but you'll put the rest of us, Kelly included, in more danger."

As I watched, all the fight bled out of my father. "Then you swear to me, Festus McGregor, on your honor, that you will bring Kelly home."

"I will bring her home," Festus said. "I swear."

While Dad stared helplessly into the fire, we revised the plan for the evening. Beau and I still had to take the orb to the cemetery. In fact, we needed to leave in about half an hour. Festus, Chase, and Tori would take Chase's car and wait for us at the head of the trail leading to the pass.

Even though he seemed distracted, Dad was listening.

"What about me?" he asked. "Am I supposed to just sit here alone and wait?"

There were two reasons I wasn't going to let that happen. I knew Dad was genuinely beside himself with worry, and I didn't trust him not to get it in his head to come up the mountain after us.

"You won't be alone," I said.

Looking toward the stacks, I called out, "Darby?"

The brownie appeared instantly. "Yes, Mistress?"

"Darby," I said, "I'd like to introduce you to my father, Jeff Hamilton."

With wide eyes, Darby said, "Oh, sir! This is a very special honor. I am delighted to meet you."

Moving in front of dad's chair, Darby bowed at the waist. Even seated, my father towered over him.

"None of that bowing stuff," Dad said, holding out his hand. "Pleased to meet you, Shorty."

Darby rewarded the new nickname with an enormous smile as his tiny hand disappeared into my father's massive paw. I knew my soft-hearted father would find it impossible not to be kind to Darby, whose simple innocence seems to exert a calming influence on us all.

"You heard what's happening?" I asked Darby.

"Yes, Mistress," the brownie said. "How may I help?"

"I want you to keep my dad company," I said. "If you get worried, or think anything is wrong, take him to the portal. Understand?"

Darby nodded. "I will guard him with my life."

Those weren't idle words. Brownies are small, but they are fiercely loyal.

"Oh, and introduce Dad to Rodney."

"Who's Rodney?" Dad asked suspiciously.

"Rodney is our rat friend," Darby said brightly. "He's black and white, very handsome, and ever so clever. Last month he was almost completely responsible for destroying the evil sorceress Brenna Sinclair."

"Was he now," Dad said, looking at me with raised eyebrows. "Why don't you tell me that story, Shorty? In fact, why don't you tell me everything that's been going on around here."

Uh-oh.

Not what I had anticipated, but at least pumping Darby for information would keep Dad's mind occupied.

I watched as my father followed the talkative brownie upstairs for a formal rodent introduction.

Before I could resume my conversation with Chase and Festus, a hissing sound from the direction of the roll top desk caught my attention. I walked over to find Glory camped out in one corner under the cubby holes. Tori had created a tiny "apartment" for the new team member using stacked books for walls. To furnish the temporary accommodations, Tori duct-taped an LED flashlight to the desk for a lamp, made up a piece of packing foam for a bed, and partially unstuffed a stress ball to serve as a miniature bean bag chair.

"Nice digs, Glory," I said. "Are you comfortable?"

"I am in *heaven*," she enthused. "You try sleeping on the side of a cup and tell me how comfortable that is."

"We'll get you fixed up with some real furniture and stuff as soon as things calm down around here," I said. "I'm sure we can find some miniatures that will work for you. Did you need something?"

"No," Glory said. "I heard about your mama and that other lady. I wanted you to know I'll be praying real hard for them to get home safe."

"Thank you, Glory."

"Also, I think maybe you better push those books closer to hide me in here. Your Daddy has had enough to deal with for one day. I don't want him seeing me and having himself a heart attack."

Good point.

"Are you sure?"

"I'll be fine, but you need to tell that good-looking

boyfriend of yours that at some point Darby needs to get your father out of the way. I have to send tonight's message to that awful Mr. Chesterfield. I thought Chase could handle all that."

"Why can't Tori handle it?" I asked mischievously.

Glory feigned innocence. "We wouldn't want to overwork Tori, now would we?"

"Of course not."

If I'd been shrunk down to three inches, turned green, and plastered on the side of a coffee cup, I might be looking for a hunky guy to tote me around too. The suggestion seemed like a reasonable consolation prize given Glory's predicament.

"Okay," I said, "I'll have Chase tap on the desk when he's ready to help you."

Glory sighed with gratitude. "You are so sweet respecting my privacy like that. I'm gonna pray extra hard for your mama."

Thanking her again, I shoved the books in place hiding her from sight.

"What was that all about?" Tori asked when I returned to the table.

"Glory didn't want Dad catching sight of her and having a stroke or something," I said, "and she specifically requested Chase take her upstairs later so she can send tonight's fake message to Chesterfield."

Chase frowned. "Why me?"

"She thinks you're a hunk."

"Oh Lord," Chase said, rolling his eyes. "Okay. She's had a tough time of it. I can fill in as her transportation."

"So," I said, "are we all set? We all know what we're doing?"

Tori eyed me closely. "We're set as soon as you and I take a walk."

I followed her into the stacks. When we'd gone several rows, she turned to me and said, "Talk to me."

"About what?"

"Oh, I don't know," Tori said, cocking an eyebrow at me. "In the space of the last hour you've seen your father almost hysterical for the first time in your life, you've found out our moms have been kidnapped by a shapeshifting psychopath, and you have a brother you never knew existed."

When I tried to answer her, the words stuck in my throat. Shaking my head and blinking back tears, I managed to croak, "Don't. I can't do tonight if you make me cry."

Tori took my hands in hers. "Just so you know, I'm scared out of my mind too."

"Good to know," I said. "Now let's go get our mothers."

Chapter Twenty-Five

Even though the killer now had two hostages to wrangle, he could still be watching us. We needed to be careful. Beau slipped off the Amulet of the Phoenix and handed it to me. Until we reached the trailhead, he would be traveling in spectral form. I slipped the enchanted bling in my pocket and put the Orb of Thoth in Tori's bowling ball bag.

"Ready?" I asked Beau.

"Lead the way."

Swallowing hard, I stepped into the evening twilight. Tori had pinned heavy blankets around the seats to hide the deep gashes, so thankfully I didn't have to look at the torn upholstery in my Prius.

As soon as I closed my door, Beau appeared in the passenger seat and gave me the thumbs up. As we backed out, I glanced toward the store and saw my father's worried face framed in the window of Tori's apartment. We held each other's gaze for a long moment and then he let the curtain fall back.

Beau and I enjoyed an uneventful drive to the cemetery. I

parked by the low wall that encloses the burial ground and followed Beau through the gate. The instant we set foot on the grounds, a throng of excited spirits surged forward in welcome. The baying of a ghostly coonhound drowned out the babble as Duke plunged through the crowd, hit Beau in the chest, and sent them both to the ground.

"Easy there, boy," Beau said, trying and failing to avoid the dog's enthusiastic licking. "Let me up now."

The hound complied reluctantly, but he didn't stray far from the Colonel's side as we made slow progress forward. Finally, Beau put his hands up. "Dear friends, this is, alas, not a social call. We are here on an errand of the gravest import. I promise to return in a few nights to hear all your news and concerns, but on this evening, Jinx and I must leave this bag hidden beneath my obelisk. Until we return, I beg you to watch over it and to come for us if anyone seeks to disturb its hiding place."

The request met with enthusiastic promises of support. The crowd made way, and I was able to quickly dig at the base of the obelisk and bury the bag. We grabbed a nearby floral arrangement, with apologies to the owner of the grave, and used it to hide the disturbed earth. Within half an hour, we were back in the Prius and headed up to the trailhead.

The vague reference to "the pass" in the killer's note meant nothing to me until Chase told me the killer was referring to the high pass at the top of the section of land known locally as Mary's Meadow. I vaguely recalled some folk tale about star-crossed lovers associated with the spot, but the important thing is that I now knew where I was going.

"Why there?" I'd asked Chase.

"Because it's one of the secret portals to the Valley. It sounds like the killer spent some time studying of Fish Pike's maps."

There was a public parking area at the trailhead, but I

pulled off the side of the road about a hundred yards away and eased the Prius down a gentle slope, so it wasn't visible from the road. We got out, and I handed Beau the amulet. The instant his hand touched the artifact, he solidified. As we walked, he tucked the amulet inside his shirt.

A few feet from the parking lot, Tori stepped out into the road. "Hey," she said softly, "how'd it go."

"No problems. It's safe for now. Where are Chase and Festus?"

"We're here," a deep voice said. Peering into the shadows, I made out two pairs of amber eyes. Chase and Festus padded out of the darkness, both in mountain lion form. They were equal in size, but gray fur outlined the contours of Festus's muzzle.

"You came shifted?" I asked.

"No," Chase said, "but we changed as soon as we got here. We need to be ready for anything."

I looked at Tori. "The same goes for us. Let's make sure our batteries are charged."

We joined hands and allowed an electric blue light to flow up our arms and light our eyes. "All systems go," Tori said. "Lock and load."

"I want to get one thing straight," Chase said. "When we find this guy, he's mine."

When I looked at him, I knew my magic still filled my eyes. I could see the azure glow reflected in Chase's golden gaze. "I want *you* to get one thing straight," I said in an even, level tone. "I don't give a damn about some werecat pissing contest. We will do whatever we have to do to save our mothers and if your ego doesn't like it, too damn bad."

To my complete astonishment, Chase growled at me. Before I could say anything else, Festus lifted one massive paw and smacked his son hard; Chase went down—only to roll to his feet with a menacing hiss.

"If you think you're big enough, boy," Festus said, his lips curled to reveal wicked fangs, "do it. Otherwise, calm down. You're letting your temper get the better of you. I didn't raise you to be this stupid."

Chase stopped, but his tail continued to twitch angrily. "I'll take point," he said, starting up the path. "Everyone stay sharp."

Beau spoke to me under his breath. "Are you sure you want me to remain behind?"

"Yes. We don't want anything coming up this path and surprising us."

As we started up the trail behind Chase, Festus fell in beside me. I looked down at him. "What the hell was that all about?"

"Just what you said," Festus replied. "It's a pissing contest. Chase's hormones are running away with him. He thinks he's protecting his mate."

"I am *not* his mate."

"I know that," Festus said. "He's giving in to his instincts, which is what I've been scared about all along. If you get a shot at that lunatic, take it. We'll deal with my boy's ego later."

"Don't worry. I will."

We reached the clearing at the mouth of the pass exactly at midnight, as the waning moon slid from behind the cover of the clouds. The scene revealed in the light made me clench my fists in impotent rage. Both mothers knelt on the dirt—bound and gagged. One of Gemma's eyes was swollen shut, and my mother had a cut on her forehead. The man standing behind them was lean to the point of emaciation. He wore a long leather duster, and each hand was encased in a gauntlet spiked with steel talons.

"Stop right here," he ordered, as we stepped out of the woods. "Evening, Festus. It's good to see you're still up for a fight."

"Do I know you?" Festus asked.

"You should. I'm Malcolm Ferguson."

"Jeremiah Pike's nephew," Festus said flatly. "Why would you kill Fish? He was your kin."

"He was a halfling bastard," the man spat. "Your father should have let the clan kill Jeremiah and his hybrid brats. They ruined our family. This was Pike territory and you high, and mighty McGregors took it. Since you took everything that should have been mine, I'm taking what's yours."

"I won't fight you over territory, Ferguson," Chase said.

"Oh, but you will," Ferguson said, "because I took pains to ensure I have incentives. Which one would you like me to kill first, the mother here or that human whore you're sleeping with?"

Before Chase could answer, I drew back my arm to hurl a ball of flame into the trash-talking scum. My eyes never registered Ferguson's motion. One minute he'd been standing perfectly still, the next he'd jerked my mother upright and was holding a single razor-sharp talon against her throat.

"Temper, temper, witch," he said. "I'm not quite ready to slit her throat, but I will if you don't put that fire out."

I closed my hand and extinguished the flame.

"That's better," he said. "The truth is that I am a reasonable man. If you fight me fair and square, McGregor, we can settle this once and for all."

"How's that?" Chase said, stepping forward.

"If you kill me, you get everything you want. If I kill you, I also get to kill all of them, and I get everything I want."

"Hell of a deal," Tori muttered under her breath.

Ferguson's sharp ears caught the words. "Oh. it is a hell of a deal. You see, your mothers are kneeling inside a closed protective circle. When I step outside the circle, the spell becomes activated. If one spark of magic is generated during the fight, they will burn to death, and there won't be any way you can stop it. After all, we do want a fair contest, now, don't we?"

"What happens to the circle if I kill you?" Chase asked.

"The moment my heart stops beating, the circle will be broken."

"We're just supposed to believe that?" I asked tightly.

"Do you have a choice?" Ferguson asked pleasantly.

Chase didn't let me speak, and really nothing I could have said would have changed what happened next.

"Fine," he said, "you have a deal."

Ferguson shoved mom roughly to the ground and took a step back. When he did, a wall of red light rose around mom and Gemma, closing over them in a crackling dome. We watched as Ferguson carefully unbuckled the gauntlets and rolled them inside a length of soft leather, which he tied with rawhide cords.

Shedding the duster, he looked toward the moon and shifted. I thought he'd be a mountain lion, but instead, a massive black panther with glowing green eyes stood in his place. Ferguson and Chase were roughly the same size, but the ebony cat's corded muscles glistened menacingly in the moonlight.

"Chase?" I said uncertainly.

He looked up at me with a regal, impassive stare, and then, without a word, went out to meet Ferguson.

As the two big cats approached the center of the clearing, they both sprang at the same moment, locking bodies in mid-air and crashing to the earth in a flurry of slashing claws and harsh shrieks. Chase used his weight to get Ferguson under him. I knew the maneuver from watching my own cats stage mock battles. He wanted to use his strong hind legs to tear at Ferguson's soft belly, but Ferguson anticipated the move and lunged for Chase's throat.

I'd like to be able to narrate every nuance of the battle for you, to describe the way their cries split the night and silenced the forest animals. I wish I could find the right words for the pain I felt when Ferguson opened the first gaping slashes in Chase's tawny pelt or my horror at watching and wanting my boyfriend to kill his opponent. But it all happened too fast—at least until the moment when the crack of splintering bone echoed through the trees and Chase fell backward favoring his right front leg, which Ferguson had shattered.

The black panther snarled and gathered himself for the final lunge. Chase's eyes flicked toward me and held my gaze. He was telling me goodbye, and there was nothing I could do if I wanted our mothers to live. A blur of motion surged past me as my mind frantically searched for an option.

Festus hit Ferguson from behind and slammed him hard against the ground, ripping out his throat with one vicious tear. As his life's blood pooled beneath him, Ferguson shifted. He seemed to be struggling to speak, but if he said anything, I couldn't make out the words.

The red dome around our mothers melted and then simply vanished. Tori and I both bolted for them, undoing the restraints and pulling away the gags. I could see Tori's hands shaking as she freed her mother. Before Tori could say a word, Gemma was reassuring her. "It looks worse than it is. He decked me when I tried to stop him from taking Kelly. I'm fine, honey, really. I'm fine."

My mother took in a gasping lungful of air once her gag was gone. She gave me a quick hug and then reached for Gemma. The two friends embraced, and Mom said, in a choked voice, "Gem, we are getting too old for this crap."

Leaving them, I made my way to Chase and Festus, laying my hand on Chase's head. "Are you okay?"

He was panting from the pain, but his eyes were remarkably clear. "It'll heal when I shift."

"Then shift."

"I don't have any clothes."

He picked a hell of a time to get modest. Spotting Ferguson's cast-off duster, I said, "Will this do?"

Chase curled his lips back. "It stinks of that murdering scum, but I guess it'll do. Throw it over me."

When his body was covered, Chase shifted, groaning as the bones contorted and reformed. Once back in human form, he sat up and slid the sleeves of the duster over his arms. He looked tired, but even the scratches on his face were gone.

"That was a hell of a risk you took," he said to Festus.

"No, it wasn't," Festus said. "You weren't listening, boy. He said magic would trigger the shield. I was already shifted, so I didn't use magic. I killed him the old-fashioned way."

Impetuously, I threw my arms around Festus' neck, oblivious to the blood staining his fur. "Thank you," I said into his neck. "I love you, Festus."

"Oh, for heaven's sake," he grumbled, but under my ear, I heard him purring.

From across the clearing, Tori asked, "Can we go home now?"

"Unfortunately," Chase said, "we can't. We have to come up with a story and call John Johnson."

You know that show, *How to Get Away with Murder*? Keep reading. I'll tell you how we did it.

Chapter Twenty-Six

So is it murder when you kill a murderer? I don't have an answer for that one yet. Staring down at a body cooling in the moonlight didn't thrill me, but Malcolm Ferguson hadn't left us many choices. We had to either get rid of the remains ourselves or explain Ferguson's death to the Sheriff in such a way that Fish Pike's murder would be "solved."

Surprisingly, my mother came up with the best suggestion. "Go home. Leave us here."

"Are you out of your mind?" I said. "Why would we leave you here?"

"Because this is where we will have been miraculously saved by a mountain lion who killed our abductor," Mom said. "For some unknown reason, it chose to leave us alone. Once we were sure the big cat was gone, we freed ourselves, rummaged through the kidnapper's pack to find our cell phones, and called the Sheriff. We will give him a slightly hysterical but believable account of how a young man who appeared to be in trouble flagged us down on the road and proceeded to kidnap us."

Who *was* this woman who looked like my mother?

"*Is* that what happened?" Chase asked.

"Yes," Gemma said. "We shouldn't have stopped, but the guy was convincing. We thought he was hurt. When we got out of the car, he made a grab for Kelly. I tried to get between them, and he decked me."

"Why didn't you use your magic?" I asked.

"Because he had one of those fake claws of his to Gemma's throat," Mom shuddered, "and he said if we went with him, he wouldn't hurt you and Tori."

"And you fell for that?" Tori said. "That's the oldest bad-guy line in the book."

"We didn't believe him," Gemma said, "or at least I didn't. I don't know what Kelly was thinking. I figured if we could stay alive, sooner or later we would be able to use our magic on him."

"Where did he take you?" Festus asked.

"It was a cabin somewhere within walking distance of this place," Gemma said. "He dragged us through the woods for about 45 minutes to get us here."

"Okay," Festus said, "I'll locate the cabin and make sure there's nothing incriminating there."

As he started to walk away, Mom called to him. Festus stopped and looked back at her. "Thank you. After all these years and everything that's happened, you're still taking care of me."

"It's my . . . "

Festus hesitated. I expected him to say "job," like Chase would have, but instead his features softened. He cleared his throat and tried again. "It's my pleasure." With that, he disappeared into the shadows at the edge of the forest.

"You sure you'll be okay?" I asked Mom.

"We'll be fine. Get back to the store and make your father go home, or better yet, tell him to go back to the river. He can't act as if he ever knew we were missing."

Chase, Tori, and I started back down the mountain. No one had much to say. I attributed the silence to post-adrenaline letdown. Beau was waiting for us. He took in Chase's appearance, Festus's absence, and the fact our mothers were nowhere to be seen and assumed the worst.

"No, no," I assured him, "the killer is dead, and we're all okay. Festus is checking out the cabin where the guy was holed up. Our mothers are set to call the Sheriff and feed him a fake story as soon as we've had time to get back to the store."

Since Chase's clothes were in his car, he started in that direction. Tori made a move to follow, but Chase cut her off. "Ride back with Jinx and the Colonel," he said.

We watched him stride away, the long ends of the leather duster flaring around his bare legs. Tori looked at me. I shrugged. Whatever was going through his mind, it would have to wait.

Dad just about blew a gasket when I told him he had to go back to the river and pretend to be fishing. "I want to see your mother *now*. Tell me where she is."

"You can't," I replied. "The man who abducted them is dead, and the Sheriff can't know any of us are involved. Mom's plan is a good one. Please do what she says and wait until we get a call. I imagine the Sheriff will want Mom and Gemma to get checked out in the emergency room."

Dad finally agreed, but he didn't like it.

Chase showed up in the lair wearing fresh clothes after my father left. His hair was still damp from the shower, and his eyes were dark with fatigue. "You okay?" I asked.

I got a short nod in response, followed by, "I wanted you to know I'm on my way to the Valley to talk to Merle, Earl, and Furl. I'll check on Myrtle and get the details on transporting the Orb of Thoth from Barnaby and Moira."

"Uh, sure," I said, more than a little startled by his curt tone.

Tori waited until he was out of sight. "Wow, fighting makes him grumpy."

"It was not the fighting," Beau said, "it was the killing."

That didn't make any sense. Chase couldn't wait to confront Ferguson. Then I started to put the pieces together.

"But Chase didn't kill Malcolm Ferguson," I said. "Festus did."

"Precisely," Beau answered.

We had now wandered into the unknown Territory of Maleness where interpretation services were required.

"Why is that important?" I asked. "Dead is dead."

"To Chase's mind," Beau said, "his father succeeded where he failed. It is a hard thing for a man of pride to swallow."

I wanted to say something snarky about "pride goeth before a fall," but decided to keep my mouth shut. Surely Chase would get over it when he had time to get some sleep and think about the outcome of the night's events.

The call from the Sheriff came in right at dawn. Tori and I delivered Oscar-worthy performances of daughterly concern, rushing to the emergency room and listening with wide-eyed horror to the story of the abduction and unlikely rescue of our mothers.

"I have to tell you," Sheriff Johnson said, pushing his hat back on his head, "they got real lucky."

"Do you have any idea why the man kidnapped them?" I asked.

"Well," Johnson said, lowering his voice, "I can't say anything on the record, but he was just as big a nut case as poor old Fish Pike. They were both obsessed with mountain lions. I'm betting this guy was feeding that big cat thinking he'd tamed it, and the cougar turned on him. Normally they're pretty shy around humans, so this fellow must have been messing with the natural order of things."

That was an understatement.

"Were you able to identify the kidnapper?" Tori asked.

"Yeah," the Sheriff said. "The guy's pack was right there. Looks like he lived out of the thing. His driver's license says, Malcolm Ferguson. Lived in Seattle, where, coincidentally, there were three killings similar to Fish Pike's a year ago. Like I said total nutcase. You can go see your mothers now."

A few steps down the hall, I stopped and turned back. "Sheriff, was there anything about this Ferguson guy in that room at Fish Pike's house you told us about?"

Johnson's face darkened into a scowl. "Damned if I know. That idiot deputy of mine must have left the back door open. Bunch of coons got in. Guess they smelled all the open cans and garbage in the kitchen. They had themselves a high old time. The whole place is wrecked. We couldn't salvage anything out of that room."

I made a mental note to buy the triplets a round of Litter Box Lager and nip nachos at the Dirty Claw.

"That's a shame," I said, "now we'll never know."

"I'm satisfied that Ferguson was the killer," Johnson said. "Those weird gloves of his with the claws have to be the murder weapon. As far as I'm concerned, it's a closed case."

Behind him, the doors of the emergency room burst open, and my father came charging through. "Where is my wife?" he demanded.

"Calm down, Dad," I said. "We're going to see her right now. Follow us."

When I opened the door of the examining room, Mom was sitting on the edge of the table. The cut on her forehead was closed with a couple of butterfly bandages. She looked tired, but she smiled at us. "Hey, you all."

Dad threw his arms around her and hugged her so hard, he lifted her a little ways off the table. "Jeff," she said, laughing, "I'm fine. Put me down."

"No," he said in a choked voice, hugging her harder. "I

knew getting your magic back was only going to get you in trouble."

Mom put her hands on his chest and forced him to loosen his grip. "You know I have my magic back? How?"

"Woman," he said, finally relaxing a little, "I've been living with you for more than 30 years. You think I couldn't feel a change that big?"

Mom laid her hand on his cheek. "Why didn't you say anything?"

"I was hoping I was wrong," Dad admitted, "but then you had to go and get yourself kidnapped and scare the holy living hell out of me. Kelly, I don't care if you brew up potions in the kitchen and grow toadstools on the roof. I love you, magic and all."

"Even with . . ." she faltered.

"Even with what happened with Connor," Dad assured her. "I'm sorry, honey, but I blurted it out. Jinx knows."

Mom looked at me. "You do?"

"I know Dad says I have a brother," I said, "but I think we have a long family conversation in our future."

"Definitely," she said, laying her head on Dad's shoulder, "but for right now, can somebody take me home?"

Chapter Twenty-Seven

So, you think all the hard stuff was over? Yeah, I did too. It turns out the mechanics of murder were easy compared to what was coming next—negotiating the fallout from the whole series of events leading up to that night in the clearing.

First, everything with the Orb of Thoth went off perfectly. The merfolk ambassador agreed to take the artifact into safekeeping at an undisclosed location in the deep ocean. He even suggested the transfer through an alternate portal so Myrtle could convalesce as long as she liked in the Valley.

Within hours of her arrival in Shevington, Myrtle knew all of us again, and her memory and perceptions continued to improve steadily. But, she showed no signs of wanting to return to the fairy mound, preferring instead to spend hours in meditation at the base of the Mother Tree.

When I expressed concern to Moira, she tried to quiet my apprehensions. "Myrtle was born in the roots of the Mother Tree. Communing with the essence from which she originated is a natural response to such traumatic events."

I couldn't argue. We were all traumatized. The only one

who seemed blissfully pleased with the outcome of events was Glory, who was newly ensconced in a dollhouse Tori found for her that is an exact replica of Graceland. They're still working on completing the furnishings, but between that and an iPod Touch loaded with Elvis hits and hooked up to Netflix, we have one happy mini witch on our hands.

Beau helped them put up a shelf in the lair complete with a tiny, ornate staircase down to the top of the desk. Glory doesn't want to go into the espresso bar any more than she has to as long as the chess set is still there. I don't blame her.

We don't know if Chesterfield hired Ferguson, so every night Glory sends the Creavit wizard a carefully worded fake report. I think she likes the idea that she's a double agent and has started trying for a femme fatale look.

The matter of her clothes has been problematic. Glory is Barbie sized in terms of height, but not figure. Tori never told Glory the red pants suit was for the Rosie O'Donnell Barbie doll. When subsequent outfits proved to be too small, Mom stepped in. She's a whiz with a sewing machine and is working with Glory to create a whole wardrobe.

One of the first items on the list was a trench coat. When we asked Glory why, she said, "Well, it is always chilly down here."

A few nights after the big rescue, Mom, Dad, and Aunt Fiona sat down and told me the story about my brother. As it turns out, the two girls killed in the high school car accident were also Fae, members of a clan of Strigoi that migrated to the Americas from Transylvania in the 18th century under the protection of a Romanian Orthodox priest named Samuel Damian.

The Strigoi aren't vampires in the sense that they don't feed on human blood. They do, however, take energy from their victims and are especially associated in the old legends with the death of infants. Damian believed the Strigoi could be cured of their hunger, and seems to have found a way to help them. The Ionescu family, the Strigoi clan, living in the area around Briar Hollow, have existed peacefully side-by-side with their Fae neighbors for generations—that is until the car accident.

Anton Ionescu, the father of one of the girls, cursed my mother to be forever parted from her first-born child, my brother, Connor. "Forever parted" translates in Strigoi speak to "drain the boy of his life force until he dies."

With help from Myrtle and Barnaby, a deal was struck. Connor would be sent to Shevington to live with Endora Endicott as her grandson. My parents were never to see him again. If they did, his life would be forfeit.

We all agreed that we had to come up with a better solution. I have every intention of knowing my brother, and my parents have been heartbroken for years over his loss. Until we can figure something out, however, trying to contact Connor would only put us all in danger. We're all in agreement there's been quite enough of that for one summer.

So far, Mom has honored the bargain. She hasn't made contact with Connor, but the mere fact that she's been to the Valley could mean Ionescu hired Malcolm Ferguson. Tori looked into the guy. He's a well-respected attorney who spends more time in Raleigh than in Briar Hollow. I think it's a long shot, but we've learned not to rule anyone out.

Barnaby and Moira want to focus on finding out what Chesterfield is up to, and I agree with them. My suspicions about Pete the Pizza Man are on the table as well. Something is up with him, and we need to know what.

In general, however, things seemed to have calmed down. We finished the sweep of the archives and found nothing unusual. Moira triple warded the fairy mound and started work with Tori and Gemma building some kind of alchemical alarm system.

I made the mistake of thinking everything was going great

until I got up on Sunday morning two weeks to the day after we found Fish Pike's body. When I went downstairs, Chase was sitting in the espresso bar.

"Hey," I said, "what are you doing here?"

"I asked Tori if she would mind going down to the lair so you and I can talk. Will you sit down?"

"Sure. Mind if I make a pot of coffee?"

"It's already made," he said. "I'll get you a cup."

My Spidey sense was screaming, but I sat down and waited for Chase to come back. When he did, I sipped my coffee and waited for him to speak. This conversation was all his show.

"Jinx," he said, "I've been thinking about everything that happened with Malcolm Ferguson and all the history behind his hatred of the McGregors."

"Okay, what have you come up with?"

He stared into his coffee cup, running his finger around the rim in slow, nervous circles.

When a couple of moments passed, I said, "Chase, if you have something to say, just say it."

"We can't be involved with each other."

The words stunned me, but I asked him to be direct, so I willed myself to respond calmly. "How did you arrive at this conclusion?"

I don't know what reaction he expected, but that wasn't it.

He blinked uncertainly and then seemed to gather his resolve. "The taboo about dating outside our kind exists for a reason. I think it's dangerous to ignore that."

"Do you now," I said evenly. "Did you have any plan to ask my opinion about this or am I supposed to accept your unilateral decision?"

Word to the wise. The bigger the words, the madder the woman.

Chase could have responded almost any other way than the

one he chose. He got his back up. "Nothing you can say will change my mind."

Bad response. Really, really, *really* bad response.

"I have no intention of begging you to stay with me if that's what you mean. If you're the kind of man who thinks he can arbitrarily make decisions for the woman in his life, I don't want you anyway. We do, however, have to work together. Did you think about that when you were designing this whole dictated break up?"

Picking up on the coldness in my tone, he said, "I assumed we could be adults about that."

"You assumed correctly," I said, "but right now, I'm very angry at you. I took you for many things, Chase McGregor, but a coward wasn't one of them. I'd like you to get out of my store, please."

It was his turn to be stung, but I wasn't the one who started this whole mess.

"Jinx . . ."

"Don't," I said, putting up my hand. "You're getting what you want, now be a gentleman and leave."

He stood up. "I had hoped this would go better."

"I'm sure you did."

As his footsteps echoed across the hardwood, I sat quietly drinking my coffee. I didn't move when the basement door opened and closed. Five minutes later, Tori came upstairs and sat down across from me.

"Hi."

"He told you?"

"He did. Are you okay?"

"I don't know if I want to throw things or cry for three days."

She reached over the table and laid her hand over mine. "If you want me to shoot him," she said gravely, "I will. I'll even wound him real bad first."

In spite of myself, I laughed. "You would too, wouldn't you?"

"Damn straight. You want me to go for the knees or the . . ."

"Tori!"

"I'm just saying there are lots of ways to hurt a man. I'm creative by nature."

"Stop," I said, laughing and crying all at the same time.

"What do you want to do?"

"I want to sit here and drink my coffee with my best friend and talk about anything other than Chase McGregor."

"Done," she answered. "Mind if I throw some bear claws into the mix?"

"Mind?" I said. "I think today they'd be considered medicinal."

So that's where we were sitting, drinking coffee and eating pastries when the second bombshell dropped.

A beam of light opened above us, and a parchment scroll dropped on the table.

"Oh Lord," Tori said. "Now what?"

I opened the scroll. It was a message from Myrtle.

When I read it to Tori, she said, "Is that what I think it is?"

"A suicide note?" I said. "Yeah, I would say so. Get dressed. We're going to the Valley."

Chapter Twenty-Eight

"I am not committing suicide," Myrtle said calmly. "I am returning to the source from which I was born."

If Myrtle felt well enough to argue semantics with me, she didn't need to be going anywhere.

"Isn't that just a fancy way of saying 'kill yourself?'"

"You are being quite obstinate about this."

Dang straight I was.

"Why are you even thinking about 'returning to your source?'" I demanded. "Moira told us you're getting better."

Tori, Moira, Myrtle, and I sat in Moira's workshop in a pool of light thrown by the picture windows behind her desk. Myrtle looked wonderful. She was her usual, radiant, golden self. Not one thing about her suggested she might be unhealthy.

Myrtle looked at Moira. "Why don't you try explaining it to her?" she suggested. "Perhaps you will have more luck."

Moira didn't look hopeful, but she tried anyway.

"Myrtle has improved," she said. "It would be a mistake, however, to think that she emerged unscathed from her brush with the Orb of Thoth. I would compare the effect to that of radiation poisoning in your world. The source of the radiation may be removed, but the damage assumes a momentum of its own."

Yeah, nice try.

"So you find a way to treat the poisoning," I said. "You don't decide to commit suicide."

Myrtle was starting to lose patience.

"Jinx, do not make me correct you again. For the last time, I am not killing myself. I plan to merge my energy with that of the Mother Tree so that I may heal."

Seizing the opening, I said, "So then you'll be back, right?"

I know. It sounded desperate, but that was how I felt.

Myrtle moved her chair closer to me and took my hands in hers. "It is possible that one day I will assume this form and return. and it is possible that I will not. I do not know where this next portion of my journey will take me, but I believe this is the right thing to do."

Desperation started to give way to despair in my heart.

"Please don't go," I whispered. "Stay with us."

"If I did," Myrtle said, "I would not be as you have come to know me."

"That doesn't matter to me."

"It matters to *me*," Myrtle said, "and I must ask that you respect my feelings."

What was there to say to that?

I'd gone cold as ice on Chase and done nothing to stop our break up because I refused to let anyone make decisions for me. Now I was trying to do the same thing to Myrtle. That wasn't right, even if I didn't like admitting it.

"When will you go?"

"Today," she said, "and I would like you both to be there."

Tori and I weren't the only ones who had received a scroll from Myrtle. When we walked with her and Moira to the base of the Mother Tree, everyone was waiting for us, including Beau and Rodney. For only the second time since I'd known him, Festus was in human form, wearing a dark suit, no less.

Word must have spread fast in Shevington. The people of the community clustered on the periphery of the square. They remained far enough back to give us our privacy, but they wanted to be present to honor the aos si.

Above us, the spreading branches of the Mother Tree sighed softly in the morning breeze. Opening my thoughts, I heard the Tree's stately voice in my head, "All will be well, child."

I didn't believe her.

Myrtle spoke to us as a group. "My beloved family, as you know, I have decided, in counsel with the Mother Tree, to merge my energy with hers and heal the damage I suffered from the Orb of Thoth. This is not so much a leaving or an end as a transition. I will be here with you still, joined with Her wisdom."

"Can we talk to you?" I asked.

"Any time you like," Myrtle said. "You need only sit here and open your mind."

Then, one at a time, Myrtle spoke with everyone present. Taking my mother's hand, she said, "Have faith, Kelly. What seems impossible may yet come to pass."

"Thank you," Mom said, embracing Myrtle. "Fare thee well, aos si."

When Myrtle came to Beau, she said, "How do you find Shevington, Colonel Longworth?"

"It is a place of great wonders, dear lady, but I am pained that the occasion of my first visit here is coincidental with your departure."

"As am I," Myrtle said. "I am trusting you to care for Jinx as I would, and to be for her a sounding board and friend."

Beau took Myrtle's hand, bowed low, and kissed it.

"I give you my word," he said. "No harm will come to Jinx under my care."

Rodney, who was sitting on Beau's shoulder, squeaked mournfully.

"Do not be sad, my little friend," Myrtle said. "You may be small of body, but your heart is brave and immense. You too, must look after Jinx. Can you do that for me?"

Rodney nodded and put his hand over his heart. When Myrtle moved past them, he dove inside the collar of Beau's shirt, seeking the comfort of a human connection.

To Festus, Myrtle said, "You old rascal. I did not expect you to appear in human form, wearing a suit, and looking so handsome."

"It's the least I could do, aos si," Festus said, and then he spoke to her in Gaelic.

Myrtle smiled. "Thank you, Festus McGregor. You are a good man, as is your son."

Chase took her hand. "If I am a good man. you have had much to do with it. May we meet again."

"May we meet again," Myrtle said.

Tori didn't wait for Myrtle to speak. She threw her arms around her neck and held on, sobbing.

"Hush now," Myrtle comforted her. "This is not a day for sadness. Your destiny is as great as Jinx's. Lean on Moira. She will guide you well."

Tori nodded, but she couldn't speak.

Then there was just me.

"I can't do this," I whispered.

"Dear child, I have trained all the daughters of Knasgowa, but only you are the true child of my heart. You can do this and ever so much more."

"I'd rather do it with you."

"I will always be with you, but at this moment I cannot be with you here in this place. Will you help me, my friend?"

"Of course," I said even though my heart was about to shatter in my chest, "what do I need to do?"

Myrtle held out her hand, and I walked with her to the base of the Mother Tree.

"Search your feelings," she directed. "Join your energy with mine."

There were plenty of emotions to pick from. Sadness. Anger. Confusion. Fear. But it was only when I settled on hope that the familiar blue light spread from my hands and my arms until the azure glow bled into my eyes.

"Good," Myrtle said, as her golden energy coalesced around her. "Hope is the greatest energy of them all."

As our magics blended, the field around us took on the same vibrant green of the Mother Tree. I felt the ground shift. Large cracks opened, revealing the massive roots under our feet.

Myrtle's form began to fade, but the pressure of her hand remained strong on mine until the last possible second. Then her essence dissipated into a sparkling fog that slowly sank into the earth as the cracks drew closed. As I watched, the blades of grass knitted over the lines until the lawn appeared whole and unbroken once again.

As my magic morphed back to blue and receded into my body, I heard the voices of both Myrtle and the Mother Tree in my mind rejoicing in their reunion.

All around us, the town folk stood silent, though many of them were weeping. I looked up and saw the dragonlets hovering above us in perfect formation with heads bowed.

"People of Shevington," Barnaby said, "the aos si and the Mother Tree are now one. *Gus am bi sinn a 'coinneachadh a-rithist.*"

"*Gus am bi sinn a 'coinneachadh a-rithist,*" they repeated as if in one voice.

Until we meet again.

Chapter Twenty-Nine

Gemma followed Kelly out the back door of the store and used a remote to unlock the rented compact SUV parked in the alley. The upholsterer would need at least a week to undo the damage Malcolm Ferguson caused to her sedan with his fake claws.

After one day with the temporary ride, Gemma had come to a decision. She had no intention of ever driving her old Chevy again. Scrap would be buying her an exact replica of the rental before the weekend was out.

Not only did she refuse to deal with lingering traces of serial killer mojo every time she went to the grocery shore, but a girl deserved a reward for escaping a kidnapping alive.

Both she and Kelly had been handling the fallout from their abduction well until they each received a scroll inviting them to witness Myrtle's transition. Now, weighed down by the sadness of that parting, neither woman spoke as Gemma drove them through the deserted streets of Briar Hollow.

Before they exited the store, Kelly gave Chase McGregor a piece of her mind for breaking up with Jinx. As Gemma listened to her friend's cold, biting tone, she knew Kelly was deflecting her grief at Chase's expense even if he did deserve her sharp words.

Given Kelly's ire, Gemma waited until they were on the highway headed to Cotterville to throw out a conversation opener. "Maybe you should have checked on Jinx before we left."

She took her eyes off the road long enough to glance at Kelly in the passenger seat. Her friend still radiated righteous maternal indignation.

"*Maybe*," Kelly fumed, "I should have gone after Chase McGregor and finished giving him a piece of my mind."

Grateful that the SUV's dim interior hid her bemused expression, Gemma said, "Oh, I don't know, Kells. I think he knew you weren't happy with him."

"He didn't even discuss ending their relationship with Jinx," Kelly said. "He made the decision without including her. That is such a *man* thing to do."

Gemma let a couple of mile markers pass before she asked, "How long are you going to stay mad so you don't have to deal with how you feel about Myrtle?"

Kelly turned away and stared into the passing darkness. Finally, in a small voice, she said, "I don't want to go home yet."

In the distance ahead, Gemma spotted the flashing arrow of an all-night diner. "Neither do I. Want to stop and get some breakfast?"

Kelly glanced at the illuminated control console in the center of the dashboard. "Breakfast? It's the middle of the night."

"That's the perfect time for eggs and bacon. Besides that's the diner we used to go to with the boys after we'd been out dancing until all hours. It'll be fun to see the place again."

Squinting into the darkness, Kelly said, "Is that really the same one?"

"How can you not know that?" Gemma asked. "You drive by it when you come to Briar Hollow."

"Most of the time I take the old way through the mountains. It's quieter, less traffic."

"And more ways to slide off the road and end up at the bottom of a culvert," Gemma thought, but she said, "It is a pretty drive through there. So, should I stop or go on home?"

"I told Jeff not to worry if we didn't get back until morning," Kelly said. "Let's stop. Maybe some food will help."

Gemma slowed and steered the SUV into the gravel parking lot, rolling to a stop in front of the diner's garishly bright windows. They could see a smattering of patrons inside occupying booths upholstered in fake leather.

"Looks like we're not the only hungry people roaming around in the middle of the night," Gemma said, peering through the windshield.

"Yes, but we're most certainly the only ones who have just come from an alternate time stream saying good-bye to an ancient Fae being before dealing with the werecat who dumped my daughter the witch."

With perfect deadpan delivery, Gemma said, "Yeah. Let's keep that to ourselves."

In spite of her dark mood, Kelly laughed and said, "Deal."

When the two friends stepped through the door, the diner's vintage decor made them both stop and stare. Well-worn pale green Formica covered the counter complemented by stainless steel trim with a diamond-quilted pattern.

The red barstools matched the booths, which were outfitted with table-top jukeboxes wedged between the condiments, napkin boxes, and tall glass straw dispensers.

A waitress in a blue uniform with a white collar and apron waved to them. "You all sit anywhere you want. I'll be right there with your menus."

Sliding onto one of the bench seats in a front booth, Kelly leaned across the table and whispered, "Are we time traveling?"

Gemma eyed the approaching waitress with her teased-up hair and retro cat's eye glasses. "No, I think time *stopped* in here sometime around 1956."

"Hey, ya'll," the waitress said, handing them sticky, laminated menus. "My name's Nolene, like the Dolly Parton song, but with an 'n.' Can I bring you girls some coffee?"

"That would be great," Kelly said. "Thank you." When the woman walked away, she mouthed to Gemma, *"Nolene?"*

"With an 'n,'" Gemma mouthed back.

The waitress returned with two vintage cups trimmed with an aqua band on the rim. "You gals decided what you want yet?" she asked, brightly as she put their coffee down.

Before Kelly could answer, Gemma said, "Two of the Hungry Man Specials."

Making a mark on her pad, Nolene said, "You want biscuits and gravy with that or pancakes?"

"Biscuits and gravy."

After the woman collected the menus and went to place their order, Kelly said, "I know where Tori gets her appetite. Why did you order that mountain of food for both of us?"

"Because it's been a mountain of a day," Gemma replied, ripping the edge off two packs of Sweet n' Low and dumping the sweetener in her coffee.

Kelly added cream to her own cup, and raised it to her lips, blowing on the surface to cool down the steaming liquid. "Why did the four of us quit going to dances?"

"For the same reason we quit going to anything social. Scrap and Jeff didn't want to have to get out of their recliners after 5 o'clock on a work day."

"I can't hold that or the endless fishing against Jeff. He had to find ways to cope. He was always there for Jinx, but everything changed after what happened with Connor."

"Do you think Connor was on the square in Shevington today?" Gemma asked.

Her friend faltered. "He must have been, but I forced myself not to look for him. I try not to think about the whole mess."

"Honey, you're going to have to think about it. Jinx will want to know her brother."

Kelly sighed. "I want to know my son, but it's still too dangerous. No matter how much I might want to hope, Anton Ionescu never struck me as the forgiving type."

Gemma grimaced. "We should have known there was something strange about that family even when we were in high school. You remember that night Ionescu and a bunch of the extended family showed up for the football game and all the lights shorted out at the stadium?"

"How could I forget it?" Kelly said. "I thought the sparks would catch the bleachers on fire."

Nolene materialized beside the table, interrupting their conversation with two heaping platters of fried eggs, hash browns, and bacon along with side plates of biscuits and gravy.

"That was fast," Gemma said.

"You picked a good time to come in," the waitress said cheerfully. "Business slows down after 1 o'clock. Enjoy. Holler if you need anything else."

As she bustled away, Kelly looked at her plate and back up at Gemma. "Anything else? Like what? An ambulance?"

"Don't be silly. You know you're hungry. You haven't eaten enough to keep a bird alive for days now."

"There's been too much going on," Kelly said. "But if I get through everything on this plate, I won't have to eat again for a month.

She picked up a crisp piece of bacon, took a bite, and closed her eyes in pleasure. "Oh, my God that's good, but I can feel every artery in my body clogging up."

"It'll be a happy death," Gemma said, breaking the yolk on her eggs and mixing the bright yellow liquid with her hashbrowns. "Kathleen always said breakfast was the most important meal of the day."

"I miss, Mama. She should have been with us today."

"She should have been," Gemma agreed. "Your mother and Myrtle shared such a close bond."

"It's hard for me to think of one without the other," Kelly admitted.

"That's the way it's supposed to be for all the Daughters of Knasgowa—two working with the aos si."

"Sometimes I wonder what we did breaking the line. These past few weeks when all four of us have studied with Myrtle, I thought we might finally be repairing the damage we caused."

"You have to stop thinking about it that way," Gemma said. "The line was broken when my mother died. Kathleen spent years alone."

Kelly looked chagrined. "I'm sorry, Gem. I shouldn't have said that."

"Don't be silly. I don't mind talking about Mama with you. Things would have been different for us all if she had lived. Thank heavens I was able to study with Mo on the sly and let her pass on her knowledge to Tori."

Kelly paused with her fork in mid-air. "You let Mo do *what?*"

Gemma shrugged. "Tori has never talked much about it with me, even after Jinx acquired her magic. She did tell me that Mo taught her to identify plants and to make healing potions, but I'm convinced the lessons went beyond that. Nothing else explains why Tori has taken everything that's happened in stride -- and I think your mother was in on the curriculum."

"Why would you say that?"

"Weren't you surprised when Mo showed up at Kathleen's funeral?" Gemma asked.

"Yes, but I assumed she was there because you and I are so close."

"That may have been part of it, but she and Fiona acted like they knew one another. If that was the case, Mo knew Kathleen too."

"Did you ever ask Mo about it?"

"I tried," Gemma said, "and she told me to tend to my own business."

Kelly laughed. "That's probably how we're going to behave when we're old women. I'm sorry I didn't know her better. She certainly went out on her own terms."

"She did that. Stubborn to the end. We couldn't get her to come down off her mountain. She liked it up there in her cabin. Thank heavens Jonas Mahoney was there to look in on her every day."

They ate in silence for a minute or two until a thought occurred to Kelly. "If Mo was teaching Tori the mountain ways, why didn't she ever talk about that kind of thing around Jinx?"

"How do you know she didn't?"

"Because I know my daughter. Jinx would have come home and told me."

"Then I would imagine that would be where your mother came into the picture. It's possible Mo and Kathleen struck some kind of deal that involved Jinx's future."

"To what end?"

"The only person who might be able to tell us joined with the Mother Tree today."

Kelly shook her head. "No, that's not true. Fiona might know."

"Does it matter now? Whatever they were up to, Jinx has her powers now. She can take care of herself."

"Yes," Kelly said seriously. "It does matter. With Myrtle gone, we have to step up and be there for the girls in ways we never have before. If Mama made some sort of deal with Mo in regard to Jinx, she had a good reason—one we need to know to ensure that we're doing our part."

"How are you planning to do that?" Gemma said, "If Mo made a promise to Kathleen to stay quiet, she took it with her to the grave."

"Maybe not."

"How do you figure that?"

"Because we can go up to that cabin, with my 'dead' sister, and hold a seance."

Epilogue

The first hint of fall cooled the night air in the cemetery and made me draw the light sweater I wore closer around my shoulders. I don't know if the shiver that moved through me came from the temperature or the sense of emptiness I felt inside.

At the far end of the graveyard, Beau stood talking with three female ghosts in gingham dresses. All the spirits still saw him as the arbiter of their problems. His visits were equal parts social call and court session.

When he finished with them, Beau joined me. I handed him the Amulet of the Phoenix. His form solidified, and I moved over to make room for him on the granite bench.

"Would you like my coat?" he asked. "There is a chill in the air."

I shook my head. "It's going to take more than a coat to warm me,"

We all felt Myrtle's absence keenly. The store seemed empty without her. That's not to say we weren't soldiering on. Beau asked Moira to train him alongside Tori and Mom, arguing that his experience of the afterlife gave him a unique perspective. Moira agreed, and now when I went down into the lair, I almost felt like I was entering a library reading room occupied by mad scientists.

Tori and Gemma's work tables sagged under bubbling beakers suspended over Bunsen burners, and Beau sat amid piles of books, his shirt sleeves rolled up past his elbows and ink staining his fingers.

More times than not they worked to a constant soundtrack of Elvis hits streaming from the dollhouse Glory referred to grandly as "Graceland East." We'd learned the hard way that asking Glory to put on something else could mean anything from George Jones and Tammy Wynette to the Pistol Annies. Tori was quietly looking into soundproofing techniques.

Technically Barnaby was now in charge of my training, but for the most part, I worked alone with the occasional suggestion or correction from Moira. The target range proved to be good therapy. I could nail a match head with an energy bolt at 25 yards every time, and my telekinesis was approaching weightlifting standards. One evening when I was feeling particularly low and wasn't paying attention, I levitated Beau's work table. He was gracious about it, but I promised to be more careful.

Chase and I managed cordial awkwardness in our encounters. I expected merciless sarcasm from Festus, but instead he was supportive and solicitous. With Myrtle gone, Tori lost her chess partner, so Festus filled in, proving to be a crafty and unpredictable opponent.

Any time Tori can get immersed in competition, she bounces back fast. It wasn't quite so easy for me. I put on a good face during the day, but at night if I wasn't crying for Myrtle, I cried for Chase and me.

Mom expressed her worry in typical Southern fashion, appearing with mountains of baked goods. At first, Darby appeared to be miffed, since feeding us was his department, but once they started trading recipes he and Mom became fast friends. They redoubled their efforts when I lost weight anyway, but I wasn't interested in food.

Rodney worked himself half to death trying to give us all enough attention to make us feel better. He also went out of his way to make amends with Glory. When she lamented to us that she had no one to dance with, Rodney promptly offered his paw and put her through a credible jitterbug, promptly initiating a strange but wonderful friendship.

Beau, who was already my stalwart confidante, was even more fatherly in the wake of Myrtle's departure. "May I offer you a piece of advice?" he asked as we sat together in the graveyard.

"As long as you're not going to tell me there's no crying in baseball."

He laughed. "I quite enjoyed that film, but I disagree with the contention regarding weeping. Anyone who has listened to Lou Gehrig's farewell speech surely could not remain dry-eyed."

"That's true," I conceded. "So what's your advice?"

"My advice," he said, "does come from a baseball-themed motion picture. 'If you build it they will come.'"

"You want me to build a baseball diamond in the cornfield so Shoeless Joe Jackson will show up and say wise things?"

Beau looked and me and actually cocked an eyebrow. Tori *was* teaching him things.

"No," he said, "I want you to pick up the pieces of your life and act as if they all have meaning until you believe they do again. This lassitude that has overtaken you must not be allowed to suppress your natural warmth and enthusiasm. You cannot afford to luxuriate in your unhappiness."

"Meaning?"

"You still face one and perhaps two adversaries," he said. "Without Myrtle here, there is no one else to step up to the plate. Barnaby and Moira are training you to be a leader, so, whether you are ready or not, you must lead."

Gazing out over the tombstones, I said, "I think I'd rather there be crying in baseball."

"You may cry," Beau said, "so long as you go on playing."

I guess that's fair enough.

CHASE SAT at his cobbler's bench resoling a pair of boots. He didn't notice Festus until the old cat jumped up beside him. "You're working late, boy."

"Keeps my mind off things, Dad," Chase said. "It's not like I can sleep anyway."

Festus picked up his hind leg and gave his ear a hearty scratch. "If that's the case," Festus said, "I might as well tell you what Malcolm Ferguson said to me that night in the clearing."

Chase looked up sharply. "I thought you said he couldn't speak."

"I said that," Festus replied mildly, "because I didn't want Jinx to know what he said."

"Okay," Chase said, "what was it."

"A name," Festus replied. "Ionescu."

A Word from Juliette

Thank you for reading *Witch on First*. Now that you've reached the end of the book, I hope you'll want to continue the adventure with Jinx, Tori, and the gang in Briar Hollow and beyond.

The story develops through a page-turning series of urban fantasy novels that take the characters into new adventures and realms.

In the next story, *Witch on Second*, Jinx and Tori have their hands full helping to organize the town's first paranormal festival, but tensions remain high after the recent killings. Still mourning the loss of Myrtle and her breakup with Chase, Jinx finds herself confronting new and unexpected foes.

Not certain you want to continue the journey? I've included the first chapter of *Witch on Second* to give you a sneak peak of the mystery, adventure, and hijinks lying ahead!

But first . . . Get Exclusive Jinx Hamilton Material

There are many things I love about being an author, but building a relationship with my readers is far and away the best.

Once a month I send out a newsletter with information on new releases, sneak peeks, and inside articles on Jinx Hamilton as well as other books and series I'm currently developing.

You can get all this and more by signing up here.

Witch on Second - Preview

The night I said goodbye to my friend Myrtle, I wound up talking to a stick.

Now, hold on before you judge me. In my world, you can't take a statement like that and assign it a face value of "crazy" without hearing the explanation first.

I'll tell you more about Myrtle here in a bit. Right now, concentrate on the fact that she was my friend and I had no way of knowing if I would ever see her again.

The rest of my family—the people I'm related to by blood and by choice—walked me home. When I announced I was going straight to bed, my mother and my bestie, Tori, exchanged worried looks, but they didn't try to stop me.

Instead, they both hugged and held me, whispering in my ear that they loved me, and then they watched me start up the stairs alone.

My new "ex" boyfriend, Chase, wanted to say something. The expression on my face shut that down fast. He closed his mouth and looked at the floor instead. We had been officially "over" for less than six hours. In good Dixie Chick fashion, I was not ready to make nice yet.

Mom and Tori must have thought I was out of earshot when I disappeared into the darkness at the top of the stairs. I heard Tori say, "Are you sure we shouldn't go after her?"

"I'm sure," Mom said. "When she's hurting like this, Jinx has to get off on her own. She'll need us more in a few days."

I hadn't intended to engage in blatant eavesdropping, but then I heard Chase ask, "Is there anything you think I can do?"

If you've never had the chance to hear your mama take up for you when she thought you weren't listening, you've missed one of life's great experiences.

As I lingered quietly in the shadows above them, Mom answered him in a clipped tone. "I think you've done quite enough."

"Kelly," Chase pleaded, "please try to understand."

"Don't you 'please' me, Chase McGregor. Breaking up with my girl would have been bad enough, but doing it today of all days is inexcusable. Frankly, I don't want to be talking to you right now."

After that, all I heard was the sound of Chase's boots walking away. Smiling through my tears, I went upstairs to be with my cats—all four of them—and broke down completely.

At the end of that crying jag, they had wet fur, and my sinuses were so clogged up I could barely breathe. I knew if I didn't get a handle on my emotions, I'd wake up to the worst post-cry hangover ever.

I wandered toward my bedroom, only to stop at the doorway. Dim light filled the room. Had I left a lamp on?

It took me several seconds to realize the glow came from the raw quartz embedded in the head of a walking staff called Dílestos. I crossed to the bed, sat down, and reached for the polished piece of oak whose name means "steadfast and loyal."

At my touch, the quartz brightened, and the pulsations thrummed with a slow rhythm I found comforting. As the vise grip on my heart loosened a fraction, Dílestos began to hum.

I closed my eyes and drank in the low, soothing melody. When I opened them again, I discovered the cats were now with me on the bed, staring at the crystal with hypnotized, golden eyes. The combined rumble of their purring struck a warm undertone to the staff's gentle melody.

My next door business neighbor and fellow witch, Amity Prescott, gave me the staff the first time I went to Shevington. She told me all the women in my line carried Dílestos. The Mother Tree originally gave the staff to my Cherokee ancestor Knasgowa.

It suddenly occurred to me that I'd never thought to ask why the Tree shared a part of herself, an idea that instantly ignited a second realization. Myrtle had merged her spirit into the Mother Tree. Could she be trying to speak to me through Dílestos?

"Is that you, Myrtle?" I asked hopefully.

Through the maelstrom in my mind, a lyrical voice answered, "The aos si now resides with the Mother Oak. Just as I can never be truly separated from my source, she whom you know as Myrtle is ever with you."

That wasn't the direct communication I wanted, but the words still comforted me. "Have I neglected you, Dílestos?"

After that first trip to Shevington, I leaned the staff against the wall beside my bed. The idea of interacting with it again literally never came to my mind until that night. Now I understand the delay wasn't my being neglectful; there was a larger plan afoot.

"Our time is as it should be," Dílestos answered. "All comes in the appointed order."

"How do you know what happened today?"

"I felt the spirit of the aos si flow into the blood of my mother."

"Does that have anything to do with why you decided to talk to me tonight?"

Under my hand, the wood warmed. "Tonight you had need of my company. You must rest. Your tears cannot undo what was done this day."

Basically, an enchanted stick told me to go to bed. Ask my mother. I was never good about the bedtime thing.

"I shouldn't have been so selfish," I said, ignoring the admonition to rest. "I've been lazy riding my bike to the portal instead of walking with you so you could see your mother."

To my surprise, Dílestos laughed. "All who journey seek to reduce their steps."

Even though my eyes were starting to grow heavy, I stubbornly kept asking questions. "Why did your mother give you to Knasgowa?"

"For the One, I create the way to the many."

"That makes absolutely no sense," I yawned, dimly aware that the staff's humming was responsible for my growing lethargy.

"Your time of joining nears. Then you will know."

Still holding the staff, I stretched out on the bed. My cats instantly surrounded me, their purring sending me tumbling farther toward unconsciousness. "Can't anyone just answer a simple question?" I mumbled.

"What is plain to the ear of one seems but gibberish to the ear of another," Dílestos said softly.

"Did you just call me clueless?"

"You are not without a clue, only lacking some. Tonight you are sad and tired. Sleep."

I think I said something about that being the story of my life. I really don't remember—but I do remember what Dílestos said right before my exhaustion claimed me.

"The story of your life is only now beginning to be told as long ago it was written."

Also by Juliette Harper

In the Jinx Hamilton Series:

ALL Books Available in KindleUnlimited!

Witch on Second

The story opens just a week before Halloween. Jinx and Tori have their hands full helping to organize Briar Hollow's first ever paranormal festival. Beau and the ghosts at the cemetery are eager to help make the event a success, but tensions remain high after the recent killings. Without a mentor to lean on, Jinx must become a stronger, more independent leader. Is she up to the task in the face of ongoing threats? Still mourning the loss of Myrtle and her breakup with Chase, Jinx finds herself confronting new and unexpected foes.

Buy Witch on Second

In the Jinx Hamilton/ Wrecking Crew Novellas:

Moonstone

Werecat Festus McGregor leads his Recovery of Magical Objects Squad on a mission to retrieve the Moonstone Spoon from the penthouse of eccentric financier and collector Wardlaw Magwilde. Festus has the operation planned to the last detail until a wereparrot and a member of his own team throw a monkey wrench in the works -- but thankfully no actual monkeys.

Join Festus, Rube and the rest of the raccoons in this fun-filled novella from the bestselling author of the Jinx Hamilton series. Filled with hysterical Fae acronyms and overlapping agency jurisdictions, Moonstone is an escapist romp you won't want to put down.

Buy Moonstone

Merstone

A werecat and a raccoon walk into a dragon's lair . . .

Join ROMO agent and werecat Festus McGregor in this second installment of the Jinx Hamilton/ Wrecking Crew novellas. Agreeing to an off-the-books mission with wereparrot Jilly Pepperdine, Festus and Rube find themselves on the Isle of Wight in search of an ancient lodestone with the power to enslave shifters.

The perfect match of whimsical fun and fantastical adventure, enjoy the latest novella from bestselling author Juliette Harper. An escapist romp in the Fae world where magic, artifacts, and laughter abound!

Buy Merstone

The Selby Jensen Paranormal Mysteries

Descendants of the Rose

Selby Jensen's business card reads "Private Investigator," but that seriously downplays her occupation. Let's hear it in her own words:

"You want to know what I do for a living? I rip souls out. Cut heads off. Put silver bullets where silver bullets need putting. You think there aren't any monsters? . . . I have some disturbing news for you. You might want to sit down. Monsters walk among us. I'm looking for one in particular. In the meantime? I'm keeping the rest of them from eating people like you."

Juliette Harper, author of The Jinx Hamilton Novels, creates a cast of characters, most of whom have one thing in common; they don't have a pulse. The dead are doing just fine by Selby, who is determined never to lose someone she loves again, but then a force of love more powerful than her grief changes that plan.

Join Selby Jensen as she and her team track down a shadowy figure tied to a murder at a girls' school. What none of them realize, however, is that in solving this case, they will enter a longer battle against a larger evil.

Buy Descendants of the Rose

The Study Club Mysteries

You Can't Get Blood Out of Shag Carpet

Wanda Jean Milton discovers her husband, local exterminator Hilton Milton, dead on her new shag carpet with an Old Hickory carving knife sticking out of his chest.

Beside herself over how she'll remove the stain, and grief-stricken over Hilton's demise, Wanda Jean finds herself the prime suspect. But she is also a member of "the" local Study Club, a bastion of independent Texas feminism 1960s style.

Club President Clara Wyler has no intention of allowing a member to be a murder suspect. Aided by her younger sister and County Clerk, Mae Ella Gormley; Sugar Watson, the proprietress of Sugar's Style and Spray; and Wilma Schneider, Army MASH veteran and local RN, the Club women set out to clear Wanda Jean's name — never guessing the local dirt they'll uncover.

Buy You Can't Get Blood Out of Shag Carpet

About the Author

"It's kind of fun to do the impossible." Walt Disney said that, and the two halves of Juliette Harper believe it wholeheartedly. Together, Massachusetts-based Patricia Pauletti, and Texan Rana K. Williamson combine their writing talents as Juliette. "She" loves to create strong female characters and place them in interesting, challenging, painful, and often comical situations. Refusing to be bound by genre, Juliette's primary interest lies in telling good stories. Patti, who fell in love with writing when she won her first 8th grade poetry contest, has a background in music, with a love of art and design. Rana, a former journalist and university history instructor, is happiest with a camera in hand and a cat or two at home.

For more information . . .
www.JulietteHarper.com
admin@julietteharper.com

By Juliette Harper
Copyright 2016, Juliette Harper

Skye House Publishing, LLC

License Notes

eBooks are not transferable. All rights are reserved. No part of this book may be used or reproduced in any manner without written permission, except in the case of brief quotations embodied in critical articles and reviews. The unauthorized reproduction or distribution of this copyrighted work is illegal. No part of this book may be scanned, uploaded, or distributed via the Internet or any other means, electronic or print, without the author's permission.

This is a work of fiction. Names, characters, businesses, places, events, and incidents are either the products of the author's imagination or used in a fictitious manner. Any resemblance to actual persons, living or dead, or actual events is purely coincidental.

EBOOK ISBN: 978-1-943516-72-8

PRINT ISBN: 978-1-943516-73-5

❦ Created with Vellum

Made in the USA
Middletown, DE
19 March 2024